THE VOICE FROM THE GRAVE

Jessica Mann

KT-164-485

Chivers Press • **Thorndike Press**
Bath, England **Waterville, Maine USA**

This Large Print edition is published by Chivers Press, England, and by Thorndike Press, USA.

Published in 2002 in the U.K. by arrangement with Constable & Robinson Ltd.

Published in 2002 in the U.S. by arrangement with Lavina Trevor Literary Agency.

U.K. Hardcover   ISBN 0–7540–4991–4   (Chivers Large Print)
U.K. Softcover   ISBN 0–7540–4992–2   (Camden Large Print)
U.S. Softcover   ISBN 0–7862–4508–5   (General Series Edition)

The text of this Large Print edition is unabridged.
Other aspects of the book may vary from the original edition.

Set in 16 pt. New Times Roman.

Printed in Great Britain on acid-free paper.

British Library Cataloguing in Publication Data available

Library of Congress Control Number: 2002106434

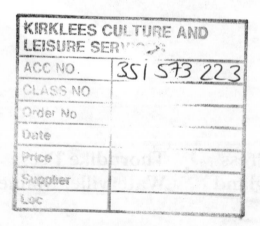

THE VOICE FROM THE GRAVE

THE VOICE FROM THE GRAVE

For R, M, S and L
and with thanks to:

Ayoola Onatade, Ben Charnaud,
Audrey Gale, Joanna Hines, Alice Kavounas,
Ken MacKenzie, Fred Taylor and
Lavinia Thomas

He has become a judge. A High Court judge. One of Her Majesty's Judiciary.

How is it possible?

It never crossed my mind that this was on the cards. Even if it had occurred to me, I wouldn't have believed it.

He's not fit to sit in judgement on other people. And I'm the only person in the world who knows it.

CHAPTER ONE

Autumn 1998

If the higher ranks of the judiciary had one thing in common that morning it was that their feet hurt. Even the few women walking in the procession, who probably had some experience of wearing nylon tights and shallow leather pumps, must surely be wishing they were in their usual shoes. And as for the rest of the obsolete gear, the sooner they got rid of it the better—at least, so the most recently appointed of the High Court judges was thinking. Collar bands and gowns had been his working uniform since day one, when he entered chambers as a pupil. God knows they were uncomfortable and inconvenient enough, but at least they did serve a purpose, being an easily recognized badge of the professional. But he could not imagine what made anybody think it was still a good idea to wear knee breeches and lace ruffles with the third millennium only two years away. Did they really suppose that a parade of eighteenth-century fancy dress, garnished with gaudy swathes of mauve and scarlet silk, would increase respect for the majesty of the law? And as for the full-bottomed wig! On a day like this, in perfect autumn sunshine and as

1

warm as it had been at the height of an (admittedly wretched) summer, sweat was running down his forehead and the back of his neck. The unaccustomed shoes slipped at the heel and a blister was forming.

As the judges processed across the square they were watched by a remarkably polite crowd: American and Japanese tourists, admiring the pageant of Olde Englande's pomp and circumstance, as well as a few local stragglers. The TV cameras were rolling as the Lord Chancellor, the Lord Chief Justice and the Master of The Rolls led their brethren in the annual show of judicial dignity, signified by red robes, purple sashes, ermine and horsehair.

Murdo Wood-Wolferstan had spent his career in the law so its pomposities were familiar. Nonetheless, the temptation to giggle or break ranks was very strong. Under the robe and the knuckle-covering lace of his shirt, he dug his nails into his palm until it hurt. Murdo was walking behind his clerk, a tall, gaunt youth in a black gown. He had pimples on the nape of his neck, below his small wig. Behind Murdo followed his attendant carrying the heavy robe's hem clear of the ground, and then came another clerk preceding her own judge, who now projected his voice forward. 'Bloody hot.'

Murdo looked round and returned a sardonic quotation. 'And my feet are killing me.'

'Your first time. Aren't you Wood-Wolferstan?'

'That's right.'

'Enjoying it?'

'Not much.'

'And just think of all the years of hard labour it took you to get here.' Individuals were hard to tell apart under the horsehair headgear and only their make-up distinguished the women from the men. Murdo did not recognize this judge, a man half Murdo's height and twice his girth who looked ancient and had probably not achieved the bench before he was in his late fifties. But they were appointing judges earlier these days, giving them a chance to earn their pensions before reaching the recently imposed retirement age. Murdo was forty-seven.

His acceptance of elevation to the bench had been a sacrifice in one way, since the pay was a fraction of his huge earnings at the bar though, with Gemma doing so well at the bank, it didn't really matter. And he hadn't relished surrendering his freedom as his own boss—since barristers were self-employed practitioners—to the impositions of the Lord Chancellor's administrative staff, who would direct his movements and control his timetable. Even in the five months since his appointment, he had already found the civil servants oppressive.

3

However, the appointment was a milestone in Murdo's career plan, and Gemma would never have let him refuse. She looked forward to his having more predictable working hours, and she was unashamedly thrilled to have a title. On the morning of the day he received the offer of appointment she had ordered a whole lot of cards engraved. Lady Wood-Wolferstan. My lady. Your Ladyship. He'd heard her trying it out behind the locked bathroom door.

Murdo didn't expect to be stuck doing routine work for very long. Two years trailing round the towns and judges' lodgings of provincial England would be as much as he could take. But he'd always been a high-flyer and was tipped for rapid promotion to the superior court. He'd never denied the accusation (made by his tutor at Oxford and repeated often since) that he was the most ambitious man anyone could hope to meet. Even his very earliest school report (a handwritten letter from the playgroup leader) remarked on the two-year-old's determination to succeed. All later assessments, including a league table originally published in a professional journal and copied in the Sunday newspapers, had invariably confirmed that Wood-Wolferstan would go far and as a matter of fact he had every intention of getting right to the top. When he did there were going to be some changes round here; he had numerous

4

ideas for shaking up the antiquated system, beginning with the flummery. No more horsehair, for a start.

There'd be no need to abolish the Lord Chancellor's breakfast and the formal inauguration of the legal year though it would only be acceptable in a less archaic form. But there was still a place for tradition, and in more sensible clothes he'd have enjoyed being part of this reverend parade with its deferential onlookers, so awed and cowed that once when they were crossing Parliament Square, a judge had called a friend's name, 'Neil!' and half the onlookers had immediately knelt down.

Someone was calling him now. 'Murdo!'

Who's that? he thought. His own guests, having attended the service in the Abbey, had gone ahead and were inside Westminster Hall with the wives—no, he corrected himself, spouses—already wearing their best bibs and tuckers; not Gemma, whose work prevented her attendance, but the children up from school for the day and Fidelis Berlin whom he'd invited because his mother couldn't come. He didn't recognize the woman who was waving at him.

'Dodie, over here!'

Only one person had ever called him Dodie. And she was just about the last person on earth he wanted to see today.

'Murdo, I need to talk to you!'

5

This was intolerable. Murdo met the eye of one of the policemen who were marching, in full fig, beside the judges. The officer nodded. The place was crawling with cops, some in sparkling uniforms but far more, one assumed, in disguise. Quite right too. As a wag remarked in the robing room, drop a bomb on us lot and you paralyse the system of justice for a generation.

'Murdo!'

He was careful not to show that he had noticed her. He kept his face impassive and eyes front, disguising from the curious bystanders that he was the one to whom this madwoman was calling. That was the fact of the matter, he thought. She was clearly deranged. Using peripheral vision he observed two people closing in on her, a man in jeans and a sweatshirt and an air-hostess type with bouffant curls, and heard the woman say, 'Let go of me! What do you think you—'

And then they were safely inside the gates. The police officers were not letting any of the public through.

'I take it that was a member of your fan club,' an elderly judge remarked with a giggle that sounded as though he'd actually said 'tee-hee.'

'I didn't recognize her. An aggrieved litigant, I should think,' Murdo replied.

'Ah, the professional hazard.'

'She was nothing compared to the one who

6

turned up at Oxford Assizes last year,' another judge remarked. 'That one had a bag full of soggy tomatoes. Luckily the stain hardly showed on my robes.'

Smiling, Murdo contributed an appropriate, if untrue, anecdote about a man with a placard who had followed his former head of chambers from court to court for a year. Smoothly, they moved into the building. All over now. But that woman—damn her. Damn her, how dare she suddenly appear after all these years? What the hell did she think she was up to?

CHAPTER TWO

Fidelis Berlin was dreading her book signing at Dillons. She had hardly felt so nervous about a public appearance since her first public lecture forty years ago. She had admitted as much over eggs Benedict for lunch at The Ivy with an American friend. Lionel was sleek in cashmere, and mopping his brow with a silk handkerchief, having forgotten how warm London could be in October. 'But you look gorgeous, Fidelis, what a terrific outfit.'

'D'you like it? This is its second outing, I got it to look smart for a friend. I knew Murdo's mother when he was a schoolboy and now he's a High Court judge, makes you feel old.' Fidelis had thought carefully about what to wear to the Lord Chancellor's breakfast the previous week, realizing she needed something more formal than she usually chose. Going into the church past the little throng of observers, and then after the service through the security booths into the House of Lords, she'd been glad that she'd conformed, and aimed not at her usual trendy/arty look, but at the dignified maternal image. She was standing in for Catriona, Murdo's mother, as she had often done all those years ago, when she'd been the Wood-Wolferstans' lodger and resident babysitter, and as she had occasionally done in recent years, since Catriona's decline began.

Seeing Murdo in his judicial pomp and glory, she was glad she'd got herself a conventional outfit. And for the book signing, the impressive label and perfect tailoring would give her confidence.

Lionel repeated his offer to keep Fidelis company but Fidelis thought she'd rather make a fool of herself unobserved by anyone she knew. She left the restaurant in good time and found the tube uncharacteristically prompt. So she walked at a slow pace through Bloomsbury, unconsciously humming a theme from the last act of *Don Giovanni*, and tried to psych herself up for the ritual humiliation that, she knew, was the lot of otherwise successful writers. Her friends had warned her of the ordeal by indifference.

'You sit at a table behind a pile of your own stuff and people avert their eyes,' the novelist Tamsin Oriel told her gloomily. 'Last time practically the only book I signed was for the shop manager.'

'It sounds terrifying,' Fidelis said, and added, 'Like some painful rite of initiation.' Her mind's ear instantly heard that lifelong companion, the internal self-regulator. Beware self-pity, beware exaggeration, beware self-dramatization. The event, however embarrassing, would be a learning experience, and an inherent part of the process of becoming a successful, money-making author. She was not used to her new status yet, although she'd been producing books and articles throughout her whole career, serious academic works that were subject to peer-review and the scrutiny of grant-awarding organizations. It was as much of a surprise to Fidelis as to her publishers when her latest book caught the eye of a feature writer on a national paper. A full page article in the Argus had been followed by interviews on *Start The Week*, *Woman's Hour* and *Newsnight*, and an invitation to appear on *Question Time*. Fidelis knew her own limitations and had the sense to refuse that one. Now she regretted not turning down today's session as well.

Her footsteps slowed as she turned on to the familiar pavement of Tavistock Square. This was where she used to bring her sandwich at lunch-time when she was working at the Institute, though in those days the garden was not so well kept. The falling leaves had already been swept from the paths. The smell of a London autumn was associated in Fidelis's subconscious with exciting new beginnings because it was at this time of year she had first arrived to live in the big city. If she had stopped to analyse the processes of her own emotions, she would have recognized that the smell was easing her apprehension. She noticed that her subliminal hum had merged into another tune, the folk song theme from Schubert's Unfinished, *'Heinrich, wo gehst du hin, wann kommst du weck, wann gehst du wieder . . .'* Her first London boyfriend had sung her the words. Whatever happened to him? Fidelis was trying to recall his surname when she bumped into someone else.

'Oh—I'm so sorry, I wasn't looking where I was going. Are you hurt? Let me—'

She was speaking to a haggard middle-aged woman, who had thick, dark hair in a long bob, deep frown and pout lines on otherwise smooth skin, and restrained makeup; she was well dressed, if too unoriginally for Fidelis's taste, in a dark blue trouser suit.

'Please, don't bother about it.' Her voice was low, her accent standard English, and her grey-green eyes were waterlogged, with tears pouring down her cheeks.

'But there's something wrong, look, why

don't you come and sit down, that's right.' On this chilly day the square was empty. Fidelis steered the way to the slatted green seat she had so often occupied, and used the familiar tool of sympathetic silence. Soon, like other psychiatric patients, the woman began haltingly to speak.

'It's awful of me, I shouldn't impose on you like this.'

'Not at all.'

'You're so caring, such a kind person, you've had enough of this kind of behaviour, I oughtn't to—but it's just that I'm upset because . . . the thing is, I've had some bad news.' She'd been coming from the direction of the hospital so Fidelis could make a good guess. This was not the first or the last time that a doom-laden medical verdict would be assimilated in this place.

'I'm so sorry,' she murmured, and the woman uttered in a kind of gasp, 'It's all so unfair, how could this—oh, it can't be true!' She folded her arms tightly across her lap and leant forward over them, shaken by gasping sobs.

She was going to make Fidelis late, which was just too bad, it couldn't be helped. Nobody, certainly no doctor and least of all a 'soul-doctor', could abandon anyone who was in this state. Though physical contact was alien to Fidelis's professional behaviour, she put her arm round the woman's heaving shoulders and

11

held her firmly. After a while, when the worst paroxysms lessened, Fidelis pulled out her cellphone. 'Is there someone I can call for you?'

'No, no, there's nobody, I lived with my mother, you know, but she died last year, she had ca—oh, God, she had *this*, and now I— why me, after everything else? It's not fair!' Sobbing, she gulped out, 'I had to nurse her myself, right to the end, you can't think how awful it was, how she suffered—and now I'm going to . . .'

'You can't be sure of that, there are so many treatments now.'

'I always told myself, I thought if this happened to me I'd finish it quickly.'

'Don't say that.'

'Would you? Would you—you know?'

'Take my own life?'

'Would you?'

'I don't think I'd have the courage or the will-power.'

'But d'you think it's wrong?'

'Not if there's nobody to be hurt by it.'

'But would you want to?'

'I've always thought life's beautiful. Even at the worst moments, things can change very fast.'

'Hanging on to the bitter end . . .'

'It might not be so bitter. Listen, you should see your own doctor, get counselling. You might need anti-depressants.'

12

'Perhaps you're right,' she said in a conversation-closing tone, alienated, as patients so often were, by the suggestion and feeling, Fidelis knew, that her unique unhappiness was denigrated by the idea of the talking or the chemical cure.

Fidelis said, 'At least let me call you a cab. You'd be better at home now, don't you think?'

She refused, mopped her face vigorously, leaving smears of beige gunge on the white tissue. 'I think I'll just sit here a bit longer. Don't worry about me. You're so supportive, so understanding, but you were on your way . . .'

'Just down there to the bookshop.'

The woman had evidently recognized Fidelis. She said, 'I didn't know it was going to be like this when I came, after my appointment I was going to come and—I'm so sorry, I can't seem to stop crying, but I'm not even your patient, please go on, you've got things to . . . thank you so much.'

'Are you sure?'

'I'll be all right,' she said, obviously knowing for certain that she wouldn't be.

'Well . . . good luck, then,' Fidelis said, conscious of the inadequacy. When she got to the corner she saw the woman was still sitting on the bench. Fidelis walked quickly back, and said, 'I must just tell you this. I thought I was seriously ill myself ten years ago.'

'Oh, I'd no idea.'

'And now I'm just fine, I really am. There's nothing wrong at all and I never think about it, it's all over. So never give up hope.' Without waiting for a response she turned away. Practised at moving on from her individual patients' troubles, she filed this sad little encounter away too.

Mortal Mothers, in its pink and scarlet jacket, was piled high in the bookshop's windows. The subject of the book, which had come out in September and quickly reached the best-seller lists, was the long-term effects of different childcare solutions on all the parties concerned. Fidelis had always taken a special interest in the subject of maternal deprivation and its effects on both parents and children. She had experienced that deprivation herself, though her life had been happy (if single and childless) and professionally successful. In the book she suggested that alternative systems could be, and throughout history always had been, guilt-free. The notion that mother and child should be all in all to each other over a period of many years was a modern one, first widely disseminated in the 1940s by a man (of course) who, probably without being aware of it, was part of the post-war propaganda machine designed to get women back to their kids and kitchens. Fidelis wrote that his exhortations represented a passing fashion, no more natural or indispensable than any of the countless ways of child-rearing that history and anthropology described. The message struck a chord with the harried, worried mothers of the late twentieth century, torn between their obligations to family and work and afraid that whatever they did would be wrong.

Fidelis was checking her reflection in the window, reassured by her long thin silhouette and the toning colours of her sharply cut steel-grey hair and the geometrical angles of the famous designer's skirt and jacket, when she saw a familiar reflection beside hers, and a welcome voice said, 'Hi.' Clodagh Byrne was Fidelis's 'un-god-daughter'. She looked bouncy and bright, wearing shocking pink, with her hair whipping round her face in the wind. Hugging Fidelis she said, 'Mum said you were nervous so I thought I'd come and hold your hand.'

'You are sweet, Clodie, I'm thrilled to see you.'

'And I need to see how it's done if I'm going to follow in all your footsteps.'

Fidelis had always loved her friend Tina's clever, charming youngest, whom she had advised on education and profession, for whom she'd written sincerely glowing references and whose successes had thrilled her. Clodie was a beauty with her mother's pale complexion and her father's red hair and long limbs. She had amassed a decent nest-egg by modelling in her teens, which paid her way through medical school. Now she was on the way to being a psychiatrist. Imitation was the sincerest form of flattery so Fidelis was duly flattered and proud. She'd added a codicil to her will, specifying that her books and papers—a huge collection by now, valuable both academically and financially—should go to Clodie.

'I'm feeling rather shy,' Fidelis admitted. 'It'll be so embarrassing if nobody comes.'

'You are silly, just wait till you see inside, it's heaving.'

Indeed, the shop seemed to be full of those very mothers, young and not so young, and their daughters, about whom Fidelis had written. And more women were still sidling in, some almost bashfully, pretending to browse or read, but all, it seemed, actually waiting for her. A banner dangling from the gallery advertised the event. The manager and the publisher's public relations man were there, and a queue of people, nearly all female, waited on one side of a table to have their five hundred page hardbacks autographed by the author.

'Please put it's for Melissa's mum.'

'To Andrea.'

'I'm Wendy.'

It was less frightening than she had feared. Unlike the audiences of professionals in the usual academic gatherings, which by this stage in her life had lost all terrors, these customers, who'd chosen to pay out their own cash for

Fidelis's work, were actually on her side.

'What you said on that radio programme made me feel so good,' one pretty young woman whispered. 'You made me think I'm doing all right after all.'

'I'm so pleased.' Fidelis smiled up at the customer, who went on:

'Because I never had any choice, I've got to go out to work and leave the kids with a minder and—'

'Dr Berlin's got a lot of books to sign today,' the publicist interrupted. 'Perhaps another time.'

'That's right,' the woman murmured as she presented the title page for Fidelis's signature. 'I only wanted to say thanks.'

The next was a bright, guiltless-seeming girl. 'It's for my friend, she couldn't get a sitter, could you put it's for Sandy?'

'Please will you say this one's for Jan's mum?'

And the next. 'For Lizzy B.'

An anonymous purchaser. 'I've got a dozen, just your name's enough, thanks.'

'You know what those are for,' Clodie whispered in her ear. 'Signed firsts.' Being a publisher's daughter Clodie was probably right, but Fidelis could hardly believe that anyone might think her book deserved the Amis/Rushdie treatment. She signed and signed. The elegant italic handwriting she'd cultivated as a teenager and retained ever since was degenerating into, not so much a scrawl, as an ever smaller and more cramped scribble. Someone had changed the tape; muted jazz was playing instead of the Cherubini. It was hot in the shop, but also draughty with the wide doors open on to the street, where a spiteful wind was blowing. Taking a moment to open and close her right hand, Fidelis glanced above her barricade of shiny hardbacks at the queue of book buyers. She could see Clodie who had wandered off and was absorbed in a Harry Potter book. Outside the open doors a crowd of students with backpacks shuffled along through eddies of dust and litter. Diesel engines spurted poison. The degraded environment of the late 1990s was far removed from the glamorous place Bloomsbury had seemed, decades before, when Fidelis first came to live in a college hostel nearby, fresh from the valleys and panting for the big city.

'Sorry, I was getting writer's cramp,' she said, smiling up at the grey-haired woman who was next in line, a comfortable-looking, mumsy person who confided:

'It's for my daughter, please will you write her name?'

'Yes of course, for . . .?'

'Oh, silly me. She's called Daisy.'

And the next and the next. Without looking up she said, 'Sorry about the scrawl, I'm out of practice at writing by hand, what d'you want

18

me to put?'

'Best wishes and your name would be fine, thanks.'

'Oh, it's you!' The woman she'd met in Tavistock Square must have followed her here. She'd calmed down, tidied herself up a bit, put on a layer of powder and a red slash of lipstick.

'Oh, you do remember me!'

'Remind me when . . .'

'I was the Medlicotts' au pair when we first met.'

A picture flashed into Fidelis's mind: a young woman in jeans carrying a platter of pudding into the Medlicotts' formal dining room. Those were the days when young wives like Anne produced perfectly cooked Elizabeth David-style dinners, while their husbands, like Gerry, did not even know how to make a cup of tea. But whether the picture in her mind was of this woman, she had no idea. It could have been any generic au pair, the girls all her friends employed for a few months at a time, more or less discontented and unsatisfactory and (to casual visitors) indistinguishable.

'D'you still see the Medlicotts?' Fidelis asked.

'We lost touch, but I heard they'd split up.'

'I see Anne all the time, we're going to move into the same building.'

'I know, I read it in an article about her,' the woman said.

19

That had been a piece in the *Argus* when Anne's latest book came out. The journalist covered the usual details in a perfunctory manner, because there was not much left to say about Anne's biography or working methods, all of which had been repetitively described since Anne, who had been writing for twenty-five years, became so successful in the twenty-sixth. The *Argus* had concentrated on 'the oldies' commune', rather to the dismay of its other residents, among them Fidelis herself.

A group of couples and singles, all nearing retirement or already retired, had decided to put into practice a long-discussed project as an advance solution to the looming problem of old age. None of these worldly, successful and in some cases famous people could bear to contemplate the idea of living in a conventional old people's home—'My dear, the noise and the people!' one had quoted, in sufficient explanation of his revulsion. None of those who had children would consider sharing homes with them. Those who were alone, like Fidelis, realized the day would come when they might need company. All those who discussed the plan had made enough money to live their retirement in comfort, but none of them wanted resident help.

There had been about thirty people in the original discussions, and most, predictably, dropped out. But the previous year nine of them, two married couples, a lesbian pair, Anne Silversmith, who had been divorced for five years after a marriage lasting for thirty, a widower called Philip Pugh and Fidelis herself had clubbed together to buy a huge house which had been built in the 1880s as a palace for a business tycoon. Fifty years later it was a downmarket hotel and one hundred years after its construction it had become a doss house for drug addicts. When the property went on the market in the mid-1990s, it had dry rot, wet rot, vermin and a collapsing roof. But it also had Grade 2 listing and a preservation order on the stone carvings. And the district was expensive. This 'oldies' commune', as the journalist had emphasized, was exclusive; the residents were rich.

The architect among them had designed and was overseeing the house's conversion into six self-contained apartments, New York style, with shared laundry facilities and storage in the front basement area under the street, a hot water and central heating system which supplied the whole building, and a rear terrace with a gate leading into the communal private gardens, accessible to all the houses that backed on to it.

The finished apartments would vary in size, from the Curzons' four bedrooms and glassed-in conservatory, to Philip Pugh's single, though enormous, studio. Some had balconies overlooking the gardens. Fidelis had bought a maisonette, the entrance on the 'lower ground' floor. She also had a private area of garden. She liked the idea of her new home, though knew she would move there nervously, hoping that her neighbours would be as anxious as she was not to impinge on the other residents' private lives. They were all, however, equally dismayed to find it described on the *Argus* features page, a great embarrassment to Anne Silversmith who sent everyone gorgeous flowers from Wild At Heart with grovelling handwritten apologies. Fidelis had been very cautious when interviewed about her own book, always meeting the journalists in hotels and refusing to talk about her private life. She cringed to think that virtual strangers, or former patients, too many and too various for her to remember as individuals but to whom she would seem like an intimate, might ever know where and how she lived.

'I read about you too, Dr Berlin, it was fascinating.'

'This book's had a lot of attention, I'm very lucky.'

'Yes, and I was so thrilled, because I'm a member of cyberbridge too.' Fidelis, who was a little ashamed of wasting her time on computer games, had let slip to the journalist that her private distraction was playing live, long-distance games of bridge at a cyber-table with people from all over the world. You might find yourself at a virtual table with three other people from Australia, California and Taiwan, and one would key in the message 'Got to get to bed' while another would be drinking their early morning tea. Only ten years earlier, it would have sounded like magic or science fiction. 'But there was an earlier article about you, Dr Berlin, some time ago, about how you solved a murder.'

That unhappy episode was the last thing Fidelis wanted to talk about. She said, 'I'll tell Anne we met.'

'And the children—they must be—'

'No longer children.'

They smiled in rueful unison, recognizing and regretting the passage of time, reasserting a normality which, for this woman, had been overturned today. She's going to behave well in public though the heavens fall, Fidelis thought, she wants to pretend everything's all right, which is probably the best coping mechanism of all.

'We really must move on, Dr Berlin,' the PR man said.

'Yes, I know—but just so that I can tell Anne about you, what are you doing these days, are you still involved in child care?'

'No no, that was only a fill-in job. I'm a writer myself.'

'Oh, under what name?'

'You won't remember, it's a while since I had a new one out and I'm not a best-seller. Not like you or Anne Silversmith.' From where she was sitting Fidelis could see that on the oval table facing the entrance doors, Anne's annual novel was prominently displayed.

'But do tell me, I'm sure they've got your books here—'

'Like hell they do. I've looked,' the other woman said, a sudden note of venom in her tone.

'Well, I can order one, if you—'

'We'd better get on,' the PR man said.

Fidelis made an apologetic face and gesture. 'You can see, this isn't the right moment. We can meet when this is over.'

But by the time the signing was finished, the woman had left the shop. Fidelis asked the deputy manager whether he'd recognized her, perhaps from a jacket photo. 'Not that they're very good likenesses,' she added, thinking of her own, which she considered a marked improvement on reality. But nobody had any idea of the woman's name.

CHAPTER THREE

I would never have dared if I hadn't been in such a state of nerves, any more than I'd have spoken to Dr Berlin. I ought to have told her about him, you could rely on her to know what should be done, after coping with other people's problems all her life, I've even got the cuttings about the murder case when she made investigations beyond the call of medical duty, like a private detective, she was the chief witness for the prosecution because she'd identified the criminals before the police did. I'd had the idea I could write it up.

Maybe I ought to get in touch with her now. I've got her number. Or should I send her an email?

I'm no closer to deciding. Seeing him didn't help. It was the first time for God knows how long. When was the last? It must have been in court down in Exeter, a grimly picturesque building that I managed to drag into the next book for local colour. I'd seen an article in the *Western Morning News* about the counsel in a murder case being tried there, and I went specially to watch him in action with his curly grey wig perched on top of his hair and the black silk flowing from his straight shoulders when he stood. From the public gallery I could only see the back view, except for a very few glimpses of his aquiline profile. It gave me a turn to hear his clear deep voice perfectly unchanged, though the acoustics were awful so the judge sat on the bench with his left hand cupped round his ear all day long, the other one scribbling away as if word processing had never been invented. In the lunch break and at the close of play I stood where he should have come out, but never caught him. I tried to make myself believe he hadn't noticed me, and

25

wasn't avoiding me, because I knew there was probably a private exit for the lawyers to keep them safe from all the people they were rude to in court, a tunnel maybe. Mem: story set in secret underground passages under courts of law.

I can't even be sure which year it was, though it must have been after they promoted him to Queen's Counsel, as his gown was made of silk, I could see it gleaming under the strip lights. Was I on one of those excursions Jeremy and I used to make from Brighton, driving round the country in his yellow Volvo, trawling the rural sale rooms to restock the shop? Or might it have been the time I took Mother on holiday to Teignmouth, just the two of us because she didn't approve of Jeremy— one divorce had been bad enough, especially as she got on well with Keith, two divorces worse although she never liked Paul, but worst of all in her eyes was my living in sin with number three. And Jeremy was in trade, which made it even less forgivable. She and I had a tetchy fortnight together in self-catering and it rained. I remember that I wore my fingertips sore playing game after game of computer solitaire, so it must have been before I discovered the Internet and cyberbridge. I know I went off without Mother once or twice, being desperate to escape the confines of a too-small chalet.

Or was it earlier, the first time I took refuge

with Mother—a temporary measure, I said and hoped, and it never so much as crossed my mind that one day I'd be back for keeps. Just after that the new agency (though I can hardly bear to write the dreaded Petra's name) found me the new publishers (may they rot in hell, agents, publishers, PR people, the lot of them) who were going to do so much for the new book—it was *The Jackdaws' Parliament*—and gave me a two-book contract and spouted a whole geyser of hot air about cracking the buyer from W H Smith and the media too, radio interviews, the *Jimmy Young Show*, *Parkinson*—I must have been mad to believe them, stark, staring mad (in fact trusting that bitch Petra was more than mad, it was just plain stupid), but hope springs eternal in the human breast—or did in mine, then.

It was about then that I took myself off to Dartmoor to research the background of *Dog Days*, I probably went into Exeter then. I ought to have written it all down, kept a record of my life, a proper daily journal. I should have written the true story of a woman who loved men. I've always got on well with men. I'm a woman who really enjoys sex. If I'd kept that journal I suppose now it could keep me like Mae West once said, but I kept it in fictional form, which has proved less marketable. Now I know what to do and it'll burn their eyes out when they read it, I'll have the last laugh, because I've always said my whole life was there in my books. And I still write, here I am writing now.

This is what I do, it's what I am, I've got into the way of writing things down to make sense of them. It straightens my head out to set down the ideas which (I whimsically suppose) seem to materialize not in the brain but in the fingertips touching the keys. How do I know what I think till I see what I say? But I know what my eventual readers are going to think this time, it'll be a sensation, because I've always had such an accurate memory for events and conversations, they scroll across my mind and on to the page transmogrified, altered by my art.

And my writing *is* art, even though it's never had the recognition I deserve, it's *good* art. I'm going to be remembered after I'm dead. Whatever publishers and agents say, in spite of their rejection and neglect, I know I deserve it as much as Tamsin Oriel or Anne Silversmith, more in fact, any really unbiased person would agree. I'm ingenious (like that one reviewer said) and I know how to manipulate the story. A school report once called me devious and manipulative and I was upset at the time, but those are exactly the qualities a novelist needs. The fact is that I've just been unlucky, my manuscripts didn't land on the right desk at the right time, I didn't know the right people. Because unless that's why, I really, truly, genuinely can't understand why they have

28

been so much more successful. Why do they make so much money and get famous and have piles of their new books on the front table in Waterstone's, when my books were never even in stock? Why are they the publishers' darlings, why do they have triumphant tours of America and appear at well-publicized book fairs and nobody wants me? Why do they always get interviewed for magazine profiles, why are their books reviewed and nobody ever noticed mine? All I wanted was to be known, to be *a name.* It was all I ever worked for, right back when I first sent for *How to Write Crime and Suspense Fiction* by mail order from Harrods book department. It simply is not fair. It's wrong.

Stop.

Back to journals.

It's never seemed important to pin down exactly when the things I remember actually happened. Maybe I should have kept the pages of my engagement book instead of throwing them out every New Year's Eve, my cleansing ritual, a habit I've had all my life. Anyway usually I can work dates out from other details if I need to. For instance, I know exactly when our trip happened because when we got to the Middle East, it was just after the Munich Olympics when the Israeli athletes were killed.

It would be silly to say he hasn't changed much since then and God knows I have. Funny—no, tragic, to think that only a few weeks ago I was seriously thinking about having a face-lift. I know that exact date of the consultation because it's in this year's month-to-a-view on my desk. June 3rd, Harley Street. I'd prepared carefully, researched the best, most skilful surgeons and arranged to increase the mortgage so as to be able to afford it. 'Very wise, Ms Cameron,' the bank manager told me. 'I told your dear mother many times that she would be so much more comfortable if she used her home as an income-generating asset.' She was of the generation that disapprove of debt, and boasted over and over again how she was going to leave me her estate unencumbered. Luckily that's not my problem. There won't be much left when I go.

While sitting in the waiting room I pulled out my pad and started jotting down ideas for a story. A short, sharp fiction. I won't write it though.

The chairs and sofas were arranged round the walls and a table was in the middle of the floor covered with brand new glossies, their cover pictures like a mockery of what the paying patients were there for; or a come-on, perhaps, images of the ideals we hoped to turn ourselves into. Everything seemed muffled, all sounds of coughs or fidgeting were softened by the thick carpet and heavy curtains. The decor was all plum and dark green, gloomy with a double layer of net on the window in spite of the glass chandelier. A couple of women were

30

muttering into their mobiles but nobody else was talking or even reading the magazines, they just sat waiting, not meeting anyone else's eyes. I looked at them all furtively, thinking that some were beyond help and others didn't took as though they needed it, and trying to recognize the evidence, scars from the nips and tucks, bulging lips, unnaturally wide eyes. One woman had a mouth like an overstuffed cushion and her skin was pulled taut, stretched over her skull like a painter's canvas before the first brushful hits it. Having got there far too early I saw them called one by one, discreetly, with the receptionist whispering in the ear so their names weren't broadcast.

When it was my turn I followed her up to the first floor, wondering if her sharp breasts and high, round bottom were meant to be an advert for her boss's skills. He met me at the door of his room with a sympathetic handshake and put his hand on my elbow to steer me to the chair facing the window. His voice was infinitely soothing and kind, and he was wearing the most perfect navy striped suit and starched shirt I'd ever seen. And of course his own face was flawless, regular, smooth features, arched eyebrows, full, mobile mouth, like a story-book hero.

He asked what I'd thought of having done, and I just said something about not wanting to grow old before my time, and then he began telling me what could be improved. He showed me my own face and body on a large closed circuit television. Size 14, as I admitted to, but 16 in ungenerous makes, and people always look fatter on the screen. The familiar eyes under the definite, black brows, smallish but a good clear green, my nondescript nose, my prominent, mobile mouth and shallow wide forehead, my unemphatic jaw-bones and invisible cheekbones. I'd been told to come with a naked face but even without the usual foundation, blusher and eye make-up, I didn't think I looked bad for my age. I just wanted to look better. And then he started pointing out every single line and wrinkle and sag and bag, my dangling breasts and sagging bottom. The problem wasn't just middle-aged deterioration but the features I was born with and had never minded before. I needed a major overhaul.

He made marks with a stylus showing how he could shave off the bridge of my nose and pull out some back teeth and reposition the cheekbone. Then he'd pull the skin back all round the edge, and cut off the superfluous eyelid folds and inject collagen in my lips and botulin in the frown lines. That was before even starting on tits and bum.

Then he said this was all the ideal, I could choose where to start, and save up till I could afford more. It must have been pretty obvious that I wasn't in the same league as those other women downstairs. Then he switched the screen off and turned to me and asked why I'd thought of having plastic surgery in the first place, was it because of the media and all the articles about it?

Actually I had found his name in one of them, but it wasn't what made me want to do it. I told him the truth, I said it was because I'd realized nobody looked at middle-aged women and I'd become invisible. Men don't *see* me any more. Then he asked me what I did and I began with the familiar, up-beat speech about being a novelist and what kind of books I write, but he seemed so caring and intimate that it tailed off and suddenly I couldn't stop myself, I'm sitting there telling this rich stranger about publishers not taking my manuscripts any more and the agent dropping me (rationalizing her client list, was what she called it) when I know my books are as good as others that do really well, better than most of them in fact, it's just prejudice against me because I'm middle-aged and mid-list and never got to know the right people. So I blurt out my plan of trying again like a first novelist, under another name with a glamorous mug shot. And then tears are washing down my face and he's handing over the tissues and somehow without my being able to work out how he swung it, I'm in a little room being swabbed down and mopped up by the perfect receptionist and a woman who doesn't need it is in there where I was sitting, discussing plastic surgery with the ideal man.

Bankrupting myself to be tortured might have been worth it. But it's too late for me now, I've missed the boat. If I'd only known the right people and had support when I was starting, like Anne Silversmith did, if I could have only broken through.

That was what made me think of M. Which is why I went to watch him. Things could have been so different, and now it's too late.

He should never have ignored me, all the same. That was a Big Mistake.

CHAPTER FOUR

Spring 1999

Gavin Rayner was finishing off a half-moon table on the Tuesday afternoon, peacefully polishing natural beeswax into the cherry wood with his bare palm, half listening to Mussorgsky's *Pictures at an Exhibition*, which Classic FM played so often that it had become one of his favourites, and keeping half an eye out front because it would soon be time for Mickey to get home from school. The door was open, so he saw the striped van labelled Tesco Direct draw up on the single yellow line outside Lesley's place and watched the driver jump out with his clipboard and go to the front door. Then he had to concentrate on the beading along the back of his table, where his questing hand had felt a slight roughness. Next he knew, the delivery man was standing there beside him.

'Sorry to bother you, mate, wondered if you'd take a delivery for number fourteen?'

'Out, is she?'

'Only it says between three and five without fail on the docket and they're s'posed to be there when I come.'

'That's cool, put it here.' Gavin helped carry the half-dozen plastic bags under cover but keeping them carefully clear of his work in progress and his tools. He used the garage built on the side of the house as his workshop but there was never enough room and Gavin was the first to admit he'd never been much of a one for keeping things shipshape. The tidiness gene was missing, his mother used to say, and in that statement, which she meant as an affectionate joke, he'd always read the whole history of their relationship. It was nature winning over nurture again.

The workshop's rectangular space was illuminated by a dirty skylight and for most of the year the wide up-and-over door was open. When he'd started up in business, Gavin had covered two walls with shelving and storage racks. His workbench stood against the third, with black lines outlining the tools that ought to hang on the wall above it, though mostly they were left lying. Every flat surface, including the cement floor, was piled high with materials or with what Gavin's wife had called junk, before she got fed up with it and him and moved in with the shithead Gavin thought of as The Pig. He did try to use the man's real name when Mickey was listening.

One pile consisted of the components of oval dressing-table mirrors on turned wood stands, a line that always sold well at pre-Christmas craft fairs. Another was of smooth, tactile bowls, sycamore as fine as porcelain and as marbled as stone. Passers-by often splashed out on those, there'd been a man on Sunday, a tall baldie in jeans, trainers and a sleeveless fleece who'd parked near Gavin's driveway, noticed Gavin watching him, and handed over the cash for a small bowl, without trying to bargain, which is what most casual customers did. There were slabs of uncut wood, old bits of furniture whose materials Gavin could put to good use, three dining chairs he was repairing for someone from the flats on the main road, plans for a revolving bookcase he was planning to make on spec, and various pieces of furniture and ornaments he was going to restore when he got round to it. What with sawdust, pollen from the lime trees that lined the road and dirt stirred up by the commuting traffic that used it as a rat run, the workshop was a mess. Which was exactly how Gavin liked it.

'That's a lovely bit of work, mind if I look?'

'Feel free.' Gavin was always pleased if people admired his work.

'Hobby, is it?'

'Was. Now it's a living. I do repairs and restoration and make things to order. This table's my own design.'

'Bet that costs.'

'Not as much as getting something of this quality from some poncey shop. Actually this one's a commission for Lesley—Mrs Cameron.'

'Hope she's back soon, some of that stuff's frozen.'

'I'll see she gets it,' Gavin promised. But Lesley hadn't shown up by the time Mickey came home and Gavin knocked off for the day so he put the frozen ready-meals she'd ordered into his own freezer and the milk and veg into his fridge and forgot about them until the next morning, when a small white car with the words 'perfect party plans' in silver cursive on its side came slowly along the road. The council hadn't yet introduced residents' permits in this part of the district, which meant the street was blocked all day by commuters who drove in and parked as near the station as they could. The white car came to a halt at number fourteen, double parked, and a blonde, bronzed young woman in a business suit got out. She was more persistent than the Tesco driver. When knocks and rings were unanswered she went to peer through the bow window of the sitting room, cupping her hands round her eyes to see inside. Then she tried the green-painted, slatted door into the passage down the side of the house, opened it and disappeared for a few minutes. Coming out again, she caught sight of Gavin and crossed the road towards him.

'I say, have you by any chance seen Mrs Cameron? The thing is, I've got an appointment.'

'For next month's do?'

'Yes, are you going?'

'Got an invite yesterday.'

'Time's quite short, we were going to finalize the arrangements today.'

'I think she's away—'

'No, she can't be,' the young woman said vigorously. 'It was only Saturday when she called and we said I'd come on Wednesday without fail, eleven thirty.'

'She must have forgotten.'

'Actually it was really difficult for me to fit it in but she was so set on me coming this morning—and now she's not here, actually it's a bit much, I'm a very busy person.'

'Want me to tell her you came by?'

'Well, thanks, you might as well, though I'm not at all sure I really want this commission actually, this isn't exactly my usual . . .' Gavin realized she was stopping herself from implying that her usual clients lived in larger houses in posher districts. Houses in Knighton Drive had become incredibly expensive in the current housing price boom. Julie and The Pig wanted to make him sell up and give her half the proceeds but Gavin's solicitor sister said not to worry, it was a try-on. The house was in his name, bought with his money—a legacy from his father—it was his place of work and Mickey's home, and Gavin had care and control. They'd be staying put, Veronica promised, sitting on a small fortune.

All the same, however much a house in this south London suburb might cost, the district was never going to be trendy and nor were semis built in the 1930s in what they called mock-Tudor style. They had triangular eaves decorated by black wood battens to mimic half-timbering, and slate hung bow windows, and small casements darkened by leaded panes.

You could see it might have been a cosy place to live in the days when housewives stayed at home wearing pinnies and the kids could play out in the street, but it wasn't any more. People weren't friendly, there was no community, or so Julie always complained. Gavin wasn't sure she was right; there were reasons why such community as there was might exclude the Rayners.

'You're paranoid,' Julie used to tell him. Blonde and plumply pink herself, she'd remind him that this was meant to be a multicultural society, but he'd respond that the idea hadn't got as far as Knighton Drive. 'Doesn't matter what colour you are when you're so gorgeous, you've got to be the best-looking bloke in London,' she'd murmur in the days when she still fancied him. Gavin knew people thought he was good-looking, but that didn't help with the neighbours. There was one family of Pakistanis living up at the far end but nobody else looked African.

Julie never did understand. She didn't get stopped when she was driving just 'cos she was the wrong colour. Least of all by The Pig. He'd pulled Gavin over three times since Julie left. 'Oh, it's you, is it, didn't recognize you,' he'd say, holding out his fat hand for the documents and making a 'ha ha' face at his mate. As Gavin turned the engine on again and The Pig swaggered back to his patrol car, the policeman spoke quite audibly. 'They all look alike to me.'

Gavin recognized all the varieties of prejudice because he was used to being the only black-skinned person in a white community. He'd been adopted at eighteen months by Kirstie, who wrote and illustrated children's books, and Alan Rayner who was an architect. Gavin and his big sisters Pernilla and Veronica had a story-book childhood, in the kind of rural setting Kirstie portrayed. They lived in a rambling converted farmhouse with two dogs, three cats, a pony and an Aga. They made dens in the orchard and had a tree-house in the copper beech. They had extra swimming, music, dancing, tennis and riding lessons and were taken on outings to museums and castles.

Wherever they went Gavin faced curiosity at the very least, revulsion or hatred at worst. He'd developed his own defensive reserve. But in his bad moments he recognized himself as the result of an experiment that had failed. Or, alternatively, as a loser in the lifelong battle to be taken for himself, no more and no less. To his parents' middle-class friends he was a sociological experiment. At school, a big comprehensive in a small town, he'd been a perpetual outsider, either on account of his colour or because he was middle class.

Gavin knew from experience that the other people who lived in Knighton Drive would never treat him like one of them and he no longer even wanted them to. Who'd want to be lost in a crowd of bank clerks, car salesmen and other such wage slaves? Self-employed, independent and creative, Gavin had nothing in common with his neighbours, so although he knew most of them by sight he had learnt few of their names. He'd only found out what Lesley's was last month, when she'd come over one day to ask if he could repair a ladder back chair, because she'd seen him at work from across the road. She left having commissioned him to make a table. She said she was thrilled, it would be a modern antique—whatever that might mean—and said the next job would be building her a glass-fronted bookcase out of some recycled mahogany he'd come by at a sale. She was going to keep her own books in it, she told him. She'd written several of them, apparently, so Gavin was embarrassed to admit that he'd never heard of her.

Gavin had seemed to see quite a lot of Lesley these days. She'd come across the road on some pretext or another, and lean against the doorway while he worked, chatting. He didn't listen really, not when he was concentrating on his work. Once or twice he'd wondered if she was making a play for him, but then he'd heard her speak to Mickey in the same kind of way, almost like a come-on, and realized it was her manner with men, or boys. Maybe she thought Mickey was older than nearly sixteen. He was a marvellous-looking kid, skin the colour of a piece of polished oak and eyes like chestnut. Lesley would look up at them, Mickey nearly as tall as his father, with a kind of appeal in her eyes. She must have been pretty, and still had a good figure, but she was too needy, you could see she wanted to be friends and Gavin didn't want to get involved. During the day he sometimes thought they were the only two people left in Knighton Drive after all the front doors had ejected and car doors admitted their commuting owners.

Lesley had been preoccupied recently, a bit vague, her voice sounding, somehow, hollow, and he'd have wondered if she was coming down with something except that the other day she'd told him there was something on her mind. Come to think of it, she hadn't come over for a while. He'd seen her go out two or three times in her car, that must have been on Saturday.

So when was it she came over last? Friday, was it, or Thursday, he could check in his work book because she'd brought over an antique writing-box she wanted repaired, and stayed to natter. It was when he was finishing a fiddly job, placing a marquetry decoration exactly right to make sure the contact adhesive stuck the pattern in exactly the right place. She hovered in the workshop door blathering on about some secret she knew and her moral duty to pass it on but would she be all right if she did, would there be trouble because there were ruthless people out there. Gavin hadn't taken much notice.

After the party-planner left he didn't give another thought to Mrs Cameron until the following day.

It was hot for March so he'd eaten his sandwich lunch in the garden but now a cushiony black cloud had dumped its load and sudden rain was battering down, bouncing off the roofs of parked cars, pouring along the gutters like an overflowing drain. Water mixed with the droppings from the trees to make a treacherous slime on the pavement and Gavin's precious tulips, newly in flower, were losing their petals before fully opening. He stood just inside the workshop watching the torrents, thinking morosely about English summers. He'd never been to the Caribbean or to Africa and neither knew nor cared where his ancestors came from, but he could easily believe that his skin belonged in a hotter climate than this. If Julie managed to force the sale of the house, he thought, maybe I'll take Mickey off to live in the sun. But he knew he wouldn't. Mickey'd never want to leave his mates and Gavin knew he'd be just as much an outsider in a black society as he felt in this one, 'neither fish nor fowl nor good red herring', as Alan Rayner's aunt had once said in his hearing. She had disapproved of trans-racial adoption long before the social services did, and who, Gavin thought, was he to say she was wrong?

Concentrating on the drawer slides, Gavin didn't notice anyone in the street till he heard thunderous knocking from Lesley Cameron's house. Three old people stood under two black umbrellas on her doorstep, a balding woman bent over a zimmer frame beside a tall, beak-nosed dowager and the sprightly little woman with a shock of white curls and a smooth, pink face. He'd seen her around, she used the corner shop.

'Young man, have you seen Mrs Cameron?' the dowager called.

'Sorry, no,' he called back.

44

'But she's expecting us!' the sprightly lady exclaimed.

'Actually I think she must be away.'

'Impossible, we've come for a game, Thursday at three as usual, she knows that,' said the tall woman, pressing the bell again. Gavin looked away, but she called again, 'Come over here a minute, will you please?'

Muttering, 'If I must' inaudibly, like a sulky child, Gavin laid his tools down and crossed the road. She shifted her umbrella into her left hand, bent forward with an air of kind patronage and said, 'I'm Mrs Roberts. My friends and I are from the bridge club.'

'Gavin. Hi.'

'Well, Gavin, have you any idea why Lesley's gone AWOL as my husband would have put it? Services slang—absent without leave.'

'I haven't seen her for—oh, it must be a week now.'

'It's really not like Lesley to let us down, she's always so punctual. I hope nothing's wrong. Have you checked?'

'Me? No.'

'She might have had a fall,' said the zimmer-framed woman.

Mrs Roberts added, 'You really ought to be keeping an eye out for her.'

'But she's not so old,' Gavin protested tactlessly.

'Accidents can happen at any age, young man,' White Curls told him. 'I was only sixty-one when I got my knee injury, it could have happened to anybody.'

'Stand under Doris's umbrella, Eithne,' Mrs Roberts ordered. 'I'm going to have a look.' She marched purposefully to try the side gate, found it opened and went through. Gavin was half-way back to his own place when Mrs Roberts reappeared saying, 'Her car's in the garage. There's an upstairs window open too. Young man! Yes, you, Kevin.'

'Gavin.'

'Come back over here. Have you got a ladder? I want you to climb up and get in.'

'No way,' he began, as White Curls protested.

'Oh Pandora, d'you think he should?' And the woman with the zimmer said:

'No no, he can't do that.'

But the major-general-manquée went authoritatively on. 'Certainly he can. I think something is really wrong. I can't see a tea tray.'

'She always makes such delicious cucumber sandwiches,' murmured Mrs Zimmer.

Mrs Roberts continued, 'Though the kitchen tap's running and there's a gas ring burning, luckily there's not a pan on it. But obviously Lesley's in there, so come along, please, there's no time to be lost!'

That's all I need, thought Gavin. There's me half-way up a ladder breaking into the Cameron house and along comes The Pig in a

46

cop car. 'I think it would be better to call the police,' he said, unclipping his mobile from his belt and handing it to Mrs Roberts.

'I don't know how to use these things,' she said disdainfully.

'I'll do it, shall I?'

'Oh, come on, we must hurry, Lesley may be in dire straits,' cried White Curls. Mrs Zimmer seemed to be shrinking as they stood, hunched further over the metal frame. At least the rain had slackened off.

'I'll give you full authority,' Mrs Roberts said firmly, her deep, posh voice issuing a firm command.

'Yes. You can blame it on us if anyone asks,' her companions agreed, and Mrs White Curls went on pleading: 'Think, if she's on the floor upstairs just waiting for us to rescue her. Please, do this for us.'

'I'm not going in there that way!' he said.

But they went on at him. It would be tantamount to murder to leave poor Lesley up there, ill, injured, dying—wouldn't he want to be rescued?

'What's wrong with you?' one asked.

He heard the smallest woman whisper, 'They aren't really like us you know, these foreigners.'

Mrs Roberts said, 'I must say it seems most peculiar that you won't do this simple service, a strong young man like you.'

So in the end he had to do it. He brought

47

his extending ladder over and the three witches, as he was beginning to think of them, followed him round to the back of the house and stood at the foot, clutching unnecessarily to hold it steady, and urging him on as he climbed up to the first floor back, where the casement was open one notch.

The house was terribly hot; that was the first thing he noticed. And it smelt like the municipal dump and then some. He found himself standing in a small, sparsely furnished back bedroom and could hear the twittering encouragement of the three old ladies. Then the authoritative voice called, 'We're going round to the front door, please go down and let us in.'

But Gavin didn't do that. Not after going downstairs, looking round the living-room door and seeing what was on the floor. At first he thought it was just mess, a bag of rubbish oozing and stinking in the heat, a toppled tumbler. Stepping closer, touching the garbage, he realized it was a body, lying contorted on the carpeted floor, the head and shoulders wrapped in concealment but with black vomit leaked from the plastic edge and a woman's legs protruding, contorted and awkward, the swollen skin purple between sock and trouser cuff.

The response car arrived quite fast, which was surprising, and was driven by Jason Hogg, which was not. Of all the cops it could have been, sod's law said it definitely had to be The Pig.

CHAPTER FIVE

Summer 2000

Fidelis Berlin lay on a slatted sun-lounger watching her toes twitch. The maid who came in for an hour every morning (officially to clean, but in fact, they all realized, to make sure the holiday tenants hadn't broken anything) was pushing a mop round the tiled living room. The owner of the terraced fields behind the villa, and presumably of the flock of sheep which had processed through the garden yesterday at dusk, was standing stock still like a scarecrow, just within sight and fully clothed, on this summer day in a flannel shirt, a leather waistcoat and a scarf. The sun was blazing in a brilliant sky and a gentle breeze stirred the leaves on fig, orange and acacia trees. The irregular, slate-blue mounds of other islands could be seen across the amethyst sea, the vista framed between huge terracotta pots of violently mauve petunias. In the foreground was the glassy aquamarine of a sea-water pool. Beyond its white railing was a grove of ancient, trunk-twisted, grey and green olive trees. Fidelis's compact disc player and its earphones lay unused on the low table. She could hear the crickets' persistent stridulations, which did not quite drown out the chattering of unseen birds. Urgent little geckos slithered across the paving stones. It was all perfectly beautiful, an idyllic place which Fidelis knew well after four holidays in the same rented villa and which she loved.

Her mind, however, was elsewhere. This time last week, she thought, I was vigorous, energetic, successful, at the height of my fame and professional success, looking—so enemies as well as friends said—younger than my years, with a full diary for months to come, with engagements for even two years ahead because experts of Fidelis's eminence had to be booked to speak so far in advance. In one half-hour in Queen's Square, she thought, I turned into an old woman.

It had taken her a long time to make herself go to the GP's surgery and then to see the specialist. It was months since she'd noticed the initial signs, the first cramped dwindling of her handwriting, the arm that did not swing when she strode along, the ache and shake of the hands. In the intervening period the symptoms had got worse. She had denied or ignored them. A medic herself, she could have made a pretty good self-diagnosis. But superstitious in this, though little else, she'd always believed that if you don't put things into words they aren't true; or alternatively, that if you take no notice of it, whatever it might be would go away.

Not this time. Now, in these incongruously dreamy surroundings she murmured her foster father's mantra, 'Beware self-pity,' and tried instead to maintain the impersonal detachment of a scientist, as she observed the textbook sign: a regular, continuous tremor of four to six cycles per second, most marked at rest. The disease was taking hold, and with its inexorable advance, self-determination would recede.

'It's not a death sentence,' the specialist had said.

'More like a life sentence,' she replied, automatically making light of it to him, averting his concern as though she'd fallen in the street and leapt up laughing, ignoring any injury.

His words were burnt into her memory like a scar. Going about her business in a daze during the week that followed, they interrupted what she should be hearing, recurring during arguments about funding at a committee convened to discuss an extension to an institution of which Fidelis was a trustee, or in the middle of an acceptance speech by one of her former pupils who had been presented with a medal for a research breakthrough, even at a concert to which Fidelis had looked forward long and eagerly. Sir John Eliot Gardiner's Bach cantata pilgrimage consisted

51

of performances of all Johann Sebastian Bach's surviving church cantatas within the single millennial year, which happened to be the 250th anniversary of the composer's death. Travelling from church to church throughout Europe, the Monteverdi Choir and English Baroque Soloists were half-way through their marathon by this time. June in the City of London was raw and chilly, but the old Church of St Giles Cripplegate, dwarfed by the surrounding skyscrapers, was heated by the attending crowd of other enthusiasts who, like Fidelis, regarded this music as the pinnacle of human achievement.

But try as she would Fidelis could not concentrate on its glory. The sounds that would so recently have transported her into another sphere of consciousness, today suffered interference like a badly tuned radio, as the doctor's voice crackled and spat in her mind. They must be words he always said at the very outset since lay patients might think the diagnosis he'd pronounced was of a disease that would be quickly fatal. 'It's not a death sentence,' he told her, and went smoothly on, ignoring Fidelis's levity. 'Sufferers from this condition can expect a normal life span,' he recited and at that moment it had sounded like bad news. Death she could face, and had faced calmly when she had cancer. But disablement? Dependence? The idea took quite some accepting, when one had always been (as an embittered ex-lover once accused) 'the cat that walked on its own', bad at accepting favours, a better host than guest, recipient of other people's worries but never wanting to share her own.

'It can progress slowly,' he said.

And, 'You may not experience marked deterioration for some time.'

And, 'It's always possible that a cure will be found,' but he didn't add, 'in time for you.'

He was not a particular friend but a long-standing acquaintance, a world specialist in neurology and an Orthodox Jew, who was known never to see patients or work on the Sabbath. His reputation was not that of a 'democratic doctor', rather of one who was bossy and judgemental with his staff and juniors. A notoriously chilly and unemotional character, at least he treated Fidelis like an equal.

'Remember what Sartre said,' he told her. 'Disabling illness removes some of the possibilities of life, but without leaving a void. The affliction creates new and entirely different possibilities which require new and different resources for them to be realized.' Fidelis was familiar with the quotation but it did not seem very comforting just now. She stared at his grey beard, the black skullcap pinned to the neurologist's scant curls, and at his long, pale face, in a kind of stupor, willing herself not to cry.

He said, 'You are a Jew, aren't you?'

'Only by birth. Not in any other way.'

'But you know there is a purpose in this.'

'I don't know anything about the Jewish faith. I'm an agnostic.'

'Believe me then. Nothing is for nothing in this life.'

Is that what Jews believe? she wondered. Fidelis had very little idea what being Jewish meant. She had once embarked on Hebrew lessons, but been too busy and, to be truthful, too uninterested, to persevere. Her former neighbour Victoria Merton completed the course in her place, which must have been predestination because soon afterwards she fell passionately in love with an Israeli and went to live in Haifa.

In a lazy way Fidelis had always been rather ashamed of her own lack of curiosity, though even if she had asked questions as a child her Welsh foster parents wouldn't have been equipped to answer them. The kind, benevolent, childless couple had done their best in every way possible when a three-year-old foreigner arrived to live with them, but they were working-class Methodists who did not know much about the world outside their valley. When she went to university Fidelis discovered that her dark, aquiline face, which did not seem specially remarkable among the indigenous Welsh, marked her out as Jewish to Anglo-Saxons. But she never took any interest

54

in the religion or the background, diagnosing her own indifference as self-protection. Her birth parents could not be traced after the war, and in adult life she always told herself she had no need of them or their culture or their identity. She stood alone. Which was, no doubt, the reason that (after a life filled with a series of uninhibited affairs and relationships) she lived alone. And now, she thought, I have to get through this alone too.

She'd shaken the doctor's hand at the door of his room and went out through the outpatients' waiting area. In the old days, as the medic, she'd learnt to walk briskly through, looking preoccupied and impersonal. On her way in this morning she'd automatically done the same, and as she was the first appointment had hardly noticed the other people sitting on those dismal benches. Now she was one of them. This would become her regular habitat. Her eyes skittered over men and women, mostly old, nearly all dressed in beige or sludge-coloured anoraks. Most were resigned, silent, long-accustomed couples. You could instantly, easily see which one was the carer and which the sufferer, effectively deformed by violent tremor, by sunken head and stooped shoulders, by all the outward and visible signs of this graceless condition.

I shall be like them, she realized in terror.

Doggerel repeated itself in her head, words read or heard, though she had no idea where.

I tremble.
I shake, I quake, I ache,
I quiver and shiver,
And I dissemble.

Perhaps, she thought, I added the last two words myself.

Fidelis was committed to the gregarious annual holiday shared with a group of female friends—intimate friends, all of whom she saw regularly. She had no family, and after months of living in 'the oldies' commune' she was, if anything, less close to the other residents than in the days when they lived apart and used to meet for jolly dinners to discuss the project. Since moving in they had all been obsessively cautious, determined not to be landed with each other's problems and not to dump their own on to their neighbours. The Curzons had already moved out. As required, their flat had been sold to purchasers who were accepted by the other residents in a secret ballot, New York condominium style, but the new owners weren't part of that original group of friends. Anne Silversmith and Philip Pugh had got married and were house hunting. So nobody was closer to Fidelis than the women she had holidays with, who constituted a group (or, as Elspeth said they now qualified to be, a coven) of mutually supportive friends. Who better to share Fidelis's problems? But she could not bring herself to speak of this one. Not yet. *I dissemble.*

*   *   *

Four of them, the advance party, had arrived at night after a delayed flight and prolonged day, too tired to have dinner and slumping exhausted into their separate beds. The others said they had slept like logs. The first day had taken its now traditional form: down to the sea, a long siesta, lounging by the pool and a late, leisurely meal in a taverna in the town where they were greeted as familiar friends. It was a feast day of the local saint, so they watched, along with a crowd of others, as his image was borne through the streets on a sort of platform-chair under a gold and crimson canopy.

The next morning they shared the lazy breakfast that had become the holiday tradition, coffee, yoghurt and nut-filled honey on the terrace.

'Isn't it heaven?' Tina said, spreading her arms as though embracing the familiar delight. 'I can't wait to get in the sea—coming?'

'Not today,' Fidelis. 'I'll stay by the pool for a change.'

'Oh, but Fidelis, you love swimming in the sea, do come,' urged Clodie. She had recently left Boston, having broken up from her long-time boyfriend, a Chinese American physicist

57

—much to her mother's disappointment, since Tina had been longing to see what their children would look like. Clodie was soon to start her new post at a Special Hospital in south London, having acquired an interest in forensic psychiatry and offender profiling while working in America, so she'd luckily been free to come to Greece at the last moment when the archaeologist Thea Crawford's first grandchild was born eight weeks prematurely.

It was Honor, of course, who tactlessly uttered the unutterable. Retired recently from a job as regulator of a privatized industry, she'd always believed in plain speaking and now showed it by breaching the unadmitted convention between the women who went on the annual 'girls' trip'. For the duration, giggling and chattering, painting each other's nails, admiring clothes and drinking a little too much, they escaped from being what they were and what the public required of senior, distinguished and important people. In this short period out of real life, they had developed a habit, almost a conspiracy, in which they behaved as if each and every one of them—all excepting Clodagh now elderly— were still the women they once had been, wrinkles and grey hairs notwithstanding. Less superficial changes were not discussed, ailments minor or major dismissed as nothing more than *petites misères'*. If one noticed a friend's problems one did not allude to them. But this morning Honor had said:

'It's too steep and slippery, Fidelis shouldn't risk it.'

'Why ever not?'

'You're the doctor, Clodie, can't you see she's—' Honor's voice was drowned as Tina and Fidelis interrupted simultaneously.

'Let Fidelis be, Clodie, if she wants to be on her own.'

'I've brought a bit of work to finish,' Fidelis lied.

'I expect she wants to play cyberbridge, as none of us will make up a four,' Tina said lightly.

'I wondered why you'd lugged that laptop along,' Honor said. 'How you can waste your time like that!'

Tina said, 'Oh Honor, it was such a good idea of Fidelis's, learning to play in good time, we should all do it. It's the best possible insurance for the old folks' home, haven't you ever noticed the only people you see having a nice time there are sitting in a bridge four?'

'What a way to spend your time on a Greek island!'

'Come on then if you're coming, Honor, Clodie, let's get a move on, let's go.'

'Fidelis, why don't you join us later, you can hang on to me,' Clodie promised.

The previous day, the first morning of the holiday, that was exactly what Fidelis had

59

found herself forced to do. She hadn't quite realized how impaired her balance had become until her feet began to slip and turn on the uneven path that led down between the fragrant bushes and trees towards the brilliant, smooth water and silvery rocks below. 'Here,' Clodie had said, holding out her hand, and something in Fidelis had cringed and shrivelled. She'd made herself smile and seem grateful. But she couldn't bear to require Clodie's physical support again. I am not that person who totters and wavers, she'd told herself. I am not 'helped'.

So today she was staying by the pool. She'd exchanged some halting pleasantries with the maid, an Albanian called Zanetta who had a few words of English, and made grateful gestures at the pool boy, who was a monoglot Greek. The travel company rep had come by to make sure everything was going well. She said a heatwave was forecast and it was already over ninety in the shade, they must take care not to let themselves get sunburnt. 'But you know the form, don't you?' she added, and Fidelis agreed that she and her friends had all been coming here for years, on and off, in various combinations.

And this will be my last time, she thought. No more holidays or adventures. No more exploration of new countries. Next time, the others will be here without me.

The holiday was shared by a loose-knit,

changing bunch of women who had known each other for years. They had marched for women's rights in the sixties, lobbied for the liberating legislation of the 1970s, benefited from the new opportunities opened up to them and now watched their daughters taking them all for granted. In private affairs, they provided mutual sympathy, support, criticism and gossip. One or other had moved in and out, away or back, but gradually a relationship had been achieved in the whole group that smacked (the anthropologist Susie Duke told them) of elderly wives in a polygamous marriage.

Every June a selection of them would gather at Gatwick, a nightmarish dawn scrum, as passengers on a dozen charter flights competed to check in. Tina Svenson organized everything. 'I like things to work,' she'd say, fiercely. She'd started her career as a secretary (as so many graduate women did in her day) but become a manager, a director and eventually, as she was now, the managing director of a publishing firm. She was the one who made the arrangements for the villa and came to it every year.

Then there might be Elspeth Scott, Fidelis's great friend from medical school, who'd gone into administration, become a medical officer and recently retired from her very senior civil service post. She took time off from admin on these trips, always willing to do, or do nothing, just as the others chose. Elspeth was due to join them for the second week. The archaeologist Thea Crawford came some years, or Tamsin Oriel, the novelist, or Meggie Lochhead, who'd been leader of the House of Lords, and her sister ('I'm just a housewife') Jinny. Last year Claire Cohen, recently appointed as head of an Oxford college, had come, and the only gay members of the set, Kaye Withers, the singer, with her agent, lover and incubus, the perpetually dissatisfied L.J. Moon. Each played a different role in the changing dynamic of the group—and not always the same or the predictable one. Tina, the publisher, hardly read a word while Thea would arrive with a novel a day plus two for each journey. Kaye made a disgusted face if anyone put music on the radio and snapped, 'Give it a rest!' while Meggie Lochhead sang along to the most unlikely pop. Fidelis, although the only practising medic, was much less willing and able to deal with minor injuries and ailments than Honor, who was an enthusiastic first-aider.

'My dear, whatever have you been doing!' Honor had exclaimed the previous day, seeing the gash on Fidelis's shin, and knees and elbows skinned like a careless child's.

'I tripped, it's nothing,' she replied dismissively. A week ago she had fallen getting out of the car to go to a meeting, cursed her own carelessness, got back in and driven to the nearest supermarket to buy dressings and new tights and arrived, only a little late, to discuss a doctoral candidate's thesis. Now she recognized the unsteadiness as a concomitant of her condition.

Knees to chin on a towel on the rocks, she suddenly thought, my car! Will I have to trade it in for an automatic? Her pride and irrational joy, a silly, impractical gas guzzler, her unjustifiable extravagance was an idiotic machine for an elderly woman, she knew, but giving it up would be anguish.

But why did she mind? What did the show-off machine represent to her? Surely not the phallic symbol it was traditionally interpreted as; or was it perhaps just that, now that she'd been celibate for—could it really be six years? Her unprecedented choice of a long, low, purring Jaguar should have told her something.

Despite having spent her career considering the psyche, other people's psyches, or possibly because she had done so, Fidelis had never thought much about her own. Putting oneself in the foreground of any picture was, she believed, a strong and probably ineradicable character trait, though whether people were born with or developed it she could not tell. It went with certain personality disorders but could also present as nothing more than introspection or vanity. Fidelis had always viewed the world objectively herself, almost (as another disgruntled lover accused) like someone who wasn't personally involved. 'Your motto should be "Lord what fools these mortals be",' he complained.

Well, now I'm the fool, she'd thought as the pebbles ground into her thin buttocks. Shifting, she stretched her legs (though cut and bruised, also depilated and artificially tanned) out on the towel. One of them was uncontrollably trembling.

She'd gone into the sea a little later and floated in the silky water with her friends, peered at the fish, golden or black or silver, and pointed out sea urchin shells which Clodie dived to collect. She'd laughed as her contemporaries pushed one another off lilos into the water like teenagers, she joked and contributed; and joined in later as they chattered through a leisurely taverna dinner. But on the following morning, alone almost for the first time since receiving the diagnosis, she could look at the emotions she'd pushed down into hiding. Despair. Terror. Disgust.

'You're going to have to live with this, Fidelis, get used to it,' she told herself, and then, characteristically contrary, thought, No I don't. I don't have to live.

Suicide was part of her professional expertise, and although her practice of psychiatry had for a long time been highly specialized she had not forgotten how to assess patients for the tendency, or how to treat those who had tried and failed to kill themselves.

She was always on the look-out for patients who had thoughts of harming themselves or others, and was used to gauging her own response. Just as the laughter and magniloquence of manic patients could be infectious so could the expression of thoughts from a depressed person. Fidelis was also aware that it was common for people who had this illness to take their own lives. Even including those who had professional understanding of the neurochemistry of suicide. I should be giving myself Prozac. Like any other patient. Quickly, before I join those others who, diagnosed with this dread condition, end it all within a few weeks of diagnosis.

What makes me different? she wondered, visualizing herself swimming into the embracing sea, out and out until there was no return. She could write herself a scrip for barbiturates and swallow the lot. She could jump from—

'Stop it,' she said aloud.

'*Parakalo?*' the Albanian maid called from the upper terrace.

'Oh, Zanetta, I'd forgotten—no, *ochi, ochi*—I don't want anything. You go off now.' Fidelis made banishing gestures, shooing Zanetta away and her own inadmissible thought along with her.

Pull yourself together, woman, she admonished herself, stop making like nobody else in the world had ever had this experience. Why should F. Berlin be immune from it? Think of all the people who live through this without fuss.

She went into her bedroom, small but luckily, this year, not shared with one of the others, pulled a thin shirt and cotton trousers from the narrow cupboard, found her purse (hidden, because no doors were ever locked here, in an empty biscuit box on top of the fridge) and walked (but should she use the word *lurch*?) down to the village supermarket, carefully, handing herself from railing to tree trunk. On the way she took note of all the wrinkled, black-clad crones she passed and told herself she was still less hunched and crippled than any of them.

The others reappeared in time for a late lunch which Fidelis had prepared. She'd intended the mechanical task to be a barrier from thought, but her clumsiness reminded her that last year she would have sliced up the huge, sweet tomatoes in half the time. She picked a late lemon, greenish, rough-skinned and aromatic, from the tree by the door and basil from a pot on the terrace, tearing its peppery leaves on to the salad. Glistening black olives in a yellow pottery bowl, chopped white cheese with grains of fresh thyme and oregano, yoghurt studded with mint and garlic, farmer's bread heated in the oven, crisp, juicy black cherries, soft, ripe peaches.

'A feast,' Tina cried, coming from the shower draped only in a towel, running her fingers through short hair dyed a soft apricot. She was younger than Fidelis and careful about her diet, a regular at the gym and beauty salon. She had been on a sunbed and was already lightly tanned.

The others were still washing the salt off, and Honor shouted, 'Start without us.'

Tina sat in the shade under the huge white umbrella, poured out two glasses of the resinated white wine and (being Fidelis's most intimate friend) said, 'What's wrong?'

'Nothing. What d'you mean?'

'Come on, Fidelis.'

'I don't want to talk about it.' So long as she hugged this secret to herself it was her own to deal with—if she chose, to finish. And she wanted no consolations or sympathy.

Tina gestured at the artful padding inserted into the swimsuit. 'Is it that back again?'

'No, there's no sign of any recurrence.'

'I'm glad. But then . . .'

At that point Honor came out in her garish sundress, her long nose sunburnt and her pepper-and-salt perm swollen into a bushy frizz. Tina and Fidelis had guiltily, privately agreed that Honor was one of those long-time friends with whom one would not become close now. What they all had in common was the past, shared days at college, in Fidelis's case, and in Tina's, shared school-runs and childcare in their neighbouring houses. In fact it was through Honor that Tina and Fidelis first met.

'The sun's very hot, shall I bring your hat, Fidelis?'

Fidelis tried to remember whether Honor would have made a similar offer in previous years. 'No thanks, I love the sun,' she said.

'Skin is less resilient as one gets older, you need to be careful,' Honor said. She had two brown moles on her face and another on her neck, which had gone a ruddy colour in two days. Fidelis's skin was always, naturally, a faint beige and it took very little time in the sun for her to acquire a perfect tan. She said:

'I never get sunburnt, thanks.'

'All the same you ought to cover up—'

Honor's lecture on the ozone layer was interrupted by Clodagh coming out of the house holding Fidelis's mobile phone.

'There's a call for you, I heard it ringing in your room.'

It was a welcome distraction. 'Thanks, Clodie. Hello, Fidelis Berlin speaking.'

The man's voice was clear. 'Dr Berlin?'

'Yes.'

'This is Hassan Mahatir.'

'Sorry?'

'Of Whitaker Pritchard, solicitors. I wrote to you.'

'I haven't seen your letter,' Fidelis said, phrasing her response with misleading accuracy as she remembered the numerous envelopes she'd felt too shattered to open before leaving for Greece.

'About the legacy.'

'Legacy?' The other women looked up from their lunch and Fidelis raised her eyebrows and shrugged her shoulders for them, before adding, 'Who from?'

'It's all rather complicated, Dr Berlin, I was wondering perhaps, could you come in to see me? I'm free much of this week.'

'Actually I'm on holiday at the moment, you're speaking to me in Greece.'

'Oh, oh I see—so misleading, cellphones—I suppose it can all wait till you're back.' Then he added incomprehensibly, 'After all this time.'

'That would be best, call me when I'm back in London in a couple of weeks. But just tell me first, who—I mean, nobody close to me has died as far as I know.'

'Mrs Cameron. Mrs Lesley Cameron, deceased.'

'But—are you sure I'm the person you're supposed to be talking to?'

'Dr Fidelis Berlin, 28 St Clement Gardens, London, W11.'

'That's me, certainly, but—did you say Lesley Cameron?'

'She died over a year ago, but there were certain problems, I'll apprise you fully when—'

'But there has to be a mistake, Mr Mahatir.

I don't know her. I've never heard the name in my life.'

CHAPTER SIX

The house looked pretty well trashed by the time Gavin got back to it. Sixteen months, near enough, it had been. One year and a third. Four hundred and eighty-six days. Eleven thousand, six hundred and sixty-four hours— no, make that six hundred and fifty-six, because it had been late one afternoon when he was taken to the station 'to assist with inquiries', and he'd been released today in the morning, in a downbeat manner, the trial having folded early on its second day, at 10:43 precisely. The barred door was unlocked and he was alone.

It was not a bit like news stories he'd watched when vindicated released prisoners emerged from the Courts of Justice, the Strand full of taxis and buses and news cameras trained on a hero, punching the air in triumph, with wife and girlfriends hanging on his arm, surrounded by a cheering crowd.

There had not been anybody to come home with Gavin. His sister Pernilla had been to the prison once and then only to say she wouldn't be able to come again because the software company her husband worked for had posted him to Indonesia. Veronica, whose specialty was aircraft leasing, was in Turkey finalizing a complicated contract at the time his case came up. She had visited Gavin in prison but Paxton Hardman did not handle criminal cases so she'd found him a solicitor called Teddy Weinstock, who was brisk and impersonal, and that morning had quickly shaken Gavin's hand, said, 'Well done, well done,' and left at a canter. Gavin's barrister, whom he had learnt to call his brief, had been looking forward to the days in court and was openly disappointed when the judge accepted his plea that there was no case to answer and directed the jury to acquit on that ground. There had also been irregularities in the interrogation. Irregularities, in the form of a beating up, whose scar Gavin still bore.

The police obtained their warrant and undertook the search while Gavin was in the station but before he was charged. He went with them that spring afternoon in the gear he stood up in, working clothes, and that was what he'd come home in now.

Nobody had put the detectives' mess right. They'd made a right job of it, the place looked like burglars had turned it over and for all he knew so they had, there hadn't been anyone here to notice or complain. He guessed he should think himself lucky that squatters never moved in, but even without them, stuff Gavin remembered had disappeared. He supposed some of it must have been taken by Julie when she picked up Mickey's things which was fair enough because Mickey'd have needed the stereo and TV in his room at the new house. The Pig's house.

Someone had spray-painted the closed door of his workshop. *Killer.* The word took up the whole width, so *murderer* wouldn't fit. But *nigger* did, under the other word, the letters parallel and rather neat.

Having let himself in Gavin climbed over the pile of junk mail and got as far as the front room, where he stood in a kind of vacant daze, disconcerted by the silence. It was a long time since he'd been surrounded by quiet, though it wasn't the first time he'd been alone since going away. He'd done solitary more than once after losing his temper.

This was the first time for all those months that he could choose what to do and he couldn't think of anything. Tidy up this mess? No point in that, he wouldn't be staying. Ring anyone? But the phone wire had been torn from the wall. Who would he have called anyway? The only voice he'd like to hear was Mickey's and there'd been no contact from him since the first week, when The Pig brought him along, already controlled and disciplined, in school gear with his hair cut, the nose and ear studs gone and his face closed against his dad.

He'd only come to say he wouldn't be

coming again, Mickey muttered, not meeting his father's eyes. He'd grown. His skin had come out in a rash. 'You shaving every day then, son?' Gavin said, but Mickey only shrugged his shoulders. It was nearly the end of the half-hour when he burst out:

'Dad, you didn't think she . . .'

'She what?'

'Her. You know. Mrs Cameron.' The name came out in an embarrassed whisper. 'You didn't think she'd—you know—tried it on with me? Was that why . . .'

'Did she? Did the old woman touch you?' Gavin's loud question brought the screws over. Mickey was on his way out the door when he twisted round and shouted:

'Sorry. Sorry, Dad.'

He hadn't visited again. Maybe he didn't want to. He was ashamed of his dad. In the long hours Gavin tried to persuade himself that it was Julie and The Pig who didn't want Mickey to come, but it was hard to sustain the belief when none of the letters Gavin sent received replies. Veronica had tried to speak to her nephew but the phone was put down when she asked for him.

By now Gavin knew Mickey wouldn't be coming back to live with him again, even after he was eighteen next year, not after all that time with Julie and The Pig. Even if Gavin put up a fight—so likely, that he'd voluntarily go near another law court, he thought sardonically

—but even if he did get it together, he knew there was no way a judge was going to give care and control to an accused murderer who'd only got off on a technicality. There wasn't even much point in trying to get access. Might as well accept it. Like being told you've got an incurable illness, he tried to make himself believe—you can't fight it. Shit happens.

After a while Gavin made himself move. The house was stuffy but dank. Veronica had paid the utility bills so none of the services had been cut off. The boiler would need servicing, but why bother? Better just get a firm of house cleaners in and put the place on the market pronto. He opened a window in the front room and went upstairs. He couldn't help seeing the back garden through the half-landing window, a jungle of docks and nettles hiding the fact that there had been flower beds and roses and lawns.

The master bedroom was a heap of splintered floorboards and mattress foam, all slashed into disintegration. Everything had been toppled out of the built-in cupboards, his clothes and shoes in a dusty heap. The only lucky detail in the whole disastrous affair was that his dope stash was so carefully hidden from Mickey, in a secret compartment he'd constructed in the thickness of the wall between the fridge and the cooker, that even the search teams didn't find it. No, correction:

the luckiest detail was that they hadn't planted any on him.

Gavin picked a fluff-covered fleece jerkin from the bottom of the pile and went into the bathroom. The lavatory cistern was broken, the lino tiles had been torn up and the medicine cupboard emptied.

Veronica had warned him the place was a mess—but this bad? There must have been intruders in after the cops. And Julie too, though wouldn't you have thought she'd have wanted to put things right a bit, given that this had been her home?

Footsteps sounded on the path and the letter box rattled. More junk mail? No, this was an anonymous letter, computer-printed. *We don't want your type round here.* Rather polite, considering. Most people would have wrapped it round a stone and chucked it through the window.

Gavin found a dented tin of own-brand baked beans in a kitchen which was smeared with grease and dust, whose sink was blocked with a scummy liquid and where the cooker had been dragged away from the wall. He swallowed them unheated. I'll have to get on, I can't stay here, he thought, wondering if his plastic cards still worked. His wallet had been in the paper package of his possessions handed over that morning, along with a mobile phone which had ceased to function a long time ago and the keys to this house. He had some money in the bank, not much but enough to rent somewhere till this place was sold and he'd found a new place. Among the many facts he'd learnt inside, most of them about the hitherto unsuspected hideousness both of human nature and of a good many human lives, he'd come to recognize his own colour. For the first time in his life he was among the majority, at least to look at. If anything could be called good about the prison experience, it was discovering what it felt like when you didn't stand out from a crowd. But in spite of that he'd still been an outsider. They called him 'a white nigger'.

He'd promised himself not to fight it any longer if he ever got out. What was the point of carrying on with his so-called integrated life? It was still him that got the blame when they needed someone to fix it on, a ready-made scapegoat. Gavin was going to move to a place where nobody would look at him twice, as he'd told Veronica more than once when they discussed the future. She'd always been upbeat, the big sister cheering up her kid brother, but he knew she was worried. What he didn't know was if that was because she thought he'd be convicted, or because she really believed he'd done it. She looked sad when he told her he planned to live in Brixton or Stockwell or any other part of London where real blacks congregated, not just Asians but proper Africans and Afro-Caribbeans.

Like Gavin.

'Pity it's come to that. Mum and Dad would have broken their hearts,' she said. Veronica always seemed uncomfortable, visiting him there, in spite of her legal training. Her only previous prison visit had been as a student, the guided tour a compulsory part of her course, and that one experience had been enough to make her specialize in a branch of the law that had nothing to do with crime.

'Pity I'm going to accept my colour, at long last?'

'I didn't mean that, don't be silly. Pity you've got to. You know they hoped the distinctions would have disappeared by the time we were grown up.'

'Yeah, like they thought there'd be no wars if little boys didn't get to play with guns. How wrong can you be?'

'So what'll you do, carry on with the furniture business somewhere else?'

But Gavin hadn't thought any further than moving house and turning himself into a different kind of person. Did he even want to go on working the wood? I dunno, he thought now, standing in his ruined kitchen, his hands heavy at his sides. I haven't got the heart for it now. But he'd better have a look in the workshop, see how they'd buggered that up.

He went in through the side door. His things were all anyhow in here too, thrown over and chucked about. It was just malice and mischief, he thought. Did they really think I'd have kept the evidence if I had been the one that topped her? Scotch of the same brand she'd drunk, some of the sleepers she'd washed down with it, a roll of dustbin bags like the one that had been pulled over her head and torso? Or the hard drive from her laptop? Or the jewels and documents they were assuming she'd had before someone killed her for them?

Perching on his filthy work stool, Gavin found himself thinking of Lesley Cameron with sympathy and even sadness, for the first time since the moment he'd come upon her corpse in her house. When that happened he must have stood there gob-smacked for several moments for he'd hardly laid his hands on the plastic in which her upper half was encased when he was hauled roughly away by the cops from the response vehicle, a butch white woman and The Pig himself, his coarse pink face suffused with undisguised triumph. 'Gotcha, you black bastard,' he muttered, twisting Gavin's arm with sadistic energy.

It was only much later that Gavin learnt from the witness statements what had happened in the Cameron house. Lesley had swallowed a double Scotch and a large quantity of tranquillizers. The glass was on its side on the thick pile carpet. Her fingerprints were on it, but so were Gavin's. 'Of course they were,' he'd protested repeatedly. 'I picked

78

the bloody thing up, didn't I?'

'You would say that, wouldn't you?' was his accusers' reply. Or, in the alternative, 'You would have made sure to pick it up, wouldn't you?' They made no attempt to explain the other prints, all too smudged to be unequivocal evidence, though there were also traces of latex on the glass, as well as on the plastic bag in which the drugged woman had vomited and suffocated. Whoever did it had worn gloves.

She must have been interrupted in cooking, as the gas was lit and the tap running. A saucepan containing two eggs was on the work surface, an egg cup and a spoon on a tray. The front door was double-locked and bolted; the back door into the kitchen had only a single Yale. She'd let somebody in through that door, somebody who was wearing Adidas trainers, like Gavin's and a million other people's, somebody with whom she had been willing to have a drink. But there was no bottle of whisky in the house, no roll of dustbin bags, nor a prescription for tranquillizers, nor a bottle of them. The cops said Gavin had brought them all over, but in fact there were other things missing too. The Cameron place had been neatly denuded. The laptop computer had been opened and its hard disk removed. The series of box files labelled in Lesley's neat writing—personal, house, tax, bank accounts, diaries—had all been emptied. She had possessed few books, but those there were had been taken from the shelf and piled on the floor, as though someone had been searching for a document. There were no photograph albums in the house; there was also no money or credit cards in her handbag, nor jewellery in her dressing table. Those valuables, the pearls and rubies neighbours used to see Lesley's old mother wearing, the stash from which she paid the milkman, were supposed to be the motive for Gavin's crime.

He knew that because the interrogators went over and over it on the first day and night before he had the sense to demand a lawyer. 'She knew you, she let you in, you robbed and killed her,' they'd insisted, saying he'd been pretending to be innocent all those days between her death and her discovery. Even the fact that he'd entered the house and found the body was turned against him. He protested, 'I'd never have done that if I'd killed her, I never wanted to, didn't the old biddies explain that they made me do it?' But the police claimed he'd been waiting for an excuse. 'Get in there first, get your prints and forensic traces scattered round in case we found any.'

'But why would I want her photos and documents?' he'd demanded, and later on, demanded why a thief—he—would have chucked the hard disk instead of taking the whole laptop. But of course they had no need to answer. As far as they were concerned, any lack of logic would have been in his behaviour, not their deductions. Knowing he was innocent, Gavin had spent hours worrying away at the facts he knew. There was no sense in it all. Gavin's solicitor had even suggested that Lesley Cameron took her own life since a combination of drink, drugs and a plastic bag was known to be the preferred method of women suicides.

But that did not fit either. She'd invited neighbours to a party and booked a caterer. She'd arranged a bridge four, and ordered the ingredients to make her guests' tea, all stored in Gavin's house because she was already dead when the Tesco driver arrived to deliver them. Information had come in showing that she'd arranged to have her sofa reupholstered, booked a holiday (a Mediterranean cruise) and signed on for afternoon classes in conversational Spanish. She wasn't planning on dying any time soon. So just because he was the handy local outsider they'd made him a scapegoat. Gavin Rayner was accused of being the man who cut her off in her energetic prime.

He knew he hadn't. But even now, nobody else did, for his had not been a triumphant acquittal by a jury which believed in his innocence. He'd only been let out because a judge said there wasn't enough evidence to prove his guilt. He was labelled as a killer who got away with it, and so it was emblazoned in red spray paint on his house. If he opened the up-and-over it would hide the words. But he switched the strip lights on instead. No need to make a show for the nosy neighbours.

Dust lay thickly everywhere. A set of shelves was still in the vice, their glue really hard dry. And there was the half-varnished table top he'd been working on when they came for him, its tidemark a permanent blemish. He could see there had been a destructively thorough search, but some of his work survived intact. Slowly he put a chair on its feet, clicked a table top on to its tripod stand, kicked some slivers of mirror glass under his bench. He'd have to clear this up, even if he left the house as it was. To accept the ruin of all his work would be to acknowledge that The Pig and his mates had finished him.

When he was teased or bullied as a kid, being one of only two black kids in the whole school, his father told him to fight back. 'You're bigger and stronger than those bullies, you can take them on with a hand tied behind your back.' Then Alan Rayner would add, 'But don't tell your mother I said so,' because Kirstie Rayner was a great one for turning the other cheek.

What would they be telling him now, he wondered, if they hadn't smashed up the old Volvo on an autobahn in '91. They'd have believed in his innocence, he knew that, though he wasn't perfectly certain that

Veronica did. And he could guess exactly what they'd be saying. They'd want him to come home, to take refuge in the farmhouse on Exmoor. But that had gone too, it had been sold and turned into a 'country house hotel'. The long low kitchen where Kirstie sat at a pine table with her watercolours, ever ready to drop the brush to hug him, or help him—that had been revamped as a chintzy bar, Pernilla had announced after torturing herself with a night in the old home. The panelled sitting room where they'd played family games of Snakes and Ladders or Ludo when tiny, or Monopoly and l'Attaque later on, and eventually, when Gavin was old enough, bridge and canasta and Scrabble, that was the dining room now with a new conservatory attached. Alan's drawing office had been turned into 'the games room', complete with pool table.

Kirstie would have opened her arms to him, warm, soft, consoling—and always on his side. But even she would not have been able to help him now.

CHAPTER SEVEN

When Fidelis discovered who Mrs Lesley Cameron had been, she was incredulous. Telling Tina and Clodagh about it she said, 'I just don't understand it, how can someone I hardly knew have left anything to me?'

'I suppose there's no doubt she meant you, Fidelis?' Tina asked.

'She only made the will a couple of months before she died and it's all there, my exact details copied out of *Who's Who* with my address and all the letters after my name, in full.'

'She must surely have left things to other people too,' Clodie said.

'That's what's so peculiar, I'm virtually the only legatee.'

'What, you get the whole lot?'

'All except something for a High Court judge and that's equally peculiar because I've known him all his life. Murdo Wood-Wolferstan's mother was—well, you could call her my mentor, Clodie. A role model.'

*　　　*　　　*

Dame Catriona Wood-Wolferstan was in the advanced stage of Alzheimer's disease. In this existence (not what one could call life) she no longer recognized even her son. But he'd been her proud achievement, brought up by her alone before the expression 'single parent' had been invented. When Fidelis was a graduate student and Catriona her tutor, Fidelis had lived in the basement flat of the Wood-Wolferstan house in Primrose Hill, in lieu of rent keeping an eye on the boy; he'd have taken offence at the idea that she was babysitting. They played chess and Monopoly. He always won. They'd had fry-ups together, and gone to the theatre. Murdo went to boarding school at eight and Fidelis moved into her own home. They saw each other less after that. Catriona talked a lot about her brilliant son and scattered pictures of him around her office and home. There had been a brief episode one summer, Fidelis by then in her late thirties, Murdo his early twenties, a 'golden boy' with tanned limbs, sun-bleached hair and startling blue eyes. They'd been picking fruit in the orchard of the weekend cottage Catriona had at the time, Murdo on a ladder, Fidelis holding a wicker basket to catch the ripe fruit. Stretching too far, he'd lost his footing and slithered down, laughing and arms flailing, on top of her. He smelt of apples and honey and sweat. They'd started kissing and touching each other in a kind of daze, Fidelis feeling guilty, which was rare because she never made love with men who weren't free and never conned those who were into thinking she cared for them if she didn't. But any quasi-maternal, quasi-incestuous feelings soon disappeared. Murdo, like Fidelis, seemed to be able to take sex without complication. They never pretended to be in love, or to have any long-term plans.

A short affair of late summer ended with the season. Fidelis went off to do research in

Philadelphia for a year, Murdo got stuck into his arduous career. They both moved on to other things, people, adventures. For long periods of time they didn't meet, keeping up at second hand through Catriona.

Tina said, 'Poor old Catriona. I never met her son, but of course you've talked about him and, Clodie, you know, he's the one Ben wrote an article about for that Internet magazine and they tried to get it suppressed.' Tina's son by her first marriage had been sued for libel twice and once prosecuted for revealing official secrets. Clodie said:

'Oh, he's that one—yes, I do, he's quite a big cheese, I looked him up on the net when Ben was up against him, Marcel Berlins in the *Guardian* was tipping him for the Court of Appeal.'

'He's always been brilliant,' Fidelis said.

'Maybe I'll lay some money on his promotion then,' Tina said. She had been brought up a Methodist, disapproving of casinos and regarding cards as 'the devil's prayer book', but had enthusiastically taken to Internet gambling on the stock market. 'Pity Ben's such a puritan, he could do with some winnings.'

'Lesley Cameron met Murdo when he was Gerry Medlicott's pupil,' Fidelis said.

'Mmm?'

'Her maiden name was Bowhill. Apparently Cameron was her third husband. Lesley

Bowhill was working for the Medlicotts and she went out with Murdo for a bit. He says he can hardly remember her.'

'In his long list?'

Tina, who seemed to have some kind of extra-sensory perception when it came to her friends' love lives, didn't know Fidelis had been on that list herself, as the two women had not known each other at the time, and it was one of the few confidences Fidelis preferred not to share. She said quickly:

'I spoke to Anne—Anne Silversmith she's called these days. I suppose I must have met the girl then myself, or at least seen her, but I can't pin her down. But Anne remembers her very clearly, said she was pretty and lively and full of fun, very good at keeping the kids amused. She taught them to set up practical jokes, apple pie beds and whoopee cushions— not really to Gerry's taste, but the children liked it. They were sorry when she left, except that Anne says Gerry fancied her so it was a relief in a way.'

'Where is Anne these days? Didn't she get married again?' Tina asked.

'Yes, to another of the oldies in the commune, Philip Pugh.'

'D'you mean the writer?' Clodie asked keenly. 'I love her books.'

'She's doing well these days,' Tina said.

'She's always been quite successful, hasn't she?' Fidelis said.

'Not really, her books didn't do much till she had a lucky break with that TV series but now she's big.'

'Back to the subject, tell us what the judge was left,' Clodie said.

'One picture, an engraving of Jerusalem, don't ask me why.'

'Have you asked him?'

'No, there hasn't been a chance, we just had a quick call. He's been in New York for the American Bar Association and now he's in California for a funeral—d'you remember Steve?'

'How could I forget?' Tina had known many of Fidelis's lovers, at least those who had been serious enough to last for more than a few weeks, but in this case she recalled, 'I introduced you in the first place.'

'So you did.'

'Who's Steve?' Clodie was always curious about Fidelis's racy past.

'One of Fidelis's many,' Tina said lightly.

'Oh Fidelis, you've had such an exciting time, all your generation—it's not like that for us, women of my age are all lying out for Mr Right,' Clodie said in pretended despair. 'Unwilling singletons who want to be smug marrieds, that's us.'

'Are you longing to settle down?' Fidelis asked curiously.

'Oh well, you know—the biological clock and all that.' Clodie was twenty-nine and,

Fidelis would have thought, highly attractive.

Tina was looking worried, probably regretting that she couldn't provide what her daughter desired.

'You've plenty of time,' Fidelis said.

'I know, I know. Me and Bridget Jones. So what happened to this Steve anyway?'

'He had AIDS,' Fidelis said. Steve went to San Francisco not long after breaking up with her. They'd parted amicably, as was usual for Fidelis who was seldom sufficiently involved with her men to make a big deal of moving on. Her relationships had been numerous and enjoyable, but she didn't ever seem to fall in love, as most women understood the words. Nor would, now.

Stop it.

She said, 'Back to Mrs Cameron, I've not got a clue why she left Murdo that picture. Any more than I know why she picked on me, because her lawyer said she was going to leave a letter with the will and she never sent him one.'

'I've done that, haven't you? My solicitor said it was called an expression of intent. Mine's upstairs, darling, in case you ever need to know, in the drawer with the certificates and my passport.'

'Mu-um!' Clodie protested.

'Lesley might have written one, but whoever killed her trashed her papers apparently. So that doesn't help.'

89

They stopped talking for a while, all pondering the mystery. They were in Tina's garden, a small patch of flagstones near the Thames on which they were exposing their limbs to the sun in the hope of retaining the Greek tan. It was a rare moment of peace round here. Not only were Tina's own three children all back in London, as well as two stepchildren and some grandchildren, but the business was ever busier. The actual profit came from non-fiction, but Tina's particular babies were obscure, highbrow novels, most of them translated from other languages and all invariably loss-making.

Visits to her home were always punctuated by telephone calls and the chattering of the fax machine, and from time to time Tina would go in because she had to check her emails. But this was the lunch hour. They'd had wine, iced coffee and bagels with lox, delivered by a boy on a scooter from a nearby deli. Pleasant shouts and encouragements floated across the water towards them as a rowing eight and its coach went by, followed slowly by two struggling scullers and a canoe. This little area was prone to flooding when high tide and bad weather combined, but on a fine day it seemed delightful. Clodie had biked over from the friend's flat she had borrowed till starting her new job the following week. Fidelis had come in on her way to Hammersmith via the detour of a full circuit of the M25, as a last fling in the

Jaguar which was being traded in tomorrow for a little car with an automatic gear change. She was to lecture at three o'clock, addressing health service administrators on 'The Bowlby half-century, burden or benefit'.

'How much will you get? Was she well off?' Tina asked.

'Oh no, not once it's all settled, almost nothing. There's a semi in Plowden and a time-expired Honda but she'd run up lots of debts and loans. As far as I'm concerned it's just a nuisance—a house with a ninety per cent mortgage, not exactly a benefit.'

'You don't have to pay the interest, do you?' Tina asked, aghast.

'No, of course not, the solicitor's dealing with it all and as soon as probate's been granted it'll be sold. He says it shouldn't take more than a few weeks now.'

'For which read a few months,' Tina prophesied.

Clodie said, 'I've been thinking, could she have been one of your patients years ago, one of those nutters who get crushes on the doctor?'

'That's an idea,' Tina said. 'But I thought you lot call it transference.'

'Oh Mum, you know how some people fall for their gynaes or surgeons, that's not transference, it's just a straight, silly, unrealistic crush. I felt like that myself when I had my appendix out, remember?'

'Darling, you were eighteen and he was dishy.'

'It was the same thing though, I fantasized that he loved and cared for me, just 'cos we were in such an intimate, no holds barred relationship. Actually I went on dreaming about him for months.'

'Isn't it a bit different with psychiatrists?'

'Doesn't seem to be, does it, Fidelis?'

'No, it happens a lot, and I suppose this woman might have been one of them.'

'Except you said she didn't have children, surely you wouldn't have treated her,' Tina said.

'Oh, I might easily after a miscarriage or abortion, puerperal psychosis is very common then.'

'Post-natal depression,' Tina said wisely.

'Yes, that kind of thing. It could have been years ago before I was at a teaching hospital.'

'Might you remember if you got some clues?'

'Oh Tina, one sees five or six hundred patients every year, and as a consultant I was responsible for nearly ten times that number in the department. I might remember their stories, but not names or even faces, nobody could.'

'And she might have had a different surname at the time, if she was married several times.'

'In any case I never kept private patient

records except for research purposes. If it was after the mid-eighties everything was computerized and one might be able to track down a patient whose first name was Lesley, though difficult unless you knew which year to try, but before that it was card indexes. They've all been put on microfilm now but still it would be a dreadful task.'

'Impossible,' Clodie agreed. 'Just imagine it.'

'So all I remember is seeing her at my book signing at Dillons.'

'It's so maddening, I came to that but I can't picture her there at all,' Clodie said discontentedly.

Tina waited to speak till a pleasure boat, festooned in streamers and with multiple sound amplification, had passed, before saying, 'You'd have thought she'd have had some relations somewhere.'

'Mum!'

'Oh, Fidelis, I'm sorry.'

Alone in the world from the age of three, Fidelis had long since forgotten to mind that she had no family or relations, and was certainly not about to be offended by Tina now. 'Don't be silly.'

'I was tactless.'

'Nonsense. Anyway, the lawyers didn't know if Lesley Cameron had any family of her own, apparently she walked in off the street to make her will and they never saw her again. She did tell them she'd inherited the house from her mother who died not all that long before her. But she didn't mention anyone else, though it's possible some family claimant might turn up out of the blue, not that they'd get much if they do but God knows I don't want to be involved.'

Tina said, 'Isn't there some way you can just say that?'

'Yes, it's called a disclaimer, I must see about it, I ought to have done it right away, when I first heard about this, but somehow I never got it together.'

'You had other things on your mind. Here, finish the wine.' Tina poured the last drops into Fidelis's glass. A large tabby cat jumped down from the garden wall, walked suspiciously round the garden and left through its gate.

Clodie said, 'She could have left it to a cats' home. People do, you know, I read about a dog in Florida that inherited millions and gets driven round in a limo all day.'

'Are you sure it's still the same dog?' Tina asked.

'I'm not going to end up with much, as a matter of fact, but I'll pass what there is on to some good cause myself, I wouldn't feel happy about profiting from a random stranger's madness,' Fidelis said.

'Wait a while before you do that, there might be some logic in it after all. Like, for instance, she could have thought you'd use it for important research. Couldn't you find out if she was interested in your work?' Clodie suggested.

'God knows how I'd ever discover that now. But she certainly wasn't professionally involved, she was a novelist.'

'Was she?' Tina asked, coming to attention. 'Under what name?'

'All I know is what the lawyer said, her copyrights were in the name of Lesley Bowhill, but nobody seems to have heard of her. I asked Anne if she knew, she might have read Lesley's books, what with both of them being crime writers, but she didn't remember any.'

'My dear,' Tina told her, 'very few novelists read novels, specially not the kind they write themselves.'

'I couldn't find her on the net either.'

'Ah,' Tina sighed knowingly. 'Small publisher, library sales, short print runs, quick oblivion and a lifetime of disappointment, it drives people to despair.'

'I certainly assumed she'd committed suicide when they told me how she died, specially as she had a cancer. Metastasized. I suppose she must have known.'

'How did she . . .'

'The lawyer said it was Scotch, tablets and a plastic bag.'

'The most common method,' Clodie said.

'Among women,' Fidelis confirmed,

blushing slightly and not meeting her friend's eyes, so she did not notice the identical expression on Tina's and Clodie's faces, both anxiously hearing the words Fidelis was not uttering. She went on after a pause, 'But as a matter of fact she didn't do it herself, she actually seems to have been murdered.'

'No! Seriously?'

'The man they charged got off on a technicality and you know what it means when the police say they're not looking for anyone else.'

'Who was it?'

'One of her neighbours. Her house had been ransacked, all her papers and computer records gone, as well as any valuables in the house, but nothing was ever found and now it never will be.'

'But surely—'

'You know what happens when the police give up on a case—if they have no hope of finding the perpetrator, or they're sure they did but he got off.'

'I suppose they close the file,' Tina said.

'No, never closed if unsolved, it's just marked NFA. No further action.'

'But Fidelis,' Clodie interrupted, 'there's new Home Office advice now, since you retired perhaps. Chief Constables are expected to run a "cold case review", go through all the unsolved crimes on their books, a cop I had coffee with at the hospital was telling me.

They're using retired officers. I might get involved, actually, I told this guy I'd been doing psychological profiling in Massachusetts and he said they could use me here.'

'It doesn't sound as if they need you on this case though,' Tina said in a finalizing voice.

'Got to go.' Clodie put on her helmet, its yellow startling against her scarlet hair and lime green shirt, and wheeled her bike out on to the tow path. Tina waved and then began to pile their plates on the tray. Fidelis stretched across with the bagel box.

'You're still so brown, Fidelis, I wish I didn't always fade so quickly.'

'We've only been back a little while.'

'And you're still shaking.'

Without replying, Fidelis thrust her hands into her pockets and bent her feet out of sight under the chair. Tina would be worried and it was good of her not to say so. Clodie, being a medic herself, would have seen, recognized and said nothing, even to her own mother.

Fidelis knew the predictable process whereby people assimilated traumatic news, the course from despair to acceptance, and she'd even written a short paper on the subject many years before. She also knew she'd need to dump the fact that she had a degenerative, incurable disease on her friends sooner or later; they had, after all, lived through her love affairs, her professional crises and all the other agonies and triumphs of a long life. But in all these relationships the support had never been exactly mutual. Fidelis was the principal adviser, sympathizer and confidante. Learning to lean was going to be another new part of the process.

CHAPTER EIGHT

Murdo and I planned exactly how we'd live one day when we were married. I wasn't a bra-burning women's libber, I wanted to spend my time looking after him and he often said that was one of the things he liked about me because there'd never be room for two high-flyers under one roof. All I wanted was a rambling house in the country, L-shaped, with low-beamed ceilings and an orchard outside. I wanted kids then too though I'd quite gone off the idea of teacher training college, which was just as well, as I don't think Anne would have given me a very good reference after a few months of having me as her mother's help. And now I don't regret not having children, I really don't, though for a while it seemed like the end of the world when I had that awful late miscarriage.

But back in those early days we thought we'd have four or even five allowing for one accident (Anne Medlicott always said that accidents happen in the best regulated families). He was going to earn enough to pay for a full-time nanny and they were going to be called after characters in his favourite books, Natasha and Emma, Horatio and Justine. Tolstoy, Austen, C.S. Forester—who wrote about Justine though? I must look it up. I did know. But that's about the only thing I have forgotten, everything else is still clear in my imagination, we were going to have dogs, golden labradors—though I don't like pets really—and we'd have kept ponies for the children but not cats because they made him sneeze. I'd design a dreamy garden and do tapestry on winter evenings, and make jam out of our own fruit and bake cakes and dry flowers on hooks on the kitchen ceiling.

Their house in Sussex is complete in every detail, it conforms to my dream though someone else is living it, I've looked through the windows when they're safely out of the way in London. They've got the dresser with blue and white china and a forest-green Aga with four ovens, and a scrubbed pine table with chairs for twelve round it. Their sitting room has red and cream chintz and photos in silver frames on the piano and through the letter flap I could see the portrait of his grandfather in the hall. They have got the lot. And a four-storey terrace house in Islington. She's something high-powered in the City, and their children are called George, Jack and Rosie. The boys are at Eton, the girl's at

Wycombe Abbey.

It's not right.

It shouldn't be allowed.

Funny to find myself writing those two phrases, they used to make me so cross when Keith kept saying them, spitting the words out of his thin mouth like venomous pellets when he read *The Times.* Disgusting, outrageous, country going to the dogs. It didn't seem like that to me, I used to read the news jealously, wishing I was there at the marches or raves. They were all having such fun.

It was the Greenham peace camp that was the last straw, listening to Keith talking about what he'd do to those harridans. Dragging them off by their messy hair was only the beginning, followed by burning their benders. Not that I had much time for them myself, it was beyond me to imagine being the kind of person who could live like that or let herself look like them, but listening to Keith spitting out his venom I could hardly believe that the elderly bigot saying those words was the sexy man I'd married. He'd changed so much. It should have been a good life for me, in my twenties and pretty, with servants galore and nothing to do all day except play tennis and swim at the English club, and bridge in the evenings. Dinner dances, coffee mornings and all that, everything expats can find to pass the time in a foreign country. Of course it was the wrong environment for an aspiring novelist, surrounded by philistine oil company executives, we didn't know people who even read books, let alone wrote them.

Keith hadn't taken much notice of my scribbling away in a corner, and I don't think he was ever a bit proud of me for doing it, not even when the first book was published and the local English-language paper ran a profile of me, printing the photo he'd once said made me look like Jackie Kennedy. Actually I'm not sure he even read the book. He said the cover was a bit soppy, but I didn't have any say about that and wasn't very pleased myself, with the busty blonde and a handsome dark man, it looked a bit cheap. But at the time I was just so thrilled to have shown I could be as good as Anne Medlicott. I didn't talk much about that time in my life, so her name wouldn't have meant much to Keith. He'd never met her and wouldn't have been impressed by what she did either. The only times he said 'Well done, old girl' to me were when I came second in the bridge tournament and was chosen to play in the mixed doubles with the area manager—we lost.

When I was ill I came home to Mum, and her family doctor and the variable benefits of outpatients. Keith wasn't at all sympathetic, ashamed more like. He just thought I should pull myself together, didn't believe in hormones or depression and sort of thought it was my fault he wouldn't be getting a son to boast about. Well, OK, so I shouldn't have gone riding in the desert that day, but who on earth would have refused when the ruler's son turned up with two white horses and servants following in the stretch limo with the lunch? And for Keith to suggest the baby mightn't even have been his—well, anyone would have had a nervous breakdown after that.

Whatever made me think Paul could be Mr Right I can't now imagine. Actually, to be honest, I don't believe I did think so. But I didn't want to go back to Keith and I certainly didn't want to stay on with Mum. Unfortunately Aberdeen turned out to seem quite as remote from swinging London as the Gulf. And at least Keith had been faithful to me. No, Paul was a bad bet. Oddly enough, I don't remember all that much about him and Aberdeen, except the details I put into *Tiger Cat*. I read it again the other day. It's good, a gripping tale, I'll never understand why it didn't do better. The publisher's reader sent a personal note to tell me the plot was highly ingenious and the second novel was always the most difficult and that was a hurdle I'd cleared triumphantly. It didn't mean anyone reviewed it though, except for a little note in the local weekly. I kept buying the Sunday papers, week after week, my heart racing when I saw there was a column of crime-fiction reviews and plummeting like a stone when I didn't see my name. Why didn't they take any notice, when I think of the other crap that gets reviewed? There must be something about me, something that makes them think I'm insignificant, not important enough to consider. They'd have noticed my books all right if my name had been Wood-Wolferstan.

Maybe I should have stayed with him after all, hitched myself to his rising star in spite of what happened. Or I should have had the courage to bring him down to earth instead of letting him off. I just disappeared out of his life. Does he ever wonder if I'll tell on him one day? Has he read my novels as they came out, anxiously wondering every time if this one was based on fact?

CHAPTER NINE

When Fidelis rang, Murdo pressed her to come to dinner. He opened the door and hugged her enthusiastically. Like faint, faded scent on a garment, there came a whiff of ancient intimacy as he met her eyes. He said, 'Come on down, Gemma's not back yet.'

She followed him down to the basement kitchen, holding tightly on to the rail of the steep and narrow stairs. 'Here, Fidelis, you liked this claret last time.' He put a glass in her hand and went on creating an elaborate meal, moving round the stainless steel kitchen wrapped in a starched white apron like a professional chef.

Murdo had put on some weight recently but Fidelis thought it suited him, lending dignity to his fair, narrow features. She noted that he was increasingly bald, the top of his head shiny and pink. He always looked like a man who had his requisite dosage of sunshine, spending New Year in Barbados, Easter in Andalucia and a summer month in Tuscany. A prosperous, well-cared-for eminence. And if, like other such men, he had dingy secrets or a darker side, inadmissible desires or unacceptable diversions, she needn't know.

They talked about his mother, still in her own home but with relays of women doing round-the-clock nursing. 'It's going to clean her out if she lasts much longer, but everyone thinks she'd be miserable if we uprooted her now. And we don't need her money, fortunately, the bonuses Gemma gets these days have become positively indecent, they make my judicial salary seem like pocket money.'

'I know you took quite a cut when you left the bar.'

'Now Gemma earns the cash and I provide the dignity. She thinks it's a fair exchange.'

'Is she coming home?'

'Hope so. If not we'll have to eat all this between us.'

Fidelis asked about the children. 'Not so

good, actually,' he said. 'I wouldn't tell anyone else, Fidelis, but Rosie's struggling academically which makes Gemma furious, but the real problem's that Jack's been getting into trouble, embarrassing—it's not easy, in my position, if the tabloids get hold of it—'

'Drugs?'

'Yup. You know the headlines, if it's a judge's son. This job—you should see me driving along, never over seventy—and not a drop of wine when we go out either. One has to be so careful.'

'Above suspicion.'

'That's right, and the lightest hint of scandal's enough. Lucky I kept my nose clean when I was a student, even youthful indiscretions can bugger everything up these days.'

'Which brings me neatly to what I wanted to ask you about—those legacies from Lesley Cameron.'

'I heard she'd left you everything when they delivered the picture for me. I never knew you knew her,' Murdo said.

'I didn't, the whole thing's a mystery.'

'What, an unknown benefactor?'

'Not much benefaction, really. But did you know her?'

'We went out together for a while, that's all, years ago, when I was a student. It wasn't serious.'

'On either side?'

'Not at all.'

'She might have thought it was, though.'

'Oh, Fidelis, it was just one of those summer holiday affairs, that's all. We never met again afterwards—the only other time I saw her was when she made a scene in Parliament Square—in fact, you were there. D'you remember, two years ago, you came to the breakfast.'

'I don't remember any scene.'

'You'd probably gone inside before she started shouting my name, it could have been quite embarrassing, but luckily I got inside before she could do anything else. Menopausal, I suppose.'

They heard the front door slam.

'Hi, darling.' Gemma's heels came clicking quickly along the passage and down. 'Fidelis, how nice, I'd quite forgotten you were coming, sorry I'm so late. God what a day.' She hooked her Armani taupe jacket on the bottom banister and poured herself a glass of wine. 'Oh darling, you are good, you've done it all.' She stood by the long, shiny table. 'But let's use the other . . .' She took the pepper and salt from the table and replaced them with a silver set, removed the paper napkins and put out white linen ones.

'I never get it quite right,' Murdo murmured ruefully.

'He cooks well though,' Gemma said. She carried a honey-coloured wooden bowl of shiny carved apples and pears from the

106

sideboard and placed it decoratively in the middle of the table.

'Pretty,' Fidelis said.

'Murdo gave it to me for my birthday last year—or was it the year before?'

Murdo gave each of them a plate of seared fish and griddled asparagus and they ate appreciatively.

'Fidelis was talking about that woman who left me a picture,' Murdo said.

'The one who rang up once, ages ago now—she sounded quite bonkers,' Gemma said.

'Did you speak to her, Murdo?' Fidelis asked.

'Did I, darling?'

'You hung up on her as far as I remember, it was ages ago. We were in the country—was that the time we had the number changed? I didn't realize she was the one the print came from. I took it down to Sussex, but I don't think we really want to hang it,' Gemma said.

'Did you know she wrote detective stories?' Fidelis asked.

'Now you come to mention it, I think she sent me one once, but I never read it,' Murdo replied.

Fidelis said, 'Have you still got the book? It would say Lesley Bowhill on the jacket.'

'No way, not here,' Gemma said. 'You've seen the serried ranks of biographies and law reports in Murdo's shelves, he never reads novels even on the beach, do you, darling?

Even his old Ian Flemings are still there at Catriona's place. Oh God, don't you dread having to clear that place out? I have nightmares about it.' But Gemma must have realized it wasn't very tactful to refer to what would happen after Murdo's mother, Fidelis's old friend, eventually died. She segued smoothly into their plans for selling the time share near Marbella and looking for a villa in Umbria. It would be fun for the children to bring their friends, didn't Fidelis agree?

CHAPTER TEN

In the end Gavin had stayed in his own house for the time being, sleeping that first night on the floor, as rough as a tramp or housebreaker. He felt dazed by what had happened, by what he had learnt in prison about the underside of modern life and by his experience of falsehoods and injustice. That was not the world the Rayners taught him about or that his previous life had shown him.

But he knew he couldn't live here for long. He might be innocent in the eyes of the law, but not of his neighbours. They used the traditional methods to indicate their hostility. The older women averted their eyes, younger ones made acid, audible remarks and children catcalled. Men's attitudes were more overtly aggressive. He was scared to confront them, knowing only too well who would be blamed and punished for any aggro in the street. Even the formerly-friendly Singh family in the neighbourhood minimart made it clear they didn't want Gavin's custom. As for the malicious attacks on his house: he couldn't tell who wielded the sprays of paint, who had manure dumped across his driveway or who was throwing stones. All he knew was that they all thought he'd killed their neighbour and got away with it—and there was no way he was ever going to be able to show it wasn't true.

He'd been existing like an animal in his rank lair when Veronica arrived. He heard her clear, cut-glass voice out in the street, though he had not heard the remark to which she was responding. 'I advise you not to repeat that statement, it's defamatory and I shall have no hesitation in suing.'

He opened the front door for her and when she was safely inside muttered that she'd better not annoy them. 'It'll only make more trouble.'

'Nonsense. What trouble, anyway?'

'Just little things, there's nothing to be done about it.'

'Your neighbours? Are they bothering you?' Veronica's eyes flashed, her muscles tensed. 'I'll see about that,' she promised.

'No, Vee, leave it, please, it'll only make it worse if you chuck your weight about.'

'The law's there to protect you,' she said, but dropped her gaze. They both knew it wasn't true now, if it ever had been.

'How was Turkey?'

'Exhausting. I could murder—I mean I could do with a coffee,' she said. But Gavin had used up the last dry scraping of an ancient jar of instant. Going briskly from room to room, Veronica nodded as though it was only what she'd expected to find. 'This just isn't on, honestly Gavin, it's worse than prison, how can you be living like this? I suppose you've been scared to face people, it takes some ex-cons like that.'

'Am I an ex-con?'

'Not technically, obviously, not if you were never convicted, but the syndrome's the same.' Veronica had never minced her words, or for that matter her thoughts. She'd always believed in confronting things, and people.

'It might be easier if I had been.'

'Stop it, Gavin, don't talk like that. Now come on, we're going to go shopping, we'll get some food and stuff to clean the place up with.'

'No, what's the point, I'm not staying.'

'You're here, aren't you?'

'Not for long.'

'Well, till you move on you need some stuff. Unless you want to come to my place now I'm back?' Veronica lived in a white space in a converted warehouse on the river. The room

110

had nothing in it that was not essential for life: a white bed which was also the one soft seat, a white table and some stacking chairs and a wall of doors that opened on to fitted cubby holes, one containing a computer and its peripherals, one with a sink and microwave, one a shower, one a lavatory. Her offer was self-sacrificing, not to say heroic.

'I won't do that, thanks.'

'Come on then.' As his drive was blocked, Veronica had parked her Mercedes sports across it beside the putrefying manure. 'Lucky it's winter,' was all she said. They drove to a hypermarket, anonymous in the uninterested crowd. On the way back she suddenly said, 'Whatever happened to your van?'

'I s'pose it's still at some police pound. But it'll have been trashed when they searched it.'

She reached into the glove compartment for a miniature tape recorder and said into it, 'Message for Mr Weinstock at Butler Weinstock and Patel. Query re Mr Rayner's van, also other property removed from his premises.' Flicking it off she went on, 'Meanwhile you need wheels.'

'Have to sell the house first. Slight cash flow problem.'

'I'll stake you. Let's do it now.'

Two hours and some sibling arguments later, they had bought an M-reg BMW 3-series saloon. Veronica thought he'd do better with a bigger estate but Gavin wanted to make a point by driving 'black man's wheels'.

'Even with Julie in the van I was always being stopped, they don't like blacks having cars,' he told her.

'Gavin, I know you've got some excuse for paranoia but there are limits. That's got to be crap.'

'Yeah? How many times did you have to show your licence and insurance in the last twelve months?'

'Never.'

'In that last year before—you know—I had to show mine eleven times.'

'Well, it's unacceptable, you should have told me about it then. If it happens again, you get on to me straight away, understand?'

Back in the dreary house Veronica was insistent on doing a proper clean. 'It's disgusting, you can't go on like this.'

'What's it matter, I'm not staying.'

'You can't stay in this mess for one more night. Come on, Gavin, hold this bag open.'

She'd bought a jumbo package of exactly the same type of plastic bags as the one in which Lesley Cameron's last breath had been stifled, heavyweight and black, with a yellow drawstring. She'd bought some Scotch too. Gavin didn't suspect Veronica of rubbing it in, she was far too practical and focused on the present to remember any tactless associations from the past.

It was hard physical labour, packing the

bags with the tattered remains of Gavin's old life. It was even harder scraping and scrubbing at the accumulated filth. But even that wasn't enough for Veronica. When they had made the house just about habitable she said, 'Come on, let's get going on the workshop.'

'You're a slave driver.'

'No, just someone who can't stand mess. Once it's sorted we can get an estate agent round too, no point in waiting. The one bright spot in all this is that the house price will have rocketed. Come on, will you, Gavin? Can you open the door and get some light in here?'

'I don't want people looking in.'

'Don't be so neurotic. We'll never sort this stuff unless we spread it out a bit.'

In full daylight the once pleasant-looking and smelling workshop seemed more ruined than anything.

'God, this is unbelievable, it's so depressing in here,' Veronica said. 'I'll make sure a bill gets sent to the police authority, they are obliged to pay for clearing up their own mess.'

'Christ, Vee, that's all I need. Do get your head round the idea, they've marked me now, the only thing for me is to get out and keep my head down.'

'I never thought you'd be so wet, little brother.'

'Maybe that's 'cos I'm not really your brother. Blood will out and all that.'

With firm deliberation Veronica put down

113

the brush and bucket. She stripped off the yellow rubber gloves and the striped apron she had bought that afternoon. Then she stepped towards Gavin and put her arms round him. She was taller and thinner, more muscular and toned, than her mother had been, but her cheek against his was as soft, her embrace comforting. It was the first time anyone had touched him in friendship or affection since a one-night stand the Christmas before his arrest. When he was inside he used to think the first thing he'd do on getting out was find a girl, any girl, but now it came to the moment he'd lost the heart for it.

Carnation-scented, soft and smooth, she stood in sexless affection, rocking a little backwards and forwards and crooning the comfort they had both grown up with. 'There there, never mind, it'll be all right . . .' He hadn't cried for years, till now. 'Don't worry, I'm here now, it'll be OK . . .'

'You ought to be ashamed of yourself, going with that blackie, d'you know what he is?' A raucous screech from outside, a harpy-like woman hissing venom. 'Black bastard, murderer—'

Before Veronica could whirl into battle for him Gavin had slammed the door down in front of her. There was no point in trying to make her understand. Self-confidence and security were ingrained into every inch, the one derived from her professional status, the

114

other from an unthreatened, loved childhood. 'I can't explain, Vee, you'll never get it.'

'I can't let her get away with it, you've got to let me—why won't you?'

'Best take no notice.'

'But it seems like running away.'

'I am going to run away. They can ride me out of town on a rail for all I care, I'm not staying here.'

'Better get on, then. Is any of this stuff worth trying to salvage?'

They made a pile for burning in the back garden. It turned out that the cherry wood table would be all right with a bit of work and so would some of the dressing-table mirrors. But the chest of drawers and the dining chairs were matchwood. Under all the other stuff they came across a hall-chest he'd been restoring for Pernilla's mother-in-law and the writing-box Lesley Cameron had brought over. It was a nice little item, walnut with ash inlay, with some tiny drawers, two silver-topped crystal ink-wells, a fold-out, sloping surface for writing and a rack of little compartments for papers and envelopes. He wiped the dust off with his sleeve. It was in good condition, he remembered being surprised at the time that she'd wanted anything done and wondering if she was inventing jobs for him and if so why.

'This was hers,' he said.

'Whose?'

'The woman who—Mrs Cameron. She wanted me to renovate it.'

'It's quite a nice piece.' Veronica opened and closed the little partitions and drawers, twiddled a screw and lifted the flap of the writing surface. 'She kept her spare floppy disks in it.'

'You'd have thought they'd have found it and taken it away when they searched.'

'I wouldn't have known this bit opened if I hadn't seen this kind of thing before, Gran had one just like it, d'you remember?'

'I don't have to pass it on to the police, do I?'

'God no, this is part of Lesley Cameron's estate. Not much of an incentive to murder, I'd have thought, but I suppose one can trust the police to have investigated the people with a motive. These houses are worth something.'

'What do I do with this then? Shall I just take it over to her place?'

'I don't think anyone's there, I noticed it's all shuttered up when I arrived. Let me take it, Gavin, I'll find out who her lawyer was, or her executor, and pass it on. You needn't worry. I'll deal with it.'

CHAPTER ELEVEN

It had been very quiet in Fidelis's home since d-day—d for diagnosis—though in normal life her home resounded to music. When planning the new flat, discussing the interior arrangements with the architect who now lived two floors up, the placing of speakers had been a fundamental consideration.

Fidelis's move into the communal house had not met with her other friends' approval or encouragement.

'I can see why you want to spend all the loot you got from the new book but you'll never feel private.'

'Nonsense. It's just a block of flats with friendly neighbours, anyway, you've been telling me for years that I shouldn't be isolated.'

But Tina had long since given up the idea that her friend might commit to sharing her life. She'd once told Clodie who told Fidelis that you couldn't expect someone to commit herself to anyone, when her first experience of love and trust had ended so brutally at the age of three. 'Mum thinks you're insecure, Fidelis,' Clodie said. 'But I told her not to analyse an analyst.'

So now Tina merely said, 'And a *garden*, Fidelis? You hate gardening.'

'I thought I'd like to try it, now I've retired—'

'Retired! You're working harder than ever.'

'Now I've stopped going out to work, the idea of growing things seems quite attractive. Roses in tubs, I thought, and lots of climbing plants,' Fidelis had replied, visualizing a statue peering from a leaf-shaded corner, and a dining table under the stars.

'And all those rooms—whatever will you fill them with?'

'I shan't. It's going to be sparse and shiny.'

'You—minimalist? You won't like that!'

But she did. The floors were wood, the bathrooms mosaic and steel, the windows had shutters and no curtains, all in contrast to the colourful cosiness of the Hampstead flat. This one had more space, containing a large sitting room with folding doors into a study on the ground floor, and an even larger kitchen-dining-sitting room downstairs. There was a bedroom and a bathroom on each floor. Fidelis had a state-of-the-art sound system installed, with speakers in every room. The garden, dug up and put down again by a fashionable designer, had built-up beds overflowing with jostling shrubs. Roses rambled through greenery in gigantic tubs. The terrace was paved with honey-coloured stone slabs. Everything was on a scale of elegance and expense that Fidelis never even dreamed of during her salaried life.

118

She'd had just about a year to enjoy this once-unimagined lavishness and to realize that she was seeing less of the friends who were under the same roof than she used to in the days when they had to make formal arrangements to meet. Now she was lucky to run into one of them in the laundry room or at the newsagent in Elgin Crescent.

Not much help from that quarter, then, even if she could have brought herself to ask for it. For the building's elegant details had turned into potential booby traps. There were smooth stone steps up to the front door and down to Fidelis's kitchen and garden. With increasing infirmity, she would find them unnegotiable barriers. The polished floors would be slippery, the sharp edges and hard surfaces unforgiving, the isolation would become frightening.

How strange, the transition from health, or temporary illness, to a permanent state of knowing she'd never be better. Only now did the woman who'd spent her life dealing with sick people fully understand what it was that divides the ill from the healthy in a society which could alleviate the minor aches and pains that must have plagued its ancestors. Healthy people think it is normal to feel well. Fidelis had to teach herself that it wasn't.

It was a hard lesson, not one a doctor was happy to learn. But come on, she adjured herself, you didn't go into medicine to make

119

everyone well, you chose it because it was just plain interesting.

She remembered it well. Or maybe what she was remembering was her foster mother telling the tale.

A good, kind, selfless woman she'd been, devoted to the clever child like the duck to its cygnet, admiring, uncomprehending and always encouraging. Fidelis was eight or nine and had a badly infected green and painful lesion on her leg. Laid up on the couch in that hot little front room with the high-banked coal fire (coal being cheap in the valleys where it came from) she had been enumerating all the body fluids she could think of.

'Pus, blood, sweat, number one, wee wee, earwax, snot—'

'That's not a nice thing to say, dearie, call it phlegm,' her foster mother corrected.

'Phlegm. Mucus, spit, that watery stuff that comes when you've got a cut—what else, Auntie Bron?'

'Maybe you'll be a nurse when you're grown up, then you'd know.'

'No, I'm going to be a doctor.'

She'd heard her words repeated that evening. 'Well, why not, why shouldn't she be a doctor, she's clever enough.' A rumble from Uncle Dai and then Bronwen's voice again. 'Maybe it's in her blood, her own da could be a doctor, lots of those people are. Were.'

That's what I'll be then, my real dad will be

proud of me when he comes, Fidelis told herself. It was the last year of the war in Europe. Grown-ups knew the truth by then but they'd kept it from the children, though it was a while since they'd promised Fidelis that the unknown, unimaginable parents who had shipped her off on a *Kindertransport* would come and find her when the war was over.

By the time Fidelis started her training it was the human mind that fascinated her more than the mechanics. But it was those body fluids, the oozing green pus that had started it, not any urge to heal the world.

It was the silence which emphasized that everything felt somehow, indefinably *wrong. As* a rule Fidelis had music playing all the time. During any previous illness she had listened continuously to requiems—Mozart, Brahms, Verdi—Bach cantatas, one after another and over and over again, hymns about forgiveness and salvation whose explicit message meant nothing to a lifelong atheist.

But never before had the future loomed before her like a nightmare.

Don't worry, her Welsh foster mother used to say in the small hours with a screaming Fidelis pressed against her plump winceyette bosom, never you mind Fiddle dearie, bad dreams never come true. But Fidelis knew better than that now. If, for instance, you're the Jewish mother of a small child in Dresden in 1939. Whoever Fidelis's mother had been, and she had never been traced, her nightmares were played out in real life. Thinking about her birth parents' fate had always been a sign of unhappiness or rare ill-health. Stop it, she told herself, snap out of it.

Physician, heal thyself, soul-doctor, soothe your soul. Occupy your brain, take your mind off the one person whom she had never scrutinized with the insight that was both innate and an acquired professional technique —herself.

And what a bore you are, my girl, she muttered, recognizing her own first step on to the path that led to acceptance or resignation, or to the decision neither to accept nor resign herself and take her own way out instead.

Almost tentatively she turned to the collection of compact discs and reached for the sound to suit her mood. Could she bear the emotion evoked by Schubert? By Mahler? Was she ready for the might of a late Beethoven quartet? No, if there was to be music again it could only be Bach; and in thinking so, Fidelis reminded herself of what he had endured, dying not after gradual deterioration but after three months of acute, dreadful agony resulting from a botched cataract operation performed by an English surgeon, whose technique included rubbing the eye with a brush and draining half a teacup of blood from the eyeball and socket. The surgeon's name was John Taylor and presumably the Christian Johann Sebastian forgave him. At least, Fidelis thought, I have nothing and nobody to blame or to forgive.

She put on a disc of the St Matthew Passion—a revelation when heard aged eight at a Good Friday concert in a Methodist chapel in South Wales and still the supreme, the only *Desert Island* sound, as indeed she had chosen for the radio programme of that name.

Hearing it induced an immediate improvement. The weighty lump—as much felt as if it were not just a metaphor—which had been fixed somewhere in the pit of her stomach was beginning to dissolve.

There was a lot of work she should be doing, articles waiting to be written or polished, a lecture and a conference contribution to prepare, but her mind still edged skittishly away from them. However, now that she felt able to face it, there was some self-interested investigation to be done. Suddenly she felt a little spurt of academic excitement, a reminder of what life was meant to be like. This would be an on-going research project with all the primary material permanently available. She would track the physical and psychological progress of a deteriorating condition. Depending on how long she stuck it out, this work, being by a patient who was also a medic, would be a useful contribution for the profession. It might also be, literally, a lifesaver for Fidelis.

It was also a long time since she'd turned on her computer. Even cyberbridge had lost its appeal in the last weeks. Opening her word processing program she created several new files: 1. Diagnosis 2. Prognosis 3. Treatment 4. Subjective experience. In the last she wrote *July, 2000, physical: left hand no longer capable of using keyboard, handwriting increasingly difficult. Mental: coming to terms.* Then she clicked on her favourite search engine, typed in, one-handed, the name of her disease, and began to read.

She had pressed replay several times as the repeated music watered her parched spirit, the sunlight had swung from the left to the right of the room, when the doorbell rang. Getting up stiffly, stretching her cramped back, Fidelis prudently checked who was there before admitting an unknown but clearly harmless visitor, a tall, self-confident woman with bright blonde hair in a loose knot and City clothes, a dark suit and tight white T-shirt, with a lot of leg showing and high heels. She came in and rested the bulky package she had been embracing on the marble-topped hall table.

Having several times been threatened by mad, bad patients, Fidelis had time to think, perhaps it's a bomb, to weigh up the embarrassment of treating it as such against the destruction it could wreak, and even to wonder if that might be the solution to her problems, before her visitor took a small card from a black tote bag and held it out. Fidelis read, *V. J. Rayner, MA, LLB.* In tiny print in the bottom corner it said, *Paxton Hardman. Solicitors,* with an address in the City.

'So sorry, this thing's heavier than I expected. You are Dr Berlin?'

'Yes.'

'Oh good—this is yours then.'

'What is it?'

'It's called a writing-box, I think, Georgian or Victorian, it belonged to Mrs Cameron.'

'I don't quite understand, surely the solicitors dealing with her estate are called—'

'Whitaker Pritchard, I know, but it seemed best for my brother to return it directly to you as he was repairing it for her when she died.'

'Well, thank you—come in, put it in here.' Fidelis led the way into her sitting room.

'Thank you. Wonderful sound.' They both listened to the disc's closing bars, and then Veronica asked, 'Which recording is it?'

'It's John Eliot Gardiner.'

'I sang it at the City of London Festival a few years ago when I was in the Bach Choir.'

'Oh, how I envy you,' Fidelis said sincerely. 'I auditioned for it once but sight reading was my Waterloo.'

'I had to give it up, I kept missing rehearsals when I was abroad or working late.'

The last notes resonated through the high rooms. Fidelis had chucked most of her old furniture, many of her pictures and all gaudy draperies when she moved. Visitors to the new flat found their eyes drawn past a polished wood floor and cream sofas and curtains to a few spots of brilliance. There was a Philipson Fidelis had bought in the sixties at the Edinburgh Festival, a tiny Joan Eardley oil presented by a grateful patient, a new abstract of geometrical blocks of colour by Barnes-Graham, a Terry Frost mobile in the window and, above the marble mantelpiece, a painting of cherries in a blue bowl.

'Is that picture a Perdita Whitchurch?' Veronica asked.

'Yes, I bought it before her prices rocketed.'

'It's lovely.'

There was a silence. Then Veronica spoke in a rush, as though she had to get it out before her nerve failed.

'Look, I brought the cabinet over myself because I wanted—that is, can I ask you something?'

'Of course.'

'Did you—was she—was Mrs Cameron a great friend of yours?'

'I didn't know her at all, I haven't got the faintest idea why she left me anything. Is that what you were wondering?'

'Yes, because—oh gosh.' This high-flying professional was obviously not the kind of person to flounder and flush but she seemed to be highly embarrassed. 'The thing is, I know who you are, I looked you up.' She muttered

126

something inaudible; all Fidelis could make out were the words 'my brother'.

'Is something wrong with your brother?'

'The thing is . . .' She changed tack, and asked a question in a legal counsel's measured tone. 'Tell me, do you believe in nurture or nature, Dr Berlin?'

'Oh, nurture, as far as behaviour's concerned at least,' Fidelis said positively.

'Not in inherited or racial behaviour characteristics?'

'No—or at least, only the most superficial ones. Appearance or to some extent intelligence, perhaps even such abilities as music, but otherwise, definitely not. Why d'you ask? Is this about your brother?'

'Yes, because he's the one . . .' She paused and took a deep breath. 'I'll start again. My brother was accused of murdering Mrs Cameron, but he's been acquitted and now I don't know how to help him. His neighbours are getting used to him being around again, but he's so depressed, he can't be bothered to make anything or look for somewhere else to live or apply to the courts for access to his son or anything. It's simply beyond me, I'm at my wits' end.'

'It's a matter for his GP.'

'I know, but he won't go.'

'I could give you the name of a specialist who might be able to help.'

'But the thing is, I've got this awful idea . . .'

She paused again, and Fidelis, resigning herself, said:

'Would you like a drink?'

'No, I'm fine, thanks, and I know I shouldn't be laying this on you, but—well, I know you're an expert on the effects of upheavals in someone's early life, so I wondered if you—I mean, your professional advice, you'd bill me naturally, but he'd have to not know I'd asked you—but the fact is I'm at my wits' end.'

'I'm afraid I don't quite understand,' Fidelis told her, at which the other woman burst into tears.

'God, I'm so sorry,' she gulped, fumbling in her big bag and failing to find a hanky, 'I've never done this before,'—sob, gulp—'I'm not that kind of person.'

Fidelis was reminded of Lesley Cameron crying on a bench in Tavistock Square. Of course, she had not been the first nor would Ms V J. Rayner be the last person to show Fidelis her misery, but she preferred to confront her weepers in a consulting room. She fetched a box of tissues from the bathroom and handed it to Veronica, who scrubbed at her eyes, took some deep breaths and said:

'I can't apologize enough. I promise you, this isn't like me, at the office my partners call me the Ice Maiden. I'd better leave.'

If it wasn't like Ms Rayner to let herself go, it was equally unlike Fidelis to change her mind, but now she felt perversely interested. 'No, stay and have a glass of wine—'

'I'm afraid I'm driving.'

'Sure? I'm having one. What would you like instead?'

'D'you have any sparkling water?'

'And you can tell me what you know about Lesley Cameron. Your brother was one of her neighbours, I believe.'

'She lived across the road from him, yes, and he was the one who forced an entrance and found her body. That seems to be the reason he was charged, simply that he was there and nobody else was. I've read the case papers and the evidence was nearly all circumstantial. But now, now I'm so worried and uncertain, the police have made it perfectly clear they think he did kill her and just got off on a technicality, and I've got to believe him, he swears blind he had nothing to do with it, but really I don't know what to think. But then it occurred to me you might be the very person for me to ask when I realized who you are—you see, Gavin was an adopted child.'

'Your brother?'

'Yes, at eighteen months. It was the early sixties, people had these optimistic notions about society and the future and how to make a better world. My parents were idealists, they thought that if enough trail-blazers brought black-skinned people into their conventional

129

families then colour prejudice would wither away.'

'I remember people saying that.'

'I'm afraid it just means poor Gavin always felt like a freak,' Veronica said sadly.

'I know the feeling,' Fidelis replied, briefly picturing herself failing to fit in with her gentle, kind foster family and their co-operative community. She'd always been too tall, too clever, too argumentative and too rebellious, always an outsider no matter how hard they tried to make her feel accepted.

'In fact, as you must know, a few years after that, transracial adoption stopped being allowed, but in those days it seemed like a good idea, and it did all seem to have turned out fine, my sister and I have always adored Gavin and so did Mum and Dad. He was the sweetest kid. He's still fantastically good-looking, actually. And I'm sure he's completely innocent, really, but one can't prove it and now he's in such a state. So this horrible thought occurred to me, just suppose there was something in his earliest months that couldn't be eradicated? Something that made him act completely out of character. Or not even that. He's got a temper on him, Gavin, it can sometimes explode almost out of the blue. But oh, Dr Berlin, could he have killed her and forgotten doing it? Might there be some violent impulse buried deep inside after an early trauma? Because I simply don't know if he was abused as a tiny baby or treated cruelly.'

'Your parents would have been given that kind of information at the time.'

'But they're dead.'

'In that case, unless Gavin himself decides to seek out his birth mother you have no way of finding out,' Fidelis said.

'I know, but he's never wanted to do that, not even when Mickey was on the way. Mickey's his son.'

'Well, it can't be done without his agreement, but really I'd have thought it was an unnecessary thing to worry about. How old is your brother now?'

'Forty.'

'And no previous signs of instability or violence?'

Veronica shook her head and made a negative mm-mm sound.

'Then if I were you I'd assume he's telling the truth and the police really did accuse the wrong man. We all know how often that does happen.'

'I'm sure you are right, Dr Berlin, but the problem is that the stigma will always be there. They run hate articles in the local paper, look.' She didn't even have to fumble for the cutting of newsprint which she drew from her bag and handed to Fidelis.

The *Gazette,* London Borough of Plowden.

A petition signed by 634 residents of the

131

Knighton Estate will be handed in to the council offices today. Local people say the return of a suspected killer to their neighbourhood puts their children and pensioners at risk.

Separated from that article by a piece on commuter trains and another about plans for a garden festival, came an apparently unconnected piece.

Police were called to the Knighton Drive home of Gavin Rayner, 40, who last month was acquitted on a charge of murdering his neighbour Mrs Lesley Cameron in 1999, when an explosive device, which did not ignite, was put through the door. No arrest was made.

'Gavin's living under siege and the police aren't interested. And it doesn't look as though they're even trying to find out who really killed Mrs Cameron, and meanwhile, Gavin's in an awful state. I did wonder about putting private detectives on to it, there's a firm we use at work, but I was frightened of them turning up evidence that might implicate Gavin.'

'I don't actually know many of the details, but was there anything to show that she didn't do it herself, had there been a struggle?'

'No, apparently not, nor had anyone forced an entry, apart from Gavin on the day he found her. The police claimed she'd let Gavin in herself. But there weren't any other signs that she'd killed herself, apart from the way she died, and several that she hadn't—she'd been in the middle of cooking something, a gas ring was on when she died, and she'd made lots of plans and arrangements for the next few months. So as she didn't kill herself, someone else must have. And Gavin idiotically touched something when he found her so as far as the police were concerned, he was the one.'

'What about a motive?'

'A mystery. He certainly didn't have one.'

'Didn't they say it was robbery?'

'It couldn't be demonstrated because nobody seems to have been sure what might have been taken. The only things that were definitely missing were all her papers and photos. According to her bridge-playing friends there had been lots of those. But some small bits of jewellery and silver were still there, and the TV, so it was a peculiar robbery. But I'm sure you know the prosecution doesn't have to demonstrate motive.'

Fidelis's reply was interrupted by the telephone bell. 'Fidelis? It's Clodie.'

'Hello my dear, how are you?'

'Just a quick call, I'm on duty, I wanted to ask you a favour.'

'Of course, anything.'

'Listen, Fidelis, didn't you say that house you inherited was in Plowden?'

'Yes, it's in Knighton Drive.' Veronica, who had got up to look at the bookshelves, politely not seeming to eavesdrop, stiffened at the give-away address.

'I thought so—it's not far from where I'm working now, and I simply cannot find a decent pad down here, you wouldn't believe how difficult it is, the flea-pits I've looked at, so I thought, how would it be if I live there till it's sold? I'll pay you a proper rent.'

'But Clodie, I haven't even looked at the place, it might be horrible.'

Veronica murmured, 'It could be quite a nice little house actually.'

'I don't care what it's like, Fidelis, I just need a roof over my head for a few weeks.'

'All right, I tell you what we'll do,' Fidelis decided. 'I'll collect the keys from the lawyers and we'll go and look together.'

The rest was left unsaid. Fidelis would meet Gavin Rayner. Veronica, of course, was far too well trained a negotiator to express her relief.

CHAPTER TWELVE

I've been thinking about Keith a lot recently. Mental displacement activity, probably, a way of putting off thinking about what happened before him and deciding what to do about it, like when I used to polish up the kitchen rather than settling down to write. Displacement activity is something one doesn't like doing, I think, so what must playing computer solitaire be then? Just wasting time? I never understood what addiction was before, the way one can feel impelled to do something unwillingly. I play one game, and another, and every time I tell myself this will be the last—it's boring, mindless, it makes my arms and hands ache, and yet I press 'deal again', and again, hating it. Hooked.

I went cold turkey a while ago, wiped the games accessory from the computer memory, but when it came to filling in idle moments, especially hanging on to the phone ('your call is important to us, please hold, calls are answered in strict rotation') I couldn't take it without the cards on the screen so I had to reload it.

Cyberbridge is an addiction too, but that's in a different kind of way because it's not just mindless, it exercises my brain. 'My hubby says this is my religion,' one of my partners typed the other day. Her playing name is Don Giovanna, and she shows a picture of a beautiful, dark girl, but her card says her name's Bonnie and she lives in Minneapolis with three cats. You could find her easily from the details she gives. People are surprisingly trusting, they should be more careful. I found Dr Berlin easily after I'd discovered she was a member, it was only a question of taking the time to run through members' names. It only took me a few days. At least she didn't put her full name on the card, she calls herself Fiddle which must be what her close friends call her,

her nickname. It's sweet, actually. And her email address is simply Fberlin@hotmail.com. She didn't take much finding. I've played with her too, though not as much as I'd like because often when I type in 'hi, nd 1, may I sit?' there's a message back saying the table's full. Of course she doesn't know it's me. I've left my picture space blank, and all I have on my card is my playing name which I chose from the sound of my initials, plus an unidentifiable email address. The people I play with don't even know I'm British. Sometimes they'll type 'where R U, Elsie?' and I reply Sydney or Singapore or wherever takes my fancy. '105 degrees today,' an opponent from Atlanta wrote yesterday, and I typed back, 'it's below freezing in Trondheim.' Well, I am a story-teller! That's one of the reasons Keith wasn't keen when I started writing, all he wanted to know was 'What's the point of just writing down things that aren't true?' And then, when I got my first contract, how much money there was in it.

Keith. Looking back I can see it was all exactly like what used to happen when Victorian men came home on leave from India determined to go back with a wife—any wife. Keith quite cynically thought he needed a wife in that little ex-pat community in the Gulf. And I wanted to get away so he seemed like the answer. He was quite good-looking, he was doing all right in the business, it would be the life of Riley. Both of us had bad motives. No wonder it didn't work out. But those few years did the trick, in the way that mattered, I got away from the likelihood of running into Murdo, I could put behind me what had happened. In fact, it seems odd now to say so, but I really forgot. I must have made myself wipe that memory-file. But they say all computer files can be recovered and this one began to flash up like a rogue picture on my mental screen a while ago, activated by seeing his name. He turned into one of those lawyers the papers expect you to have heard of, he appeared in prominent cases, he was photogenic even in a wig.

I've just had to break off and do a few rounds of solitaire. Thinking about him gets me all het up. No way is that game random like it's supposed to be, the program's got to be fixed to not come out, the machine hides all the sevens, or turns up nothing but blacks.

Come on, Lesley.

Murdo.

It still wouldn't matter if they hadn't made him a judge, we could have carried on as before. I always told myself it was perfectly OK for him to be a lawyer working with criminals, they'd be perfectly matched. But I was brought up to respect the judiciary, Dad used to be pompous about what the army was for, and he'd talk about maintaining the common law in his list of the good things about England. The rule of law, he'd say, that's what we fought for, the rule of law protected by Parliament and the judiciary and the army.

But Murdo isn't good enough. There was his picture and an article about how young, ambitious, brilliant etc etc he is and destined for the very top, the next Lord Chancellor or Chief Justice or Law Lord or all of those things. Murdo Wood-Wolferstan. The man I went on my travels with.

How is it possible for that man to be a judge, for him, of all people, to sit in judgement on others? It isn't right. And I'm the only person in the world who knows that. So what do I do about it?

Back again. The computer was on my side this time, the games of patience came out three times running. Is that a positive sign?

I wish I had someone to ask what to do, but it's not the kind of problem one can take to the Samaritans or even the Citizens' Advice Bureau where Mother helped out for so many years. I can just imagine her consternation if I plonked this quandary down on her desk. I can't even go to a solicitor, lawyers stick together, I remember Gerry Medlicott saying so. Might have been a joke, I suppose. Should I ask him—not that he'd remember me after all this time. Or some newspaper? Create a public scandal?

I ought to get in touch with Murdo first. If I didn't think about it for years myself, maybe he's forgotten the whole thing. It would be the decent thing to do, get in touch and remind him about the summer of '72.

CHAPTER THIRTEEN

Cleaners had been sent into the crime scene, paid for out of the police budget, according to Hassan Mahatir of Whitaker Pritchard. When Fidelis collected the keys he assured her there would be nothing in the house to distress her, but that was not quite accurate, for when she opened the front door the smell of industrial-strength chemicals was powerful enough to knock her backwards, stepping hard on Clodie's toes.

'Nobody'll buy into that!' Fidelis gasped as they fled out of range across the road, followed by an almost visible cloud of fumes.

The property opposite looked derelict, boards across its downstairs front windows, the letter box screwed up, the front patch a mixture of straggling weeds and patches of mud. Words had been spray-painted on to the closed door of the garage. They went up the short driveway to look. *Nigger. Wog. Paki bastard.*

Staring at the hideous graffiti, Fidelis suddenly realized she was hearing the roar of a car as it swerved at high speed off the road and into the drive. 'Look out!' Clodie cried.

The driver's teeth were bared in a furious snarl as he hunched furiously over the steering wheel. Fidelis tripped hard on to her knees, as the vehicle skidded to a halt and a tall, black man jumped out shouting, 'You stop it, don't you—'

'Stop what?' Clodie said in a patient pacifying tone, spreading her hands wide. 'We weren't doing anything.'

'I thought you . . .' He peered at the painted words and said in a quieter voice, 'I thought you were adding to it.'

He was tall, broad-shouldered, narrow-waisted, thin, with tight curls on a perfectly round skull and small ears set high; his nose was narrow and short, his mouth full but sharply outlined. He had tired eyes, their whites yellowed and bloodshot, and he did not meet their gaze. His skin was as black as milkless coffee.

'Gavin,' Fidelis said.

'Who's asking?' he snapped, every muscle tensed. She spoke gently, soothing him with a leisurely, low tone.

'I know your sister, my name's Fidelis Berlin. Didn't Veronica mention me? I've brought my friend Clodie, she might be going to come and live here.'

'Over there?' he asked with a jerk of the chin at the house across the road.

'Yes, for a short while.'

He didn't answer; but confronted with the matching skills of Drs Berlin and Byrne, mute hostility was ineffective. Within a few moments the two women were in the hall and chatting amiably: the weather, residents' parking arrangements, which day the dustbins were emptied, did a milkman deliver, what time did the mail arrive. Clodie said she was a doctor without admitting to her specialism. Fidelis said the houses looked cosy, and admired a table, asking if it was one of Gavin's, and a small wooden bowl. He unbent enough to say that had been one of the sycamores in the back garden that came down in the great gale, wood he'd saved to season for years. But he didn't invite them further in.

'Come on, Clodie, the place should have aired a bit by now,' Fidelis said.

Walking back across the road Clodie waited till he was out of earshot and then said, 'So that's the famous Gavin.'

'So it seems.'

'Well, I wouldn't have thought he had "the look".'

'The look?'

'People who've been inside, it always shows.'

'Does it, Clodie? That doesn't sound exactly scientific.'

'It isn't, obviously it's only the first impression, but my boss in the States was keen on them.'

'That's unexpected.'

141

'I don't mean when I was in Boston, it was the elective I did on the West Coast, I worked with a laid-back Angeleno, very touchy feely, and he was a great one for vibes. He said they were the automatic interpretation of subliminal signals and perfectly capable of definition and explanation but why bother.'

'It certainly sounds labour-saving,' Fidelis remarked.

'You're making yourself be non-judgemental, I can tell,' Clodie said.

'Tell me more about this interesting technique then, and I might make a judgement.'

'It's not a technique, Fidelis, merely a professional aid. But he was a good teacher by example, it was watching him that made me interested in the forensic side. The first time I was on the acute ward with him, it was all so different from anything I'd seen, he didn't *do* anything, he just *was*, watching and listening and not being in a hurry. We had a really long list and I asked him why we weren't getting going on taking histories, and he answered that it took too long for patients to describe the salient psychological events of even a single day—'

'Ah,' Fidelis interrupted.

'What?'

'Did he go on to say it took James Joyce several volumes to describe just that, in *Ulysses*?'

Clodie was disappointed. 'You mean he was just spouting an old saw?'

'No, just defining a familiar problem. How are we to hear the words the patients don't say? I remember a professor when I was a student who told us, "When you come to the bedside, don't do anything at once, just stand there." For some people who've got a particular set of human skills, his way is probably the best and you'll be a good doctor if you can do what he does.'

'Or maybe it's all crap, which is certainly what my consultant here would say, he's definitely one of the old school, every problem is chemical, every solution pharmaceutical.'

'Ah, that kind.' Fidelis tried to keep any disapproving note from her voice.

'And as far as he's concerned, any penetration of the criminal mind depends on mathematical systems and computer programs. The very idea of investigative psychology or offender profiling—I wouldn't dare even say the words when he's around.'

'Are you doing any of that?'

'I'm working on my contact in the local CID.'

'Well, go carefully with your boss, you'll need a decent reference.'

'Don't I know it. I certainly won't be suggesting a patient has any particular look if he's listening. And you needn't tell me I could be wrong about that guy across the road. He could be an axe murderer for all I know.'

'In which case, if I were your mother I'd say you weren't to move in within miles of him, but as your godmother, I'm assuming you can cope if anyone can. Though it would be interesting to know why the police seem so sure he was their man.'

'Actually, I've got quite matey with this woman from the local CID, I might get access.'

'Good. Come on, let's have a look at this house.'

The smell had almost gone when they stepped inside the front door, into a narrow hallway from which steep stairs led up towards a landing window obscured by dull green glass. A mess of papers was overflowing from a metal cage hanging on the inside of the door. Fidelis took them out and leafed through the special offers and circulars.

'Look at this one!' she exclaimed. Clodie read it as Fidelis held the flaming red paper. *Red for Danger. Warning to residents. Miscarriage of justice. Help make the Knighton Estate safe.* In imprecise but unmistakable language, the writer was stirring up trouble against 'murderers in our midst'.

'That's actionable. D'you think Gavin's sister's seen this?' Clodie asked.

'No doubt she'll come out fighting if she has,' Fidelis said drily. 'Come on, let's go round.'

The ground floor contained a front room

144

and a dining room just big enough for its four-seater table; from it a door led into the corridor-shaped kitchen along the back of the house. In the sitting room there was an overstuffed three-piece suite covered in a harsh floral print.

'I thought you said everything was stolen, Fidelis.'

'Did I? What I meant was that the place had been turned over and all her papers had gone. And the hard disk out of her computer.'

'Sounds like they were looking for a document or something she'd written.'

'Why would anyone have bothered?'

'She must have known where the bodies were buried,' Clodie suggested.

'As far as I know the authorities always believed it was murder in the furtherance of burglary, but not with any specific motive.'

'It might let Gavin Rayner out, though.'

'Could be. Come on, Clodie, let's look upstairs and get the hell out.'

There was a bathroom on the half landing and two bedrooms on the first floor. Someone had slashed down the grass in the small oblong back garden but it still looked shaggy and unloved. Each bedroom had a single bed with a mahogany frame, a freestanding wardrobe and a bare dressing table. The floor coverings had been removed, presumably torn away when the house was searched. Nail-studded strips for fitting carpets were left round the

145

edge of the floors.

'It's too gloomy,' Fidelis said, shuddering in the dim light the leaded casement windows allowed.

'D'you think I should light the boiler?'

'If you can.'

Clodie could always deal with gadgets; in a moment Fidelis heard the satisfactory pop of the pilot light igniting the gas, and then, almost at once, the creaking and gurgle in the radiators as water began to circulate through them. Hanging on to the banisters and watching her feet, Fidelis went down to the kitchen where Clodie was opening her satchel. 'Look, I brought coffee filter bags, I know you won't drink instant, and milk, let's hope there's some cups here somewhere.' There was a cupboard full of china, a matching set with six of everything, in an ugly maroon and gilt pattern. 'So what d'you say, will you be my landlady, Fidelis?'

'But it's such a gloomy place, the atmosphere's really depressing.'

'You of all people, superstitious!'

'No, not that, just the dinginess and the district, I can't believe you want to live here.'

'It would be perfect for the next few months. How about me moving in till Christmas?'

'Christmas—I can't think so far ahead.'

'Yes, well, I want to talk to you about that.'

'Christmas?'

146

'No, about thinking ahead. Mum's worried sick about you, and so am I.' Fidelis got up abruptly, the kitchen chair she had been sitting on skidding backwards with a screech on the tiled floor. Clodie went on, 'I know you don't want to talk about—about what's wrong—'

'No, I don't.'

'But you can't go on hiding from—'

'Listen, Clodie, drop this subject, will you?'

'No, you listen to me, Fidelis. I'm a medic, remember? Of course I know the trauma you've been going through, hearing the diagnosis I believe you've been given, you've obviously got—'

'Don't say it.'

'There you are, Fidelis, doesn't that just show the problem? You of all people, a physician, a scientist, you can't even bear to hear the name of—'

'Clodie.'

'OK, OK, but honestly, I've got to say this, it's time to come to terms with this thing, get a grip. You've needed the period of mourning, you've lost a lifestyle and the future you'd expected but this is like a bereavement, one has to move on after a death.'

Fidelis heard the girl parrot the phrases all doctors had learnt. Fidelis had said them, or words like them, to other people in her time and to herself too, ten years ago and in the last weeks. But there was still a wound over which scar tissue hadn't grown. Clodie's words were

147

true but stung like salt. Now she was producing the other, equally familiar facts. 'There's a cure on the way, they're going to find how to regenerate brain cells once the embryo research gets going, and you've got time till that's on stream, remember the condition can progress really slowly, it could be years before you're seriously impaired—'

'Clodie.' Fidelis was shaking uncontrollably and unconcealably. 'Drop this, will you? I must say if this is what your touchy feely doctor taught you, trampling in where you're not wanted, then I'm shocked.'

'But I'm just afraid you're giving in to it, colluding, conniving—you've got to accept it before you can fight it.'

'Back off, Clodie, d'you hear, spare me the sermon. I'm not your patient, you aren't responsible for me and you never will be, not you, not Tina, not anyone.'

'Of course I'd never talk to a patient like that.' The girl was nearly crying now, her cheeks blazed, clashing with her red hair. She muttered, 'It's just I've got this horrible feeling—just promise me you won't do anything stupid. I couldn't bear it if you ever . . .'

'Believe me, Clodie, I am as well informed on this subject as I can be. Actually,' she added, forgetting to be angry, 'd'you know, it's very interesting, I'd no idea what developments there have been in treatment and management.'

148

Fidelis met Clodie's blue gaze, knowing that she would have looked up all the published information about this condition and tracked down all internet references. She would, like Fidelis herself, have pored over every possible prognosis and treatment, the effect and side effects of the drugs, the success (or, actually, the almost invariable failure) of the attempts at surgical intervention, the life expectancy and quality of life, and—this was the sub-heading that made Fidelis cringe in the context of this beloved goddaughter—the role and problems of the carer.

Fidelis took a deep breath, shoved her shaking hands into her pockets and said, 'I'm not ready to discuss this, not even with you, but I promise that I'm applying a properly scientific objectivity to the problem.'

'I suppose that's a start,' Clodie muttered.

'Now, let's change the subject. What about this place? I can't believe you can really face living here, it's got a terribly depressing atmosphere.'

'Nothing that some paint and primping won't cure, if you'll let me. And Fidelis, you don't expect me to wimp out of this house with that man across the road?'

'But suppose he's dangerous?'

'I seriously doubt it. And he has to be, without exception, quite the most gorgeous-looking human being I've ever seen.'

CHAPTER FOURTEEN

The summer of '72. I was nineteen. Murdo was twenty-two, a prodigy who'd started at Oxford at seventeen and was now already through his professional finals and apprenticed to Gerry Medlicott, though that's not what barristers called it. Mr Medlicott, as I always addressed him—no first names between unequals in the early seventies—was Murdo's 'pupil master'. The night Murdo came to dinner I hadn't been invited to eat in the dining room so had early supper with the children and disappeared up to my bedsitter.

Pure fluke, then, that I'd crept down—careful not to let either the kids in their bedrooms or the grown-ups in the dining room hear me—to fetch some coffee and snacks, and was standing in the kitchen scoffing chocolate digestives when Murdo came out with the main-course dirty plates. I can see him now, a very tall, broad young man in a severe suit and a wide flowery tie. His straight, fair hair was below his collar with a smooth curve falling forward on to his forehead. He had little round, black-framed spectacles which seemed to magnify his bright blue eyes. He stooped like someone used to hitting his head on doorways, and he was carrying the stack of crockery awkwardly, his thumb in the gravy. I went forward and he smiled down at me with large, very regular teeth, and said, 'Hi.'

I took the plates off him and put them on the draining board. Then, although I didn't have to, I busied myself washing them and clearing up the mess Mrs Medlicott had left in the kitchen. She'd made kipper pâté with toast, lamb with garlic and rosemary, wrapped in puff pastry, with ratatouille and mashed potatoes. I was always interested in her menus, which were so very different from anything Mum produced, and remembered them too. I reproduced some when giving dinner parties with Keith a few years later.

I took a long time scraping congealed fat off the plates, and taking the Magimix and mouli-légumes to pieces and washing all their parts and drying them carefully. So I was still in the kitchen when he came through with another lot of plates, sticky with lemon mousse, warm apricots and cream.

'I'm Murdo,' he said in a low voice.

'I'm the au pair,' I said, though it wasn't technically true because I worked full time looking after the children and cleaning up while Anne was shut up in the dining room hammering her first book out on a portable typewriter. And I was paid a proper wage, rather than pocket money. But calling myself a 'mother's help' sounded more menial.

When he brought the cheese board out I

handed him a silver tray already laid with pretty demitasse cups and the silver thermos of coffee Anne had made earlier, and he bent close to me and said, 'Want to come out for a drink afterwards?'

Which was how it started. He took me to the movies. We saw *Cabaret* and Murdo said I was prettier than Liza Minelli. We went shopping in Carnaby Street. I would go along to his college friends' parties, where, please note, the future judge had his fair share when the joint went round.

Anne wasn't best pleased when I gave in my notice for July, less than a year after I started working for her. In fact we parted coolly and they only kept me on the Christmas card list for a year or so, though I couldn't help following Anne's career. The book she wrote when I was with her came out a couple of years later and I ordered it through the British Council library. It was a 'historical mystery' set in the nineteenth century with a heroine who was a photographer. Reading it I could hear Anne's voice telling what seemed like a quite simple story and what I thought was, If that's all there is to it, I could do that myself. And I could. I did. And I still can. But unlike Anne, I didn't go to Cambridge and meet all the right people, my husband isn't a famous barrister and I don't have a daughter who married a very rich lord, as the Medlicotts' right little madam of a daughter did, so no wonder Anne

Silversmith is famous now, while I've been dropped by publishers and agents.

I did wonder if I'd run into Anne at meetings of the Crime Writers Association when I started going to some of them after I was living in Brighton with Jeremy, though by then I suppose she was too grand and important to associate with people like me. But I didn't want to get in touch with the Medlicotts myself, because it still seemed more sensible to steer clear of their friends. By which I mean Gerry's colleagues—or to be precise, Murdo himself. I'd had no contact with him after what happened that summer. Not a word.

It was July when the six of us set off in an old VW van with sliding doors. You didn't need to wear seat belts in those days so three or even four people would cram on to the front bench-seat. We had a tent for the nights we weren't in hostels, and a Calor gas ring, so it wasn't exactly luxurious especially in bad weather. But as we got further south we slept on beaches or hillsides. In Rome, I remember, we entered an apartment block, crept up to the roof and slept out there.

There was Murdo and a medic from New Zealand called Don Pritchard and Geoff who was doing a doctorate on some incomprehensible subject to do with ancient music. There were two girls whose surnames I forget, Linda and Sue. Dolly birds, which I suppose is exactly what I was too.

We drove along with Led Zeppelin and Carly Simon blaring out. I only have to hear a phrase, or to smell L'Air du Temps, which Sue treated herself to in the duty free and sprayed on three times a day, or to get into a certain state of heat, prickling with sweat, to be transported right back to that time.

I'm making it sound idyllic and it wasn't. Sure, there were some moments of happy freedom, barefoot on a sandy beach or floating in the Mediterranean, but we were too close together for too long. We girls scratched irritably at each other, snide or catty. At any given moment one of us was grumpily pre-menstrual or had the jitters about a late period. I got cystitis, which didn't clear up for ages, and Linda came out in a really ugly heat rash. We were all eaten alive by insects.

When we got to the heel of Italy Don and Linda split, saying they wanted to go to Spain, although the plan had always been to carry on eastwards. Then there was a message waiting for Geoff at the poste restante in Trieste about being interviewed for a university job he was in the running to get if he made it back to Oxford by the end of that week. As the van belonged to Geoff, he and Sue turned it northwards that very day and Murdo and I were left to hitch on alone. That was the best time. Even though my memories of it are clouded by what happened later.

He had money so we could have taken public transport and once or twice we did go by bus, but it was easy to get lifts. We must have been an attractive-looking couple with our tanned skin and long hair, his blond in the bright sun and mine so dark, a couple of minutes of thumb-in-the-air was sure to net a lorry driver or businessman. We wandered down the Dalmatian coast which is the most beautiful place I've ever seen before or since. Murdo was thrilled by the archaeological remains, which were admittedly picturesque. Of course I never wanted to spend as long examining them as he did, but I was madly, idiotically in love, so if he was happy I was too. We went on leisurely down across Greece, which was beautiful but boiling hot, and reached Athens in the middle of September.

We slept out with hundreds of other backpackers on a grassy space at the port of Piraeus, where everyone congregated, hundreds of people of our generation milling round and discussing where to go next. Ferries went all over the Aegean and eastern Med. We debated the Greek islands or Egypt or Crete. Murdo was keen on Cyprus, but I remembered it from when my dad was stationed there and didn't have very fond memories. We'd settled on Rhodes along with some Cambridge undergrads we'd chummed up with. We were in an endless ticket queue for the ferry when I noticed that the ship in the next berth, with no queue, was going to Haifa. So Murdo and I went there instead.

CHAPTER FIFTEEN

The phone rang at ten to nine. Fidelis had been listening to herself on the *Today* programme. She was on second, after the lead item, which was an anguished, circular argument about what to do with paedophiles once they came out of prison. A tabloid paper had published names and photographs and effectively incited concerned citizens to lynch any of the men rehoused near them—which residents of what was freely described as 'a sink estate' in Southampton had promptly done.

Fidelis had recorded an interview the previous evening, commenting on the merits of a new policy for childcare that was being discussed before the Secretary of State formally announced it. She was amused again, as she'd been at the time, by the terrier-like attack of a reporter who was trying to create contention where there was none.

'Hi, it's Clodie, I just wanted to say you stood up for yourself well.'

'Thanks, darling—but it's so late, aren't you at work?'

'On my way, in the car. Fidelis, the house is

perfect, I'm making it really cosy.'

'Good. Though I still think it's pretty dismal round there.'

'It's fine—and I've made friends with the gorgeous guy.'

'Gavin?'

'He's not a bit like I'd expected. I'm going softly softly, he's very suspicious and sometimes puts up the barriers, but he's really nice. He's a craftsman, makes brilliant furniture and stuff. That's how he met Lesley Cameron, she gave him commissions,' Clodie said, and added, 'I'm going to get involved, actually. My friend in the CID worked on her chief and I'm going to look at the case as an independent consultant. They want me to build up a psychological profile of the killer.'

'Have you got the time?'

'I'll make time. I do want to get Gavin off this hook and if finding out who really killed Lesley Cameron's the only way, well then—'

'Be careful, Clodie, won't you?'

'You too. But you certainly sound much better. I could hear it on the radio. I'm really, really glad.'

Yes, Fidelis thought, I did sound OK on the air. I'd be able to tell if it was any different. Fidelis had done a lot of broadcasting and, in pre-computer days, dictating, so she knew her own reproduced voice very well, calm, contralto and with a hint of Welsh lilt that, she had been told, wasn't noticed face to face. She would hear the change, if it were there to be heard, so its absence was a confirmation that she was indeed better, that she'd recovered from the initial shock and done the necessary 'coming to terms' with the prospect of a different future from that planned. Back on an even keel.

She smiled to think what her stuffier colleagues would make of her aural self-diagnosis. Crap, they'd say, total tosh, Fidelis is losing it.

But this was a trick she'd used all her professional life, though it had taken many years of rigorously scientific work before she acquired the confidence to admit that she ever used techniques and abilities not measurable by science; that to some people they came naturally. She'd been interpreting expressions as long as she could remember and even once dashed off (though left unpublished for fear of her colleagues' ridicule) a treatise on the art of reading faces. It was a useful knack for a practising psychiatrist, perhaps one with which anyone who ended up choosing to specialize in that branch of medicine might have been born, an ability instinctively to understand what less sensitive people might never perceive. But it was only a trick, not susceptible to description, analysis or explanation; and it was fallible, for Fidelis was not always right. But she often was. Her insights would once have been called intuition, with the disapproving adjective 'feminine' attached.

Which came first, the interest in the human psyche or the ability to understand it? And was that innate, or an ability learned (in Fidelis's case) by a frightened little girl who had lost her mother and father and desperately needed to predict the reactions of the people around her, in case something she did might drive them away too?

Voices were as significant as body language and facial expression, and Fidelis had read with interest a recent paper describing them as a diagnostic tool. A researcher at Yale, more willing than Fidelis to risk his colleagues' ridicule, had published an article that very summer revealing that she was not the only psychiatrist who trusted their ears as well as their eyes. He had recorded interviews with depressed people, and later compared the recordings with those patients' subsequent histories. And he discovered what Fidelis always believed, that in patients who were suicidal, who actually meant to carry out their threats, the voice became slightly hollow and empty. There was a recognizable change in quality. Fidelis had privately thought of the changed vocal timbre as a death knell, a serious warning that this particular depressive seriously intended to do what so many patients talked about. She used to mark her own notes with the obscure initials DK. Dr Silverman from Yale had another name. He said the doctors and nurses called it 'the voice from the grave'.

So, as she pronounced about adoption policy, Fidelis listened out for, but did not hear in her authoritative sentences, the voice from the grave or even from the sickbed. The tone was vigorous and self-assured. She sounded like the expert she was rather than some poor old bag on her way out. And Fidelis was looking forward to the future again, to plans and projects. She ran the cursor down the index, uninterested in the files she had opened to record her own introspection. No more of that. Instead, documents labelled Edinburgh, Adelaide, Oslo reminded her of lectures due or given to audiences of international experts. Projects, articles, the proposal for another book lay people would want to read. Back to work, even if she trembled and tottered, even though she'd need a walking stick. Diminished, maybe, but not, any longer, disguised.

Fidelis had missed meetings in the last months. But her engagement book was still full with reminders of her status as a governor, a trustee, a committee member, an adjudicator, an examiner, a referee—all the useful, unpaid functions that were heaped on senior members of her profession. Fidelis had become a member of 'the great and the good', wheeled out to serve on committees as the token woman or academic or shrink. On one table lay a pile of the brown, A4 envelopes in which agendas and minutes arrived daily through the post, all disgracefully unopened. There were dozens—no, hundreds—of emails unattended to and a stainless steel basket overflowing with unpaid bills.

Oh Fiddle, she thought, Oh Fiddle dearie, as her foster mother used to say in her kind Welsh voice, where have you been, what did you think you were up to, *what are you like?* A kiddologist, that was what she'd been like, kidding herself along for weeks. She'd never been going to end it all—not yet, not for years, not till there was no, absolutely no alternative. She'd always known that she had a strong will to live, part of her inborn personality, and later on, intellectually justified. Given the gift of life by her rescue from the gas chamber to which other girls of her age were delivered, Fidelis would never throw it away. Every extra year or even day was a victory against those who would have killed her.

Right, then. Let's get on with it.

She'd become clumsy, her left hand infuriatingly weak and no longer obedient. Coming across and flicking (right-handed) through a stack of news magazines, Fidelis cut out an agonizing photo of children in Sierra Leone, their black arms terminating in stumps because enemy soldiers had lopped off their hands. *And I'm complaining.*

She had to walk carefully. Unless she thought about picking up her feet at every step, she tripped or stumbled. But she wasn't on a zimmer frame—yet.

She wasn't in agony. Who should know better than this particular patient, that her sensations were only what, in the trade, they called 'discomfort'?

No self-pity. Just accept that tasks she would have polished off in half an hour would take twice as long. This condition might be seen as nature's retribution, she told herself, the impatient speed-addict, a lifelong fast worker (as she'd always been) forced to take things slowly. And she tired easily. You and everyone else your age, she reminded herself. Why should F. Berlin be immune?

She would tackle the pile of unanswered mail: bills to pay, references to write, invitations to respond to, condolences to write. She must tell Lionel that she wouldn't be getting to New York this year, and answer Victoria Merton's invitation to go and stay with her in Haifa. The two women had been neighbours in Hampstead until Victoria emigrated and Fidelis moved. Before her marriage to a boisterous Israeli, transmogrified into Yoshua Lang from the English public schoolboy Justin Lang had been, Victoria had been a reserved, bashful woman. Now she wrote long letters, much more intimate than the two women's previous acquaintanceship would justify. But then, Fidelis had had a lifetime of breaking through other people's reserve and, she supposed, did it unconsciously and unintentionally too.

Victoria's invitations were literally pressing. She was putting the pressure on, a kind of moral battering, beginning with the fact that Victoria's husband, Yossi, couldn't any longer fly. Doctor's orders. It was an awful warning for them all, Fidelis really had to come before it was too late. Don't be put off by news stories about the troubles, life is perfectly safe and normal here. At least promise it'll be '"next year in Jerusalem", like the ancestors said.'

Fidelis had heard the phrase. They said it at the Passover meal, the only one she'd ever been to, when she was a research student. She'd been invited by an American colleague who assumed she knew what was going on, but she'd sat at his laden, decorated table like an anthropologist, an uninvolved observer.

Ratcheting up, Victoria added, 'Yossi says you'll be denying your dead family if you don't at least visit the Jewish homeland.'

Crap, Fidelis thought. Or hoped.

In her early years in London she'd met lots of other people who were, like her, dark, intense, talkative, excitable. But then so were the Welsh; and musical, too. She did not believe in racial characteristics. Her training denied them. And in the post-war decades it was felt that only Hitler and his Germans defined human qualities in that way. And yet, and yet . . . she did recognize that something

163

connected her with the Jews she met. The feeling was not liking (indeed it was more often disliking) nor sympathy; not even any kind of affinity. Fidelis had nothing, less than nothing, in common with Orthodox seminarists in the gear of the ghetto. When she saw a group of men in black coats and hats, with white high-buttoned shirts but no tie, with locks of black hair dangling down their pale faces—the archetypal targets of Nazi race-hatred—a wave of dislike and even fear blotted out her otherwise universal tolerance. She felt a subliminal awareness of a Dalek-like command. Assimilate, assimilate. Otherwise *they* will exterminate, exterminate.

That's really why I've never been to Israel, she thought now, remembering the excuses she'd given for nonattendance at psychiatric conferences, for turning down a winter break with a scuba-diving boyfriend, and for not yet visiting Victoria. Not just that I don't like the sound of it, not just that there are so many other places I'm longing to go to first. But something else too. I'm afraid of it. The difference was that now she had something worse to fear. The prospect of encountering all those people, to whom she belonged yet did not belong, was like scratching one's skin to distract from a pain in a tooth. Maybe I should go. It could be now or never. But an instinctive unwillingness remained. She would tell Victoria she couldn't make the trip. Not yet.

The mail included two death notices, acquaintances not friends, but reminders of mortality. There was a sad letter from her friend Gary in Los Angeles whose companion of thirty years had liver cancer. *Count your blessings,* said her foster mother's remembered voice in her head.

It was evening before the apartment was back to its proper state, tidy and ordered. Finally in the hall, she noticed the package Veronica Rayner had delivered weeks before, which had been on the floor under a table ever since. She took it into the sitting room, poured some whisky, changed the music to an undemanding Handel concerto and got out her trusty Swiss Army knife to cut the tape and slice the brown paper.

Mr Mahatir had sent a reckoning explaining that Lesley Cameron had been massively in the red when she died. She'd taken out a mortgage on the house, she'd acquired half a dozen credit cards in the last year and run up huge debts on all of them, she was substantially overdrawn at the bank. All she owned was the house. 'I'm glad to say that you won't be liable for any of the debts,' the solicitor said in a reassuring tone when Fidelis rang to enquire. 'But the sale of the property will not satisfy them.'

'She must have owned her copyrights,' Fidelis suggested, remembering Anne Silversmith explaining that she had given hers

165

away to grandchildren as they were born.

'She did say something about writing, yes indeed, but I'm afraid they are quite worthless.'

'Frankly, Mr Mahatir, this whole episode is a complete mystery. Why on earth did I ever need to get involved at all?'

'Well, now, Dr Berlin, how could I have known that my client's testamentary dispositions were to a putative beneficiary to whom she was unknown? But I don't want you to worry, not at all. You told me the bequest came out of the blue, and into the blue it will vanish,' he said, and added, 'in poetic terms, that is to say.'

So this parcel would be Fidelis's sole, and still inexplicable, legacy from the unknown Lesley Cameron. In fact if the contents looked as though they were worth anything, it would be tiresomely necessary to ensure they were sold to lessen the debt.

No, not worth anything. Which was lucky and also rather depressing. What on earth am I going to do with this? she thought. A cabinet, about the size of a crate of a dozen wine bottles, made of polished wood with inlays and curlicues. A lid opened at the top, releasing a desk top, which came down horizontally, and revealing a collection of compartments intended for writing paper and envelopes. Deep down in the foolscap size slot there was a gleam of coloured plastic: a floppy disk.

The cabinet was archaic, awkward, *not my line*—at least, certainly not Fidelis's line now that she'd got rid of most of her accumulation of clutter. There had been a period in her life, after she began to earn a steady salary and had her own first flat, when she'd persistently acquired antique objects and ornaments. Haunting salerooms and junk shops on Saturday mornings—for in those days nothing was open for the rest of the weekend, or after 'closing time' at five thirty on weekdays—Fidelis had developed the instincts of a hunter. Searching, sighting, stalking, followed by fury at the one that got away, when she couldn't afford to buy it, or that delightful rush of triumph when she could, and bore her trophy home.

In her middle years that emotion had been evoked when Fidelis tracked down the perfect dress or sweater. That Mary Quant dress from her first shop in the King's Road, the first Jean Muir, second-hand from a 'dress agency' near Sloane Square, an early Vivienne Westwood at a closing-down sale in Marylebone High Street, all of them beautiful examples of original modern design. And in those days the other objects Fidelis gave herself were modern too, paintings, pottery, glass, things to tether her to the world.

She hadn't needed a friend to diagnose it for her, though several had, because it was perfectly obvious that Fidelis was providing

167

herself with the material possessions that other people inherited from parents and grandparents. In those early days she still vaguely expected to lead a conventional life, sooner or later turning into a one-man-woman, marrying, settling down, having her own children. How old was she when she realized that wasn't what she really wanted or was capable of? In her thirties, by which time she knew herself to be a sexual butterfly? In her early forties, when she realized she simply didn't have and hadn't ever experienced those maternal longings which she'd always expected to hit her before it was too late? No, it couldn't be pinned down. But Fidelis had never regretted her single state, never, she really honestly believed, not for one minute. Single, alone, but not lonely.

Lesley Cameron had apparently been all three of those things. 'She hadn't got any friends!' Clodie reported when she rang again after work to give Fidelis a blow by blow account of her extra-curricular work.

CHAPTER SIXTEEN

Knighton Drive looked surprisingly cosy in the mellow light of an autumn evening, like an English version of a Norman Rockwell picture. Clodie, who aspired to a high-tech loft, did not see herself as someone who belonged in a suburban semi, and Lesley Cameron's house was unarguably dreary, but it was exactly what she needed during this six-month contract and she returned to it from a testing day (a patient having managed to find the means to go in for a spot of self-mutilation) with relief and even pleasure. Changed out of work clothes, she ran five miles round the blocks of the six parallel streets. She was interested, indeed impressed, by the way owners had managed to give their homes, which had been built by a 1930s developer to identical plans, personality and individuality, with plain, coloured or leaded glass, with paint, rendering or timber, with flat, panelled or glazed doors and above all with glimpses of interiors that showed how infinitely various the domestic imagination could be. She had already found markers for her run. Five minutes to the house with the life-size plastic reindeer on its roof, ten to the front garden set up for an assault course, fifteen to the one whose lighted windows revealed an enthusiast's picture gallery inside.

Clodie had noted the witnesses' addresses from the Cameron inquest report. Mrs Doris Flynn had moved out into an old people's home in Kent but the remaining two of the bridge four were still in the neighbourhood. Mrs Lieutenant Colonel William Roberts (as she introduced herself), who was actually called Pandora, was of the age to say she shouldn't really speak ill of the dead, but believed in candour so described Lesley as a sad little person, who didn't have enough outside interests and was disappointed with life.

Pandora Roberts had a Union Jack sticker on her front door. Inside, her house was filled with relics of empire: brass trays, ostrich feathers, japanned and rattan furniture and dignitaries' silver-framed photographs with cursive signatures at an angle across the bottom corner. She explained that she had first met Lesley's mother at the local bridge club. 'Not an easy character, but she played well.'

Old Mrs Bowhill was a loner. Few as the neighbourhood activities were, she'd never taken part in them, no pennies for the guy or door opened to kids on the trick-or-treat campaign, no posters in her window about neighbourhood campaigns, no contributions to the occasional jumble sale. She wasn't a churchgoer, didn't go to evening classes or bingo, was never known to have a visitor. Her front windows permanently shut, her expression dour, the only social interaction she was known to partake in was the Thursday afternoon bridge game at the community centre.

Lesley Cameron had moved in with her mother in the early nineties, presumably when her third marriage broke up. After the old woman died Lesley inherited the routine of the bridge game, rotating between the four members' houses. She didn't play as well as her mother, but well enough.

'If only she'd been more cheerful. She never tried to put on a good show, one should always do that, keep up the shop front, as you'll discover in life,' Mrs Roberts told Clodie. 'Lesley rather despised this neighbourhood. Well, I'm not saying it's what I would have chosen. I shudder to think what my late husband would have said if he could see where I ended up.'

'I suppose it is quite a mixed neighbourhood,' Clodie murmured.

'Mixed! What with the Africans across the main road—I know it's some way away but look what came of having that man living opposite poor Lesley.'

'But he's not African!'

'My dear, if the cat has her kittens in the stable it doesn't make them into horses, as you'll discover, the leopard can't change its spots. It's the same with all of them, the Indians, the Jews—my poor husband would have had a fit, I can tell you, he was never very fond of the chosen people, though he was quite an Arabist in his way, when we were stationed in Aden he . . . but there I go, rambling on.'

'So you haven't lived here very long then?'

'Not quite twenty years. My husband passed on in '82 and I couldn't stay on in Malta without him. But you see, my dear, I always say one has to make the best of things, be satisfied in the station of life one's called to, it doesn't do to grumble,' the colonel's widow announced.

Lesley, on the other hand, believed she deserved better and made no secret of it. Lesley, she said, always used to have an air of grievance, behaving as though she were in some way the innocent victim of a cruel fate. 'I tried to interest her in helping those who are less fortunate than ourselves, there's nothing like doing your bit for charity to make one count one's blessings—can I interest you in collecting for the animal hospital, my dear? No? Of course you're very busy. Oh thank you, that's very generous. Poor Lesley, she couldn't manage to think that others were worse off than herself, if you know what I mean. I found her irritating if the truth be told, too introspective. But you'll probably find Eithne's more sympathetic. She always tells me I'm too critical.'

Miss Eithne Browne lived with her bedridden mother in a flower-sprigged pink bower. She put her finger over her lips, gestured Clodie to follow her down the passage and carefully closed the kitchen door before saying, 'You must forgive me for entertaining you in here but I'd rather Mamma didn't hear that there's a visitor. Let's have some tea, would you like that? You wanted to talk to me about poor Lesley?'

'You were in her bridge four, I believe.'

'I don't know what I'd do without our bridge games, you know, my dear. I sometimes say they're the only thing that keeps me sane!' Her tinkling laugh had an undertone of desperation.

'And did they keep Lesley sane too?'

'Well, it's a very absorbing occupation,' Miss Browne replied evasively. She set out table mats, milk in a jug and sugar in a bowl. 'Earl Grey,' she announced, pouring out straw-coloured liquid.

'Thank you, that's lovely,' Clodie said, wondering when she had last drunk tea out of a porcelain cup.

Poor Lesley'd been very unlucky, she explained. Miss Browne remembered her from years back, when she came to stay with her mother if things were going wrong. She'd been so pretty when she was young, jolly and jokey, a laugh you could hear two streets away. She liked to have fun, you understand? A natural, normal, lively girl. She should have found a steady, reliable chap and had a family instead of frittering her days away, filling in the time. She even tried to write books! But poor Lesley had married rotters, one after another, they'd all treated her badly, it was a terrible shame because she wasn't the kind of woman to thrive alone, some women needed a man to lean on, wouldn't Clodie agree?

Clodie nodded, but insincerely. OK, so she

hoped to find a man herself one of these days, but you only had to look at Fidelis to see how OK you could be without. As far as Tina knew, Fidelis hadn't had a serious relationship in her sixties. She found what she needed in her coven, now she was past actual sex. If she was past it. I wonder if Fidelis is lonely and frustrated after all, Clodie thought, but at the same time she was taking in what was being said about Lesley.

'She was left without any income, none at all, so she was absolutely forced to move in with her mother. And then old Mrs Bowhill got ill and took a long time to die. Everything went wrong, it was all such bad luck, such a good-looking woman too, she must have been very attractive. Well, she did have three husbands. So you can understand why Lesley wasn't happy. Embittered, you could say,' sympathized kind Miss Browne.

'Did her ex-husbands keep in touch?'

'D'you know, I really don't think so, poor thing, she was all alone, not many friends apart from all of us, and apparently no other family. And the worst of it was she was dreadfully short of money too.'

After her mother died Lesley went for one or two jobs—a tearoom, the bridalwear shop, Miss Browne had written out a character reference—but there was so much competition these days, you have to have certificates.

'I don't really know how she managed, to

174

tell you the truth. At least I've got my pension, and then there's Mother's disability allowance—she's quite bedridden, you know—but Lesley wouldn't qualify, she wasn't old enough. So of course she was lonely, you could quite understand things were difficult for her.'

Clodie said, 'But she must have had some friends, Miss Browne. She sent out party invitations the very week she died, didn't you get one?'

'I did, my dear, so did we all, the bridge set, but we were the only ones from the community centre to be asked, and nobody else came to the crematorium at all, only the three of us and the solicitor, not another soul in the world, it added to the tragedy, standing there alone in that chapel.'

'Gavin Rayner got an invitation to her party.'

'Don't mention that man to me, we're not safe in our beds with him there in the next street. Pandora Roberts is getting up a petition, perhaps you'd sign it, let me see, where did I put it?'

'I don't think I—'

'It doesn't bear thinking of, a pretty young thing like you, with that monster living right across the road.'

'Goodness, is that the time? I must run,' Clodie exclaimed. As the door shut behind her she heard a cracked voice calling from the upstairs front room and what sounded like a stick thumped on the floor. The suburban evening smelt fresh after the mixture of sickness and potpourri in the Brownes' house.

Clodie ran on faster, conscious of her own strength, health and freedom. There'd be no dwindling into the kind of life those women led, not for Clodie. Well, for a start, her mother would die sooner than be looked after by her children and luckily had enough money to ensure they would never have to. But Clodie wouldn't be alone. Smug in the intolerance of her generation, Clodie disapproved of Mrs Roberts and Miss Browne. Why didn't they move in together, or set up an oldies' commune like Fidelis lived in, or—or something. What was the point of being alive if you didn't have some pleasure in it? Clodie laughed at herself as she ran, and pigeon-holed her thoughts into 'impermissible' and 'unrealistic'. She'd seen enough psychiatric casualties to know that life didn't turn out the way you wanted it to at twenty-nine. I might end up old and poor and disappointed and lonely on the Knighton Estate in Plowden, she thought, but I'm sure going to have some fun first. At which, a man's image popped into her head and the hairs on her skin rose. It was a long time, several months, since she'd had sex. Too long.

Gavin didn't work with the door open these days but he raised it when Clodie tapped out a rhythmic knock and she slid under into the workshop. He was gradually thawing towards her. She'd been careful not to let slip that her speciality was psychiatry, thinking it would frighten him off, and had implied she was doing obs and gynae.

'Hard day?' he asked.

She wiped the back of her arm across her sweating face and nodded. Chit-chat flowed more easily each time they met, but Clodie was treading hyper-cautiously. But she knew where she wanted to go. As she'd told Fidelis, 'He could have done it. Technically, I mean, motive, opportunity and all that routine stuff.'

'But you really want it to have been someone else,' Fidelis remarked. They'd met unexpectedly the previous evening at a lecture at the Royal College. Afterwards, clutching tubes of acid sherry, they sat whispering together on a hard little sofa upholstered in slippery yellow brocade. Fidelis kept slipping forward and sliding herself back. Clodie perched like a horsewoman on a side saddle, her red head high, her eyes vivid and excited. She said:

'I don't just want, I know. Gavin isn't capable of killing, he's the most gentle, unaggressive, sensitive man I've ever met.'

'Clodie—'

'He's the kind of man my mother says is wet.'

Clodie liked men who were at once gentle, exotic and mysterious. She found Gavin

177

fascinating.

First he had to trust her and then—well, she knew what she wanted after that. So while his hands swooped and swept across the smooth wood, she told him her godmother had suggested she could make enquiries about Lesley Cameron, her mysterious benefactor.

'It's all so peculiar, I can't visualize her life at all, on her own without a job or anything, it must have been lonely. What was she like? Did she have boyfriends? Women? Girls? Or boys?'

'Boys? Why d'you say that?' His face momentarily contorted in a kind of snarl and he backed away. Making a mental note that she'd touched a sore spot—could Lesley Cameron have made advances to Gavin's son?—Clodie hastily went on.

'It seems so peculiar that nobody mentions any friends, even her bridge partners weren't, not really. You must have seen who came to visit her though, didn't you?'

'Don't think she had many visitors apart from the bridge players, and there was some guy came a few days before—you know—he bought one of my bowls on the way.'

Clodie said, 'I suppose she used to go out to see other people, but we'd never find out who they were now.'

'She wasn't out much.'

'I suppose you'd have noticed that.'

'Yeah, well, she hardly ever used that car, I

178

know that 'cos I kept having to jump start it when she did, she wouldn't buy a new battery and it never got charged up. Just that last week, before she—you know.'

'Mmm.'

'She went in and out then, lots of times, never for very long, but she locked the Honda in the garage every time in between. Like she was running a delivery service or something.'

'Any idea what that was about?'

'Well, I knew there was something on her mind, but not what it was. Could have been to do with that. She had worries, that much I do know.'

'Worries?'

'She was scared of something. I'm sorry now that I didn't listen properly, but she was always in here rabbiting on, standing there where you are now, I used to tune it out.' His eyes turned back to the wood sphere from which he had begun to shave delicate, curled slivers. Gavin was tuning Clodie out too.

CHAPTER SEVENTEEN

This was far worse than a funeral or visiting a grave. The life that was left in Catriona Wood-Wolferstan was physical only, like a paraplegic on life support, without a flicker of brain activity. The fierce, cultured, knowledgeable intelligence, the intuitive sympathy, the honed critical faculties—all gone into a mush of infantile sensation.

Fidelis made herself sit with the carcass that had housed her friend. She held the withered, clammy hand. She murmured inanities.

The team of expensive carers looked after the old woman well. She was kept clean, with her nails cut and sparse white hair trimmed and washed. She was dressed in the clothes human beings wear. But everything that made her human was gone.

What was it that Orthodox Jewish neurologist had told her? *There's a purpose in this. Nothing is for nothing in this life.* Catriona was a lapsed Catholic from the Western Highlands. In the days when she'd believed, she would have said there was a soul still there, within, precious and to be protected.

And I've been lamenting my physical decline! Fidelis thought. I should be transported with relief that it's only my body going. I've been—yes, she thought, I've really been lucky. So far.

Fidelis had sent the afternoon nurse off early. The night nurse came in at eight o'clock. 'Oh, hello, Dr Berlin, I didn't know you were coming. How does she seem to you then?'

Fidelis gently put down Catriona's purposeless hand and got up. 'Further gone,' she said. As though at the sound of Fidelis's voice, Catriona gave a little, chesty cough. If only she'd get pneumonia, Fidelis thought. She kissed the soft hair and said:

'I'm going to look for something in Sir Murdo's old room while I'm here, I won't disturb you.'

Catriona had moved to the sprawling mansion flat when Murdo was about eleven. She'd filled it with vivid colours, big oil paintings by the Scottish colourists, tapestries from the Edinburgh Weavers, gorgeous-coloured Persian rugs and rich velvet curtains. It was quiet, four floors up and with street sounds muffled by figured lace over the sash windows. Murdo must have moved out a quarter of a century before, but there had never been any need to clear out his bedroom, though visitors occasionally slept in it. The posters Fidelis vaguely remembered on its walls had been taken down, but the fleet of Airfix planes still stood ranked on a glass shelf and a stack of long-playing vinyl records was heaped in the mahogany cupboard along with an old pair of tennis shoes and a tartan dressing gown. Shelves were built into alcoves on either side of a wall, once a fireplace but now with the bedhead against it.

The books represented a record of intellectual development, Beatrix Potter at the top left, out-of-date legal textbooks far right. The very few novels were on the bottom shelf. Tolkien, Ian Fleming, *Jennings at School*. Squatting in the corner, Fidelis pulled them out and found others in a second row, mostly soft porn. *The Story of O, The Tropic of Cancer* and—here it was. *Cat Walk.* The author's name, Lesley Bowhill, was printed in much smaller letters and the cover picture showed a busty blonde with an expression of terror in her outsize eyes.

Sitting on the bed, Fidelis opened the book and saw it was inscribed *Murdo, remembering. From Lesley.*

She looked at the blurb. *When famous star Hermione Elphinstone learns she has only a short time to live, she determines that her death will not be in vain. She plans to take her own life and do it in a way that ensures that the man who used and spurned her, the villainous Sir Gervase, is suspected of committing murder.*

Fidelis was practised at filleting a book and quickly found the operative part of the plot, a plodding denouement with a police inspector explaining what had happened to the assembled suspects. Hermione had fixed up misleading clues to make it look as though she'd been attacked, swallowed an overdose of seconal and put her head in a plastic bag.

But for the fact that she'd used temazepam rather than a barbiturate, that was exactly how Lesley herself had died.

CHAPTER EIGHTEEN

None of us had been reading the papers that summer as we travelled round Europe, and although we did have a tranny we only listened to music on it, so we hadn't heard any news. Someone would have told us soon enough, if there'd been anything we needed to know.

We slept the whole way from Piraeus to Haifa and woke up when the ferry was docking under Mount Carmel at dawn. It took ages to disembark, edging forward in a slow queue through what we both thought was extremely over-the-top security—Murdo's guitar was literally dismantled—before we could set off through the harbour and up towards the town centre. We were in a crowd of other foot passengers, lots of students (which is what I pretended I was too) of course, and some people I can only describe as pieces of human wreckage who must have been immigrants.

Murdo was wide-eyed and bushy-tailed and if I hadn't inhibited him would probably have knelt down to kiss the ground, being a well-brought-up public schoolboy who'd been through a pious phase in his teens and dreamed of setting foot in the Holy Land. I was tense for some reason—no, for two reasons. One was that my period was late. The other was because my father had often talked about his time here, before I was born when he was serving in Palestine and came to hate, or was confirmed in his preexisting hatred for Jews, who he said were stroppy, cheeky and dangerous. One of his mates was wounded in a Stern gang attack. The Stern gang were freedom fighters or, depending on how you looked at them, terrorists but as far as the Brits who served in the Palestine police were concerned the whole lot were vermin and men like my father might sometimes say, if they didn't think any unfriendly ears were around, that when it came to the chosen people Hitler had the right idea.

Some Palestinian terrorists had had the same idea that September though we hadn't heard about it when we arrived so we didn't know what the rows of half-mast flags signified or why so many people looked quite so glum. Of course we discovered soon enough that the Israeli athletics team had been wiped out by gunmen at the Munich Olympics a few days before. In fact people hardly talked about anything else, in the hostels, in the kibbutzes, on buses, the drivers who gave us lifts, everyone went on and on about the massacre. Well, it was awful, we could understand why they were so upset but as outsiders we got less emotional about it. We took a few days to look round the north of the country. Murdo really surprised me by quoting the Bible all the time, he even bought a bottle of Jordan water and said he'd have our children christened with it and in Jerusalem he was ostentatiously moved by walking where Jesus had walked. He kept asking if I didn't feel the vibes too and I did pretend to because it seemed to be expected of me, but actually I was getting pretty fed up with everywhere being so hot and crowded.

Some of it seemed kind of familiar, because Dad was stationed in Cyprus when I was a small kid. In an unspecific way I recognized the dust and light colours, the old women in black, donkeys, palm trees, cypresses and noise. Traffic and men quarrelling incomprehensibly —the sound of a hot country.

But then we decided to go down to Eilat, crash out on the beach, and Murdo suddenly produced some money I never knew he'd been saving for emergencies and said we'd hire a car to drive down through the desert. I must say, I was relieved. Like I told him, if I never heard another speech about progress it would be too soon. Everyone who came within range banged on about how this field had been barren and that flourishing orange grove had been planted in the desert, how the whole place was derelict until the Israelis came to irrigate the land and farm it properly. And all that talk about the past—the recent European past, and the historical facts recorded in the Old Testament. There'd been ancient gods in Cyprus too, I seemed to remember, but the Greeks didn't still think Jupiter or Aphrodite mattered. Over here, people were so unrelaxed. Boys twirling their army rifles like City gents with their umbrellas. Everyone so tense. I couldn't be doing with the politics of it. I wanted to concentrate on us. Murdo and me. A couple, a pair, a unit. I believed he was Mr Right.

Until Sde Boker. It's pronounced Seddy Bockair. A place in the Negev desert.

And now I'm scared to write down what happened there. I'm frightened of someone reading what I've said. He won't let me screw things up for him. And he's ruthless.

CHAPTER NINETEEN

When Fidelis got round to looking at the floppy disk, she found it was in Microsoft Word. Fidelis had gone over to an Apple when she retired on the unworthy ground that the hardware was elegant, but she managed the conversion and brought the floppy's file list up onto her screen. The names were simply letters—A, T, U, B, W, Q—there were six files in all. This was Lesley's back-up floppy which she had put somewhere apart from her laptop for security. It was what Fidelis did herself and so did any other computer user with a grain of caution. Fidelis kept one floppy disk in her car and another in her Filofax, marvelling when she caught sight of the fragment of plastic, that on it could be stored a whole unpublished book. Lesley Cameron had used the old-fashioned writing-box.

The files were copies of indispensable information. One was an income tax return for the year 1997 to 1998. Embarrassed to be looking at it and embarrassed by her own silly embarrassment, Fidelis scanned the figures. How pitifully little money the poor woman had lived on. She certainly did not make enough to pay tax, indeed might have qualified for some supplementary benefits if she ever brought herself to apply. From her work as a writer the only payment listed was from Public Lending Right, which had brought in £127.

One file was copies of letters. To Thames Water demanding the installation of a meter, to British Telecom, registering for a low-user tariff, to the local council explaining that Lesley lived alone and was entitled to a single-person council tax discount.

The file labelled B was about the bank loan or mortgage Lesley had raised when she inherited the house. And the next one was W: her will.

The bank says I've got to make a will if I don't want anything that's left when I die to go to the Chancellor of the Exchequer, which is what happens if you're intestate and don't have any relations. I've never felt quite so alone as when that well-groomed young man told me that. I'd thought he was quite attractive until that moment, it felt like we were friends chatting, but then I realized he saw me as an old bag, absolutely out of his sphere, a poor thing raising her pitiful little loan to avert destitution. I nearly wept; but it would only have confirmed his opinion. At least I hadn't told him I was going to spend some of it on plastic surgery.

He suggested I should leave everything to charity and gave me a printed list of good causes. I read the names. Animal charities—but I've never been keen on pets. Environmental ones; not for me, as far as I'm concerned it's *après mois le déluge*, why should I care if I'm not going to be there, it's not as though I've got any descendants to worry about. Then there were a whole lot of organizations devoted to being nice to other people but I just wondered who'd ever been nice to me? Look at me, all alone, unappreciated, with nobody to love me or for me to turn to— why the hell should I? It's like what happened to my books. Now it's me. Rejected.

I could count on the fingers of one hand the people I've had kindness from. Mum and Dad. Keith, for a while. Jeremy, ditto. Paul wasn't ever kind and neither were any of the other men I've known.

Not kind.

Dr Berlin was kind. When I'd just heard about what was wrong with me and thought everything was all over—one does, at the first shock, it's natural to fear the worst, you think straight away that nothing can be done about it, that no treatment will help. I was in despair and she was really kind. Just like she'd been the previous time though she was far too professional to mention it. That was real tact, very considerate not to let on. You don't want someone to remind you about being mental a long time ago. I thought it was really nice of her to pass over that without a word.

So she was a patient, after all, Fidelis realized, it must have been post-puerperal trauma.

And we've had conversations since then. We've become friends. When I manage to find a seat at her table at the cyberbridge game I always feel a warm glow, like heat's coming off the computer screen, there's this benevolent presence, in infinite space and in my own room. Hi, Elsie, she'll write, nd a pd? I tap in, Rehi, F, or hello again, yes I do need a partner. And then we exchange pleasantries. She says it's raining or I say it's hot. We play well together, almost as if there's some kind of telepathic understanding.

Actually she's the only person in the whole world who's ever been disinterestedly kind to me. Dr Fidelis Berlin.

Good Lord, did I really play bridge with her? thought Fidelis. She wondered who else she knew might be disguised by the codenames of play and realized that she must immediately change her playing name, Fiddle, to something by which nobody, having learnt that Dr Fidelis Berlin was a member, could possibly identify her.

She hadn't played cyberbridge for a long time. Her mind had been on other things. But with the music the intellectual restlessness had returned too, a mental energy that was perversely rested by its total concentration on the play of the cards. I'll log on when I've seen to all this, she thought. But Fidelis had never played bridge seriously, either in real or virtual life. At the cyberbridge club, her habit was simply to click on any 'table' that had a vacant 'seat' and she never remembered the coded identities of her partners or opponents from one session to the next. In the very middle of a game she couldn't remember whose table to rejoin if her computer crashed and she had to log in all over again. She felt no awareness of the other players as people. It was one of the reasons that the game was so pleasurable.

Total impersonality was a holiday for someone in Fidelis's profession, though she knew other people did make insubstantial friendships across the world, she'd seen their typed, curiously intimate conversations. Some players even posted their email addresses along with their convention cards.

Was it possible that Lesley's legacy had been made on such illusory and flimsy grounds?

Patients did sometimes leave tokens of gratitude, or give them, or ask what Fidelis would like. She'd always been grateful for anything that could be consumed: wine, whisky, chocolate, a basket of fruit, a truckle of cheese or, once, a year's supply of organic eggs. Cash she passed on, usually for whatever item of equipment her nearest hospital was at that time raising funds to buy. Everything else she politely refused.

'If I'd only known she was a patient I'd have refused to have anything to do with the late Lesley Cameron,' she muttered aloud. There was plenty wrong, almost certainly clinically wrong, with that woman. The diagnostic phrases sprang into her mind, but this was not the occasion for them. In these circumstances Fidelis was allowed the normal human reaction—that the woman, quite simply, was a self-pitying, lonely mess.

She scrolled the page down, seeing that the will she'd already read was copied on the screen. And at its end, another sentence.

She'd know what should be done about Murdo. She'd give me the courage to tell someone about him. I'm afraid of what he might do if he thought I was going to tell. I daren't tell a journalist. First off they'd ring him up, and he'd know straight away it was me, and then—well, I know how unscrupulous he is. I'm the only person alive who does know. And I really don't think I'd stay alive. He'd kill me. I really really believe he would, he'd do anything to keep me quiet. But my conscience is troubling me. I managed to put it behind me, out of my mind, for years. But now they've made him a judge. It's not right. He's not good enough. He's got to be exposed.

That was where the file ended. Fidelis went back and read it again. She thought, there can't be two judges called Murdo. Then she printed the document out but thought better of it and shredded the pages. This stuff was dynamite.

If true.

She could hardly bear to click on to the next and final file. Its initial was Q.

Q for quandary. Q for question.

This was a longer document. It was not continuous but fragmented, each section separated by page breaks. Lesley had obviously written it in emotional spurts as a form of thinking aloud, or, as at some point in it she said, thinking at the tips of her fingers.

He has become a judge. A High Court judge. One of Her Majesty's Judiciary.

How is it possible?

It never crossed my mind that this was on the cards. Even if it had occurred to me, I wouldn't have believed it.

He's not fit to sit in judgement on other people. And I'm the only person in the world who knows it.

Fidelis made herself read on, but reluctantly. Her professional and personal judgement was that she was looking at a sick fantasy. But could she rely on that? Her instinctive revulsion from this voice from the grave was probably all the more reason to take it seriously. Never let friendship cloud your judgement, she'd warned students in her time. But she really didn't want to know what Murdo was, or had done, or was capable of.

If only I'd never found the disk. If only that woman had left me out of her fantasies. I could just chuck it away, she thought. Nobody would ever know. Make it as though this legacy had never been.

But she was constrained by a lifetime of taking responsibility for others. Even if the record was destroyed it would stay there in

Fidelis's head. She couldn't stop now. But no wonder the woman hadn't any friends, Fidelis thought viciously. And no wonder she was so unsuccessful as a writer. Lesley Bowhill Cameron clearly had little internal perception of other people as existing except in so far as they impinged on her. Dislikeable or not, she had a story to tell.

She wasn't telling it to me, Fidelis thought, but she knew I knew him. Was leaving me the problem some kind of insurance—or just a ghastly coincidence? For it was horribly clear. On her travels with Murdo Wolf-Wolferstan he had done something so dreadful that Lesley was afraid to utter it all these years on. And the woman had indeed been killed. Killed in a way she'd invented herself years previously—and if that complicated concoction, fiction or not, didn't show her mind was sick and disordered, what else would? A nutter, a nasty nutter. Not words that a psychiatrist would normally use. Nor were 'crazy' or 'bonkers'. But, she was bonkers. Anyone who'd read her disgusting fantasy would remember it, stashed unlabelled in the lumber room of the mind, to be dragged out, unidentified, years later, and put to use.

I'm going crazy myself, Fidelis thought.

She got up to change the music, putting on Verdi's Requiem. She was trembling almost too much to hit the right button. The left hand would not obey the signals from the brain. It was increasingly difficult to press the computer keys.

It's because I don't want to read what he did, she thought, I don't want to know the worst.

Oh Murdo, what have you done?

CHAPTER TWENTY

On the second weekend of half-term, a dark, damp evening, three Plowden kids were struggling across the spongy recreation ground with an old dressmaker's dummy that had been left behind the water tank in the attic of their new home. Their mother had screamed at the sight of it, thinking in quick succession that the dim shape was an intruder, a body and a ghost. Then she told her Kevin to get the disgusting thing out of there, do it now! It was Emma who had recognized that the female form was just the thing for a guy. She'd made a head out of a balloon covered with fabric and pinched a baby-buggy from a shed some dorks two roads down had left unlocked.

'Penny for the guy' had been really really good, far better than trick-or-treat. Who wanted sweets when they could pull in real money? The three of them were taking a short cut across the rec, on the way to East Plowden station to shake down the angry crowds of delayed commuters, when Emma stumbled against an obstacle and fell flat on the mud, pulling the chair and guy over with her. Into the squelchy grass. Kevin was yelling at her when she realized what she'd fallen over and let out a screech that drowned his voice. This one really was a body.

CHAPTER TWENTY-ONE

Sde Boker was in the middle of the Negev desert. It was a horrible drive there. Actually I wasn't enjoying the trip at all by this time, mainly because I was pretty sure I must be pregnant and didn't dare tell Murdo. I didn't know how he'd take it.

But even if I'd been perfectly well, I wouldn't have chosen to spend my time in that hot, horrible place. The first day was OK, we found an oasis with a natural waterfall and bathing pool, and although there were far too many other people there, lots of rowdy kids and shouting parents, it looked like something out of a romantic film so I felt like a film star twisting and turning my body under the spray and feeling my hair plastered wetly to my back and visualizing the drops of water on my bronzed face and hanging from my black eyelashes.

Murdo insisted on going up to the top of the Masada, which is a grim rock in the dry desert where lots of besieged Jews jumped to their deaths rather than be enslaved by the Romans. That was crowded too, full of teenagers chanting in Hebrew, words a guide told us meant 'never again'. Murdo said it was because of what happened at the Olympics, which had put everyone on the defensive. Fair enough, I thought, I would have felt like that too, but not being Jewish it all seemed apart from us. Eventually Murdo agreed to carry on. That night we slept in the hired car under the stars, which sounds more romantic than it felt at the time, since neither of us had any idea it could get so cold, but we dropped off eventually. When we woke up, it was hot again but we were in a howling gale, with dust blowing into the car and our clothes and eyes and hair, horrid. The guidebook said this wind happened occasionally, bad luck on us to get caught in it. It was called the khamsin and was blowing up from Africa. Men could be driven mad by it. If they killed their wives in a fit of rage they'd be let off if the khamsin was blowing.

We didn't think it would last long, not after such still, hot days as there'd been; and we couldn't stop where we were, so we drove on southwards, looking forward to plunging into the Red Sea at Eilat. But you couldn't make much progress in that weather. Far from being down in the south near the Red Sea by the late afternoon, we were just near Sde Boker, where the book said there was a hostel, so we decided to stop there. We were driving through the dirty fog on the outskirts of the town when it happened.

I hadn't been watching the road, so the first I knew was a thud, and Murdo stamping down on the brake and the car skidding to a stop.

He leapt out and ran back, behind the car. I got out more slowly because my door opened into the wind and I had to lean really hard against it.

There was a child lying at the edge of the road behind us. About six, with brown arms and legs, black pigtails, a gold hoop in each ear, a full-length, dirty white caftan-type dress. Blood was pooling under her body.

Murdo knelt on the dusty ground. There was a keening noise coming from him, a kind of high 'no no no' sound. He put his fingers round the child's wrist and then put his ear to her mouth. I touched her skin. It was smooth, damp, cooler than mine. He said, 'She's dead.'

'No, she can't be,' I protested.

'I think she is.'

'But look, her chest's moving, let me find my mirror, I can see—'

'What are we going to do?' he said.

I said, 'There must be a hospital. An ambulance.' I looked wildly around, but other people had more sense than to be driving round in a sandstorm. There was nobody and nothing to be seen in the swirling sand and dust, except that the shapes of goats or sheep began to loom up out of the gloom. One or two of them came close and I tried to flap them away.

'She can't have been all alone out here,' I sobbed.

He said, 'She must be the shepherdess.'

'Oh, why doesn't anyone come? Please God let help come!'

Murdo got to his feet and moved to examine the car. He called, 'There's no mark.'

'Oh, what does that matter?' I was crying by that time, here was this poor little girl like a broken doll sprawled at our feet. 'We've got to get her to hospital, lift her up.'

'We can't do anything for her. You know she's dead,' he said.

'Oh no, she can't be, her parents, her poor mother.' I'd never seen a dead person before. 'But I don't think she is dead, come on, Murdo, take her legs.'

'This means prison,' Murdo said.

'What does that matter?' I tried to make him hurry up. 'Quickly, hurry.'

'That would be my whole future,' he said. 'All done for just because of one Yid kid.'

I'm probably making most of the exact words up, like I did when it was stories I was writing, but the sense is accurate and that last sentence was engraved on my mind, because I'd been so careful ever since we got here not to talk like my dad or think like him either though it was difficult when the Israelis were mostly so rude and aggressive. Murdo hadn't said a single word that showed he harboured anti-Semitic thoughts, not till that moment. *All because of one Yid kid.*

'That'll be curtains for my career,' he said. 'The bar, my future—I'd be done for.'

And still nobody came along. And there the poor child lay, limp and still, with blood spreading from her body on to the road. Dust settled quickly on its scarlet gleam, dulling it as it flowed.

I've got to remember how young I was. Ignorant. Inexperienced. I didn't know anything. I thought we could save her and he was sure it was too late. He forced me into the car, twisted my arms behind me, shoved me down, started the engine, did a rapid three-point turn and drove away.

That was a dreadful thing we did, I say we, because I'm guilty too, although it was Murdo who drove the car that injured the child and Murdo who insisted we should leave her there where she lay. He said it wouldn't help her to have him punished, the girl was dead and there was nothing we could do for her, what was the point of ruining his life for an accident? He was persuasive. It's his metier.

Veteran of real-life horror stories though she was, Fidelis was brought up short by the image of a child bleeding to death on the dusty road while Murdo—*Murdo!*—drove away.

I don't feel well enough for this, she thought. She had started thinking herself a bit better recently, taking new medication, *coping*. But now it came to her that there was no improvement, not really, in fact a deterioration. It was just that she was getting so used to her condition she didn't notice it when she felt poorly, her limbs weighted down by non-specific aches. It had become normality.

But she didn't feel up to reading on. Perhaps now was the moment to give way to illness, let herself off the hook of duty.

'Fidelis Berlin, pull yourself together,' she said aloud, and turned back to the intimidating screen and its hateful text.

201

The sand and dirt were falling like a blanket on the windscreen, visibility was down to almost nothing so Murdo had to inch along with the wipers labouring and groaning. We can't have gone even a mile. My head was in my hands, I was sobbing my heart out.

We hardly spoke, just enough to say we'd give up on the idea of Eilat, we'd make straight for Tel Aviv and Murdo would use his credit card to buy us air tickets out.

It was a Mexican stand-off because I couldn't tell anyone what we'd done for fear of what would happen to me, his unwilling, ashamed accomplice. My period started when we were in the air. So there was no unfinished business between us and I never spoke to Murdo Wood-Wolferstan again.

CHAPTER TWENTY-TWO

The Plowden local paper, *The Gazette*, was a freesheet that was delivered to every letter box in the borough once a week. On the second Thursday after half-term it led with a factual report about the body in the recreation ground, which had been that of a middle-aged woman called Janine Robertson, who had been coshed and robbed of her purse and jewellery. It was not the attack that killed her, but a stroke, not her first, that she had suffered afterwards. But the Plowden Action Group called for more severe penalties for criminals and proper police protection for local citizens. A spokesman said, 'We've got known wrongdoers living among us, violent criminals with clever lawyers who know how to cheat the system. The government must act. If it doesn't honest citizens will be forced to take the law into our own hands. Otherwise our wives and children can't sleep safe in their own beds.'

CHAPTER TWENTY-THREE

Fidelis would have thought it an unlikely story if a patient had told it. She'd have put it down as the fantasy of someone who'd read (or even written) too many novels—if it hadn't been about Catriona's Murdo.

Fidelis remembered the year he went travelling. It wasn't quite so common in the early seventies, students didn't all disappear for a 'gap year' with their backpacks. But Murdo wasn't a student by then, was he? It must have been after university and law school when he was a trainee. He was lucky to be allowed the whole long legal vacation off. His mother knew he was somewhere in southern Europe, as the postcards trickled in, but she didn't know he was alone with a girl. No, correction: she didn't know which girl he was alone with. Fidelis had been working with Catriona that summer on a government-commissioned study of foster care, so there had been lots of proud talk of Catriona's golden boy.

Fidelis remembered his homecoming too, as he came up the lane to Catriona's cottage, a perfect early autumn day. Fidelis had been gathering blackberries and looked up to see the tall, smiling youth and to feel his brotherly hug. It must have been the very next day that hugs turned to sexy embraces and brotherly to loverly affection in Catriona's orchard. Not allowing herself the diversion of analysing the fruit symbolism, Fidelis asked herself whether she had taken Murdo away from Lesley? Had she kicked off the series of disappointments that made up Lesley Cameron's life?

Unlike Lesley Cameron, Fidelis had never recorded her own thoughts or experiences, but she used engagement diaries, though entries were gnomic and most of them incomprehensible even by her when she checked back. What did a large S enclosed in a circle mean, why had she put asterisks here and there, who was the Oliver she'd met for dinner at the Coq d'Or? It gave Fidelis a pang of grief to see her own firm black handwriting.

She could hardly write her name so that a bank clerk would recognize her signature now.

No, there was no entry to remind her of the detail of that distant time.

Try another tack. How come I'm reading this anyway? By pure chance. Lesley 'thought aloud' by writing on to her screen. She saved her files on to security floppy disks. One she put, and accidentally left, in a cabinet given to Gavin to restore. That one remained after all Lesley's documents and her hard disk were taken from her house by her killer.

And why did it come to me? *Think!* she admonished herself.

Lesley Cameron read that Murdo had become a judge. She wanted to talk to him, maybe she thought she could tell if he was a reformed character, maybe she intended to make him resign. She must have tried to speak to him. Gemma said she'd phoned and Murdo hung up on her. Why would he do that if it wasn't true, if he didn't know she'd got something on him? And then she went to see him in the flesh at the procession, she'd have known he'd be there, at the beginning of the legal year in 1998. The year he'd become a judge. But he wouldn't acknowledge her then either.

But that's where I come in.

Lesley happened to see Fidelis standing with him as a guest and recognized her as the doctor who had treated her for puerperal psychosis many years earlier, when as a patient she'd been temporarily fixated on her doctor. Having read an article which mentioned that Fidelis played cyberbridge, Lesley then sought her out on line.

Not long after that Lesley met Fidelis in Bloomsbury. Was it a coincidence? Not perhaps a remarkable one. Lesley had probably noticed an advertisement for Fidelis's signing session. That was probably on the Internet too. Typing Fidelis's name into a search engine would have done the trick. Lesley planned to turn up at it, being in the neighbourhood for a hospital appointment. Fidelis's apparent concern for her distress had revived that old feeling of dependence and that old illusion of a nonexistent personal relationship between the two women.

So in her mind Lesley built Fidelis up as the one person who could help her—and as the only person she wanted to benefit if she died, though she wasn't expecting to die, as far as one could tell from her ramblings. Funny, Fidelis thought, that she doesn't even mention the diagnosis. I don't even know which organ was affected. Perhaps the test result had given a false positive. She may not have been ill after all.

But Lesley was frightened about Murdo, and by pure chance left this information about him in a form and in a place where one of Murdo's friends would find it when she was dead. Dead not from her fatal disease but because someone killed her. Someone who had a motive for silencing her. Someone who used a method that was intended to make it look as if she'd killed herself—a method Lesley herself had described in her long-forgotten novel. A novel Murdo had owned and denied reading.

Where Lesley Cameron 'thought at the tips of her fingers' on her keyboard, Fidelis sometimes clarified her thoughts by speaking them aloud, or dictating. It was a rare fine day so she went out to sweep up leaves, muttering as she worked. The disadvantage of having a garden backing on to a communal one was that the ancient deciduous trees, which filtered the sun in summer, emptied a dozen bagfuls of 'garden refuse' on to her flagstones in the autumn. It was as much a question of scraping as sweeping after the wettest autumn on record. It was difficult to work up a rhythm when one side of her body was so disobedient, which perhaps contributed to the unaccustomed disjointedness of her thoughts.

What does A do next?

Where did that old quotation come from? Was it a school test paper? What should F do next? Go to the police? You've got to be joking. About *Murdo*? Regard him in the same light as all the others, those patients who told her about horrendous acts, often about crimes, which of course she'd kept to herself as a physician must, repository of the soul's dread secrets.

I want to forget it, she thought, just as Lesley Cameron herself had managed to do for years. But her crisis of conscience had been well founded. If one knew a judge had committed a crime one had to do something about it. Especially such a crime. I'm not more shocked about killing a Jewish kid than any other, Fidelis told herself, but that story has pressed all my personal buttons. And murder. Her mind briefly wandered into an enumeration of the patients who'd admitted, or claimed perhaps untruly, to have killed. Not so many, over the years. And none of them set up to pass judgement on others.

But perhaps none of this was true. Perhaps after all she'd used the method she'd invented for murder to kill herself. And how reliable was a witness who, after all, was a professional, if awful, novelist? A story-teller. Someone whose job was making up lies.

'Fidelis, you're talking to yourself, is it really the first sign of madness?' Seeby Curzon had paused in his daily walk round the communal garden. The secretary of the 'gardens committee', he took his responsibilities seriously, often picking up litter or cutting off suckers the contractors had missed. 'You look worried, nothing wrong, I hope?'

'No, thanks, Seeby, I'm fine, I was just pondering a problem.'

'Trouble? A trouble shared is a trouble halved.' He took any chance to keep the boredom of retirement at bay.

'What would you do, Seeby, if you knew someone in a responsible position had committed a crime in his youth and never been suspected?'

'A serious crime? Or a traffic offence?'

'Very serious.'

'Tell the authorities,' said the former civil servant.

Asked over the next days, Fidelis's other friends proffered advice that matched their own preconceptions.

'Write up an in-depth investigation,' said Esmond Smith after his lifetime in newspapers.

Tina said she'd offer the unnamed person a book-contract.

Honor said Fidelis had enough on her plate without dredging up other people's gossip.

And Clodie asked, 'How d'you know it's true? I'd tackle him or tackle the story, or both.'

CHAPTER TWENTY-FOUR

But Clodie, who had called late, when Fidelis was thinking of going to bed and wondering if she could be bothered to move, wanted to tell Fidelis something else.

On Saturday, her day off from the hospital, she'd gone to the police headquarters where the CID had shut her up in a windowless room and given her access to all the material in the Lesley Cameron case. The material was disconcertingly extensive. Every little scrap of information from the very first moment the police were called to Lesley Cameron's house was recorded and preserved. Much of it was computerized: the incident room logs, the index of those interviewed, the witness statements, the pro formas from house-to-house enquiries, the summary sheets in which every drop of information was digested, itemized and cross-referenced. In this case there had been no surveillance, video footage or phone taps, but other physical evidence was stored in plastic and paper bags, while the forensic material was stored in the lab.

Then there was the hard copy material. The Senior Investigating Officer's log was a large hardback lined book in which he wrote down every policy or practical decision that he or anyone else had made during the investigation—whether to drop or pursue a line of enquiry, and the reason for any action taken or ordered. There were periodic résumés of the case so far. There were copies of reports made for the force's chief officer. In this case there was a note of a review of the case papers by a Detective Chief Superintendent and the Chief Constable after the acquittal of Gavin Rayner, and of their agreement that 'further investigation of the case was unlikely to be fruitful.' The file was marked 'NFA' for 'no further action'.

It took Clodie a little while to find her way round the English version though she had seen the equivalent records in America and understood the rationale behind keeping this mountain of material, because justice required that the evidence had to be seen to be fair and truthful and to have been obtained with proper legality. The defence was entitled to full disclosure of every single little detail, even those the prosecution would not be relying on in court. The investigators had no discretion here, they were not permitted to decide what might be revealed. Gavin's lawyers could have seen the whole lot—and been as bored and daunted by it as Clodie, whose mind kept sliding away to the bright day outside.

She'd seen Gavin across the road as she left her front gate. Gavin had come out of his shell in the last days, encouraged as the neighbourhood grew used, or resigned, to his presence. There had been other things for the householders of the Knighton Estate to worry about as the rain continued to fall, in this wettest autumn for a century; the Plowden clay became saturated, house foundations loosened, the park turned into a pond and floods washed away part of the embankment that carried the main commuter railway lines.

In watery sunshine, Gavin called across:

'Want to go to the match?'

'I'd really love to but I've got to work.'

She hadn't told him she was going to try to clear his name.

It was uncomfortable to find herself fancying a man who might be a murderer though in fact it was an occupational hazard, one she'd been warned of when starting to specialize in forensics. Some patients exerted a perverse attraction on the psychiatrist, especially, an improperly candid male doctor said, if the psychiatrist was a woman. His lack of caution only went so far. He didn't dare to voice his politically incorrect feelings about Clodie's appointment, but he moved around in a cloud of disapproval that a pretty young woman should have been given a job working with violent, unbalanced male patients. A nurse interpreted in a whisper. 'He thinks it's dangerous for you and unsettling for them.'

Well, perhaps there'd been something in it. Clodie was treading a thin line. She came to know the patients in such intimate circumstances, with none of the usual intellectual or emotional holds barred. There had been one serial killer, a man with sea green, hypnotic eyes . . . Clodie understood only too well how he'd charmed and seduced his victims. He'd appeared in her more embarrassing dreams.

Was Gavin one of those? Intuition wasn't

enough. Clodie needed to know if he could really be, as the police still believed he was, Lesley Cameron's killer.

Motive? Theft, the police had said, which never seemed terribly plausible. Rage? Clodie still remembered the vicious expression on Gavin's face at the notion that Lesley had any kind of sexual appeal for Mickey. If he'd discovered his son with her . . . the boy had been only fifteen, but tall and handsome, probably, if his father was anything to go by. There were plenty of women who fancied very young men, who slipped between the sheets of their sons' school friends on a sleepover, teachers who seduced their pupils. It could easily have happened, a lonely, sexy, disappointed woman and a young neighbour. Would it have driven the boy's father to murder? Yes. It might. It could. Clodie could almost believe it—but only if the killing had been violent, brutal, the act of a man who'd lost it, not something calculated and sly. No, she told herself, she wouldn't suggest that to the police. But she knew she ought to. It was relevant. She shoved the unwelcome thought into a back recess of her mind and turned to opportunity.

Yes. The victim had let her killer into the house, gone to the door, opened it—and? The path report said the body showed no signs of a struggle other than infinitesimal traces of fabric under her fingernails. Someone wearing a navy fleece could have grabbed her from behind. The scene of crimes officers reported that the carpet showed indistinct marks from the sole of an Adidas trainer, not sufficiently complete to size accurately, and scuff marks and black shoe polish. Lesley was wearing well-cleaned black leather lace-up shoes. There had also been some hairs on the carpet—Lesley's dyed hairs, white at the root. There were unidentified prints in the sitting room, and on a coffee mug in the kitchen, but the house was not scrupulously clean and those prints could date from months back. Some crockery and door handles showed the prints of Lesley's bridge players. And beside the body was a glass with her own prints on it, naturally enough in her own house, and smudges of latex from other hands inside surgical gloves. And Gavin's fingerprints.

The police thought Gavin had grabbed her hair from behind, pulled her head back in a simple, disabling hold, and with his other hand held the glass to her mouth, though without leaving scratches or bruises. Dribbles of drugged alcohol had dried on her chin and jersey. The attacker had then pulled a plastic bin bag over her head and shoulders and left her to suffocate. The outside of the bag showed smudged marks but no fingerprints.

The autopsy report showed the remains in the glass matched the stomach-contents analysis: temazepam and whisky. Other irrelevant details were noted. The victim was well nourished, but had not eaten for several hours before her death. She had been pregnant at least once. She had crowns on her front teeth. She had broken her left tibia and fibia in childhood. Her hair was dyed. She had bunions, corns and a Morton's neuroma on her feet; walking would have been painful. There was early arthritis in the left hip. More seriously, she had pancreatic cancer which had metastasized into the liver and bowel. There was no physical trace of treatment, with no chemotherapy traces in the analysis, no radiation burns or hair loss on the body. The immediate cause of death was suffocation while sedated.

Motive, opportunity, means. Well, this was a very peculiar murder method, perhaps even a unique one, being both uncertain and inconvenient and more suitable to the pages of Lesley's junk fiction than to her real and dreadful death. What a comeuppance for a novelist! But it was the most commonly used and widely known means of suicide among women. *Perpetrator F not M?* Clodie wrote on her pad. Or had that perpetrator expected the death to be taken as suicide and tried to make it look like that? Because otherwise, once inside the house it would have been much easier to hit the victim over the head. Or use one of the kitchen knives to stab her. Or cut her throat.

Devious, Clodie thought, unphysical, indirect. She underlined the 'F' and crossed out the question mark. But would any woman have left the water running and the gas on? It had wasted away for days. But if Lesley let a friend or acquaintance in, why hadn't she turned the kitchen tap and the gas off at that stage herself? Or had someone else turned the taps on? But why would the killer want to give the fact away by showing Lesley had been interrupted when preparing her lonely lunch? Yet in a pretence of suicide there would be no traces of a meal under preparation, the eggs set out for boiling, the toast popped from the toaster. Women who make careful arrangements to die don't bring it about on impulse, having planned a neat little meal.

But where was the bottle of whisky, the pot of tranquillizers? Gone with the word processor and paper files. A careful perpetrator then, who knew the house well enough to come round to the back, and then left the same way, slamming the back door shut on the way out. The front had been double-locked and bolted from the inside.

Her visitor can't have left her time to turn everything off, pushing her straight through into the sitting room as soon as he or she came in and afterwards, perhaps in a panic, or maybe simply with hands too full of gear to bother with the taps, rushing away. Unless somebody else had been there too.

If not a woman, then a man who was not used to physical violence. A man with access to temazepam. His wife's? A man who didn't get his sexual kicks from violence. This was an unusual case for the psychological profiling techniques she'd learned at Quantico and begun to use in Boston. Nearly all her experience was in cases where the victim was a woman, usually several women, who had been subjected to unimaginable cruelty and suffered from perverted sexual practices.

She'd tried to imagine what turned someone into a serial rapist, torturer and killer. What could have motivated the unknown man to do these dreadful things to a woman, what childhood experiences, what imagined adventures, what misunderstood signals had driven him on?

But no sexual component had been identified in Lesley Cameron's death. The only detail shared with those other cases was her gender, and assuming her killer was not the man accused, it could perfectly well have been a woman. Or, an intellectual man in a sedentary profession who'd dressed up in sports gear. Nobody in the street had noticed anyone or anything, but then nobody but Gavin had been at home. Anyone could have driven up in a delivery van. Or a car. Or walked there.

And why? Any of the other houses in the street would have been as easy to enter. There was a reason for choosing Lesley's, and it can't have been the obvious one because she didn't have anything worth stealing. No, her killer wanted those files and whatever was on the computer. She (and Clodie still inclined to think it was a woman's crime) or he had a secret that Lesley knew and intended to make sure she never had a chance to tell it. And that, Clodie told herself, having managed to bring herself to the conclusion she'd hoped to reach, couldn't have been Gavin Rayner.

CHAPTER TWENTY-FIVE

The Langs' phone rang unanswered for much of the day. They didn't call back in response to Fidelis's message until evening, by which time she'd finished reading Lesley's screed, and gone over it again trying to find gaps or implausibilities. It can't be true, ran a refrain in her mind.

Explaining to Yossi what she wanted checked out was less of an ordeal than she'd prepared for, having forgotten that his training and experience were not only of reading between lines and hearing the words people didn't say, but also not asking questions. She visualized his dark, sun-spotted face, his intelligent brown eyes and the expression of someone who has seen it all. His voice was weaker than when they'd last met, but clear.

'OK, got it,' he said. 'Was a child killed in a hit-and-run, September '72. That it?'

'If you could, Yossi, I'll send you the text as an attachment, you won't mind if I delete the names.'

'No problem. I'll get back to you.' The laid-back languor of the public schoolboy he must once have been was overlaid by a brisk, brusque, 'don't waste time' attitude that, Fidelis knew, was not meant to be unfriendly. It was how all the Israelis she'd ever met just were. He cut her thanks short and had rung off before she'd finished the phrase, 'love to Vicky'.

CHAPTER TWENTY-SIX

A leaflet about the meeting to be held the following week was put through every letter box on the Knighton Estate except for one. Gavin was in his front room trying, for the umpteenth time, to make Julie see sense and let Mickey come round. He saw the woman who delivered the leaflets, in and out of garden gates, up the far side of the road and down his own. She went quickly past his frontage, eyes averted, a stout, pink, mumsy figure in a shiny pink anorak and track suit bottoms, moving like someone who was scared. I did that, he thought. My enemy. My victim. Funny, that, when the real victim was Gavin himself. His new-old car had been vandalized so many times, even if he parked it half a mile away, that he'd given up on it; the useless hunk of metal and broken glass sat up the road on its collapsed tyres and could stay there till it rotted. Mickey had not so much as called his father. The Pig had been transferred to North Hendon so Mickey was a two-hour journey away. If he came it would have to be for a night and Julie wasn't having that. She claimed that Mickey didn't want to and he couldn't come to the phone either. Gavin asked for Mickey's mobile number but Julie wouldn't tell him that. He didn't even know if his son had got a driving licence yet.

It would have to be legal action in the end, like Veronica said, but it didn't seem a very good way to win the boy's affection back. Maybe when I move, Gavin thought. If I move. If I ever find anywhere to move to when I don't even have the get up and go to do any house-hunting. I'm good for nothing now.

Veronica thought Gavin was clinically depressed. It's like post-natal depression, she told him, you can't expect to get over an experience like that without help. She'd offered him a holiday in the sun or a private-medicine visit to a shrink. 'There's a woman I know . . .' she'd murmured. 'Maybe all you need is Prozac.'

Gavin couldn't be bothered with any of that. He didn't even think about sex. He just slept a lot instead, at least by day, when his eyelids would fall closed over a kind of stupor. At night he had bad dreams.

He knew that two things would make him better: getting together with Mickey again was one, having a chance to make him realize his dad was still the same person. He worried so much about the lad. What was he learning about life from The Pig? Were they making him study for his A levels? Did they know who his girlfriends were? Did they understand him at all? Were they protecting him? He didn't feel strong enough for confrontation and rejection yet but one of these days Gavin would go up to Hendon and see Mickey. Maybe when he'd got himself together by spending gradual, peaceful time with the wood. Making something in the sweet smell, feeling a smooth, imagined object emerge, tactile and organic. So far he'd only been able to doodle. He had no energy for anything. All the same, he kept a look-out for the red-haired knock-out who'd come to live opposite. She was careful about drawing curtains at dusk and never even took milk off the doorstep in her dressing gown, but catching sight of her on the way in or out was about the only cheerful spot in the whole dismal world.

221

CHAPTER TWENTY-SEVEN

In an apocalyptic November week, when heavy rain incessantly fell and ground water rose, when thousands of homes were flooded and Britain's railway tracks were washed away, roads were blocked by processions of lorries whose drivers were protesting about the price of fuel, scores of young skiers were burnt to death in a fire-swept tunnel under the snowy Alps and the votes of billions of American citizens were so close in number that neither candidate emerged as President of the world's only superpower—in such a week as this it was only proper that torrential rain, horizontal in a gale force wind blowing straight up the Thames estuary, should greet Fidelis as she emerged from the underground at Canary Wharf to walk the few steps to the Light Railway. Her umbrella blew inside out immediately. Soaked as though by a power-shower she stood in the steaming carriage and emerged on the south bank of the river where she decided there was no point in trying to protect her hair or clothes; lie back—or rather, stride forward—and enjoy it.

Fidelis's foster mother would have said it was 'raining stair rods' though it had taken Fidelis a long time to understand the phrase, since no house she'd seen in the Wales of her childhood had a stair carpet held down by shiny metal rods. The watery silver stripes enhanced the view. There were the archaic masts and rigging of the clipper ship the *Cutty Sark* silhouetted against the night sky. Then one came to a destination worth struggling towards. It was a place of extremes, as though crossing under London from the tame west had brought her to an alien place. How monstrous, but how glamorous, was the highest tower in the country, Canary Wharf, on the far side of the dark, streaming Thames with lights blazing in every window. And the old Royal Naval College at Greenwich must be the most beautiful complex of buildings in England, if not in Europe. When Fidelis had come here for the first concert in the year's programme the previous January, her companion, Philip Pugh, had remarked that sitting in the cream and aquamarine chapel was like being right inside a gigantic piece of Wedgwood pottery. 'Not with that up there,' she'd responded, shuddering at the vast, murky painting above the altar, a *Preservation of St Paul after shipwreck* by Benjamin West.

The cultured middle-aged groupies who regularly turned up to the Monteverdi performances looked as bedraggled as Fidelis felt. She had come by public transport because she was meeting Tina, who had driven up from a visit to an author in Kent. Tina was waiting in the lobby, dry but anxious. 'I shouldn't have let you come by train, it's far too wet!' she wailed.

'Don't be silly, I'm waterproof. In fact I quite like it. Look, isn't this place worth the effort?'

Their seats were near the front, so they could see that, with the Bach cantata pilgrimage nearing the last lap of its millennial marathon, the players were weary, one violinist snoozing when not playing, another mopping her nose and brow. But the conductor's expressive gestures evoked brisk, toe-tapping Bach, serpentine lines and dance time rhythms, a fresh interpretation of familiar music. The counter-tenor produced an unearthly clarity of tone, and the harmony was glorious. To hear the soprano and flute conversing gave Fidelis a spiritual charge she could not explain.

The last time she'd sat behind this frock-coated conductor, facing these white-bloused singers, she had hardly heard a thing. But now the music caught her up into a state all her skill could not analyse and while the instruments and microphones were rearranged she congratulated herself on the change in her own mood since that day in June when pessimism and terror had consumed her. Five months on, the tremor was worse, the weakness increasing. Infirmity inexorably loomed. But, for the time being at least, she'd emerged from the fog that had engulfed her. Now she had too much to do, too many more urgent things to think about.

There was no interval in this concert but in the pauses between cantatas Tina and Fidelis told each other how lovely it was. Baroque music was a taste they had always shared, a counterpoint to their long friendship. In the second gap, Tina whispered:

'Look. Isn't that Wood-Wolferstan over there, a few rows back?'

'I didn't see him.' Damn, Fidelis thought, why did he have to be here to spoil this for me? Can't I have one single evening without worrying? But a deep, dragging fear made her hunch into herself.

'Have you found out why that woman put him in her will?' Tina whispered.

'They went out together for a while.'

'So it was just for old times' sake?'

'She wanted to remind him of something.'

'Something nice, one supposes.'

'She didn't mean it at all kindly.'

'So why a print of Jerusalem? Did they go there together? It must have been ages ago, hasn't he been married for years?'

Tina had always been perceptive, able to hear the things other people didn't say, and she made accurate leaps of understanding. Not an easy person to keep secrets from. Even Fidelis's affirmative murmur was probably some kind of giveaway

'I suppose something went wrong there. Have you asked him what?'

The conductor, his thirst quenched and brow mopped, came to the front again.

'Fidelis? What's the matter, what have I said?'

The lovely noise began. But Fidelis could feel Tina shifting around, and her own concentration was broken by the idea of Murdo back there, unseen behind her. We'll dawdle leaving, she planned, so we needn't speak. But she was waiting for Tina to get her coat when she felt an arm round her shoulder and smelt a faint, astringent citron.

'You're the one who first taught me to like Bach,' Murdo Wood-Wolferstan said.

Trained not to show her feelings, she managed to greet him calmly.

'And how *are* you?'

She could tell immediately from the solicitous, intimate tone of his voice that since they last met he'd heard there was something wrong. Gemma had noticed that evening at dinner. Bristling, she said, 'Fine thanks, and you?'

He told her exactly how he was: the bad cold he was recovering from, the sciatica that plagued him, and then his wrist, still causing trouble after a sprain. He thinks he's entitled, she thought. If you can't tell a mother-surrogate your troubles, who can you tell? But she didn't want to know, she wished she hadn't met him, it was too soon—she needed to decide what to do first.

'How's Gemma?' she asked.

'Oh, she's fine, just getting her coat—there she is. Sweetie, here's Fidelis.'

'Fidelis, how lovely.'

'It's our anniversary, nineteen years, can you believe it?' Murdo said.

'Yes, and look what he's given me, isn't it gorgeous?' Gemma stretched out her hand to display a gold bracelet.

Looking and smiling, Fidelis thought irritably, Is this woman going to boast about her husband's presents every time we meet? Last time it was a wooden bowl—oh my God. It was a sycamore bowl, highly polished, delicate, patterned like tortoiseshell—one of Gavin Rayner's bowls. Suddenly faint, she felt the blood draining out of her cheeks. No no no, it can't be! her mind screamed, lots of people do wood turning, it's not unique, it can't be. But she knew it was the last card in a trembling edifice. Murdo had been to Knighton Drive. When he said he hadn't spoken to Lesley, he'd lied.

'Fidelis, are you all right?'

'Yes, yes, I'm fine.' She leant against the stone doorway.

'Shall I fetch a glass of water?'

'We'll give you a lift home.'

'No, I'm with Tina Svenson, she's got the car.'

Gemma said, 'Murdo, I've just had such a good idea, why don't you invite Fidelis to

Ferriby? Fidelis, he's on circuit in the Midlands later this month, and I'll be in Jakarta—couldn't you go down for a night or so and keep him company, stay in the judge's lodgings?'

They stood to one side, letting others plunge before them into the waterfall outside.

'Good idea,' Murdo agreed heartily. And sincerely? Of course he was sincere, she told herself, why would he have any idea that she'd been the unwilling recipient of Lesley Cameron's leavings and ramblings? How should he know that Fidelis had learnt of his crimes? A vision of the little girl, bloody on the road in a sandstorm, flashed into her mind; and of the young Murdo, running away. If Lesley had decided to tell the secret she'd kept for so many years, then that would have been a cast-iron motive for Murdo to need to silence her.

'We'll wait with you for your friend, shall we?' Gemma offered solicitously.

Could he have been the intellectual man in a sedentary profession, dressed up in sports gear, whose existence Clodie had postulated?

'No,' she said aloud. Not Murdo, not Catriona's boy.

I can't believe it, she thought. Fidelis pulled herself together and said Tina would be there any minute, Gemma and Murdo should carry on. Gemma said there was a long queue for the loo, pressed her scented cheek against

228

Fidelis's, and said, 'Come on, Murdo, we'll make a dash for it.' The Wood-Wolferstans left Fidelis in the shelter of the great door.

She had seldom felt so indecisive. She felt her mind quivering as badly as her limbs. Had this disease affected her brain too? With forced determination, she turned her thoughts to the music she'd heard. And as though its power had switched the points in her brain, she realized that in fact she literally couldn't believe it of Murdo.

She'd had a whole long lifetime devoted to interpreting other people, from the time when an anxious little girl felt the need to understand what strangers wanted of her, till the peak of a career devoted to human interaction. It simply wasn't possible for her to have got so wrong a man she'd known all his life.

As she struggled into her macintosh, her disobedient arm fumbling for the elusive sleeve, and then fought with the recalcitrant catch on her umbrella, Fidelis's mind clicked through a series of consecutive yet almost instantaneous thoughts: her suspicion of Murdo, of His Honour the judge, or of the boy she'd known back in 1972, was unsustainable. He simply couldn't have been the one who killed Lesley Cameron—or anyone else.

I'm not saying anything to anyone, she decided. It would do him too much damage. Until I'm utterly certain, I'm keeping quiet.

Tina talked about Murdo. What had his connection been with Lesley Cameron, did Fidelis have any idea, had Murdo explained it? Eventually Fidelis said:

'Oh, Tina, don't!'

'Sorry, I know he's one of your old protégés.' They lapsed into silence as Tina negotiated the long journey from south-east to north-west London, past floods and overflows and drunken fights.

Fidelis closed her eyes. I don't have to believe it, she thought. The woman was a novelist, she wrote fiction not fact. Her trade was inventing things. Writing down lies. The whole Israel episode could be a figment of her imagination, or at least an embroidery of the truth. Even if Yossi finds that a child really was left for dead by a roadside, it might not have been the way she described. She might even have been driving herself.

CHAPTER TWENTY-EIGHT

Clodie found the word-processed paper when she came in that evening. *Protest meeting. Action group. Neighbourhood watch. Make Plowden safe for our kids and pensioners.* She thought, they can't really think of Gavin like that. Phrases like lynch mob, or run out of town on a rail, or tarred and feathered, came to her only to be banished. Ought I to go across and get him out of here before it's too late? No, come off it, this is England, she told herself, not the Midwest. This is a civilized society. There's a rule of law.

She'd finished work late after an unsatisfactory day, on which a patient who she'd thought was learning to trust her took fright at a figure only he could see at her elbow, and had to be forcibly sedated and removed, but she took off her work clothes and tucked her give-away hair into a baseball cap before jogging off on greasy pavements to the community centre. A neat old gentleman in a regimental tie held out a clipboard for her to sign in. He whispered:

'So glad you've come to support us, but you've missed the speeches, it's question time now.'

'Sorry, maybe I'm too late to—'

'No, no, go on in, it's a good turn-out, we've even got the TV news here.' Her heart sinking still further, Clodie wrote her name with careful illegibility at the end of a very long list. A good many people had come before her. She tiptoed through double swing doors into a single-storey oblong built of breeze blocks, with an airport-style studded rubber floor. Premature Christmas decorations were dangling from wooden roof beams, coloured paper chains and tinsel stars. Children's paintings of Santa Claus were stuck on the rough-cast walls. There were rows of flimsy-looking folding chairs, nearly all taken, and at the far end of the room a low platform, on which three people sat behind a table covered with a brown cloth. The place smelt of wet material. Most people still sat in their anoraks, but some coats were draped, steaming, over a stack of folded green baize tables. Two men with a camera and a mike on a boom stood in a corner looking bored. Clodie looked for, but didn't see, any black, Asian or Chinese faces.

She was reminded, not so much of a town-meeting she'd attended in America, as of the political gathering she'd gone to with one of her early boyfriends, a fiery young socialist in those days but now a conformist New Labour MP. But those had been less well attended than this meeting; and there'd been less passion about. This audience was well worked up by the time Clodie came in. Sliding unobtrusively on to a seat, she suddenly found herself with a tune in her head—which was unusual for her, since Fidelis had failed to pass her passion for music on to her god-daughter. But Clodie was remembering a school concert from her teens. At her school, all education was based on nonconformity, egalitarianism and social conscience. Games never had winners nor exams top marks. It made it difficult to teach anything in hierarchies. Why should Agatha Christie be less worth reading than George Eliot, when both writers had done their honest best? Or what made Beethoven better than his contemporaries? Which was probably one of the reasons the music department put on an obscure Belgian opera by Daniel Auber. On the opening night in 1830 of *La Muette de Portici*, a heroic epic about rebellious Neapolitan fishermen, the audience was so stirred by a duet calling for freedom from the shackles of foreign oppression that they swept out of the theatre without waiting for the end of the performance, began rioting and thus inaugurated the Belgian Revolution. The story had made a great impression on the fourteen-year-old Clodie, and ever since she had been frightened of crowds and what they could do, deeds which individually few of its members could imagine. She had done a dissertation on neuro-chemical changes in the brain as a result of mass hysteria during her very first psychiatry elective.

Not that one could see Miss Eithne Browne succumbing. She was standing up in the front row.

'It's really very upsetting to be here, it's a painful reminder, she used to come to this very place every week, poor dear Mrs Cameron was a leading light of our little bridge club, and when you think what happened to her, I—I can't . . .' Her breathy voice dwindled into sobs. A stout woman came and helped Miss Browne to sit down and smoothed her permed hair back from her forehead with kind but disarranging pressure.

The chairman was in a dog collar and therefore, presumably, the local vicar. He said in a sonorous bass, 'I'm sure we all sympathize very sincerely with Miss Browne and her friends in their sad loss. Now, friends, our time's nearly up, we've all had a good chance to have a say and there's only time for a few more, Mr Hancock, I think your hand was up?'

More men spoke, though there were more women in the hall. Most people repeated what previous speakers had said. Shock at the murders in their peaceful suburb. Dismay at the failure to convict a perpetrator. Useless authorities—from social services to the police. Winding up, the ward councillor said the council would act without specifying how, the third man in the platform party turned out to be the local MP. He said what everybody else had said, at greater length and with more accurate grammar.

It looked, to Clodie's relief, as though the event was nothing more than a hand-wringing exercise and was fizzling out when a tall, posh-looking couple in toning tweed jackets stood up near the front of the hall, chorused, 'This is a waste of time,' and turned to leave. Galvanized by their uncooperative example, other people, this time more women than men, began to shout or bang their heels. Some people unfurled banners, or waved pre-

234

prepared poster boards, which were emblazoned with slogans. *Mothers for safety*, and *Keep Knighton Klean*.

In the sudden cacophony, Clodie could make out some intelligible phrases.

'String him up.'

'We want action.'

'Out out out.'

The vicar banged uselessly on the table. Little Miss Browne was cowering with her hands over her ears.

A huge, burly man pushed his way forward to the platform. His roar followed an ear-bending screech from an umpire's whistle. This was evidently a well-known local figure, for quite quickly the noise subsided to let his voice be heard. 'Listen up, folks. We all know what we think. Hanging's too good for scum like that. But we can't take the law into our own hands—no—' He shouted over a protest. 'Peaceful picketing comes first.'

'Run the bugger out of town,' shouted a woman in pink leggings and fleece, showing a manic gleam of overlarge dentures.

'There's a right and a wrong way to do things,' the big man asserted.

'We'll petition the council. And Parliament.'

'Give it time, it'll sort itself out,' a motherly, posh woman said.

'Time's running out.'

'Friends, we've made our feelings known, I've no doubt the authorities will listen, but we can't do anything else for the time being,' the vicar said soothingly, and then called that the meeting was closed. Lip-reading, Clodie could see he was offering a prayer, but his words were inaudible as the audience pushed out into the wet, dark night. She took shelter in the doorway of a chippy across the road to watch them go. The crowd looked curiously cheerful after all the cathartic emotion, like people coming out of a cinema. Most got into parked cars and drove away. Very few were on foot. And running back to her house along Knighton Drive, Clodie was relieved to see that very few other people, and those all householders going peaceably home, were going in the same direction.

CHAPTER TWENTY-NINE

Fidelis was infuriated by her own weakness. Even a handbag or briefcase was a burden, even the extra weight of a mobile phone or a Filofax made a difference to her ability to carry it. Why had nobody ever explained to the practising medic, why was it only now that she understood, how debilitating her condition could be? Not every day. Sometimes she was fine—but unpredictably; she never knew when she'd falter along with limbs that ached and trembled, a body and mind that felt so heavily weary that dragging herself around was an effort she could hardly make. Nor could she tell how long it would last. This time she felt better by midday. She wondered why it wasn't possible to predict this cycle. Was there a pattern she hadn't observed, or a cause? Could the failing impulses of the damaged brain cells be mapped or traced? That would be a research project that was both interesting and useful. At least she'd have the raw material handy by.

Fidelis spent the afternoon at the board meeting of a charitable trust. Life must go on, and she was outwardly her usual sensible, trenchant self, but all the time fighting with demons in part of her mind. She kept visualizing Murdo, the brotherly boy, the brief lover, the middle-aged man for whom, in recent years, she'd been an intermittent mother-substitute—and the monster he might be. A selfish, careless, ambitious man whose only concern was his own advancement? A man who lied?

He could even have forgotten reading Lesley's silly book, she thought, just remembered the murder method, the way to make it seem she'd killed herself. In fact, if he did kill her—oh God, it was unbearable to have to think those five words together!—but if he did he must have forgotten her book or he wouldn't have left it in full view in his mother's apartment.

She told herself, You've got to stop this. Until Yossi lets me know whether there's any serious basis for the story. But there won't be. He's going to call and say there's no record of any such event.

And meanwhile, life must go on. She decided, rather regretfully, that she was up to going out that evening. Not for the first time Fidelis, who regularly walked under ladders, spilled salt and refrained from touching wood, regretted her only superstition, that she should not say she wasn't well enough to do something unless it was true. As she waited with her umbrella at the ready for Tina to double park at her door she tried to remember whether, after all, she'd broken her own rule and brought this illness on herself. 'Don't be silly,' she said aloud, and went carefully down the steps to Tina's Saab. She had hardly slammed the door and fastened her seat belt before Tina launched into her complaint. 'I'm so worried about Clodie.'

'Why, what's wrong?' Fidelis asked. 'She sounded fine this morning. Careful!'

'I saw him,' Tina said crossly, steering round a man in dark clothes whizzing along the road with one foot on the board of a scooter. 'It's that man. Gavin Rayne.'

'Rayner.'

'Whatever. The one who could be a killer. That poor woman, I've been wondering about her now I've seen where she lived, I went down to supper with Clodie, it's a pretty dreary place.'

'It'll go on the market next year, Clodie's only staying there for a little while.'

'I hope you're charging enough rent,' Tina said, pulling in to let a boy racer and his trail of spraying surface water flash by. Then she said, 'Funny, I've hardly ever been to one of my own authors' homes and you don't really visualize a novelist living somewhere so dismal.'

'Not the successful ones, anyway.'

'That's very few of them. Most earn peanuts.'

'Even the ones who go on getting published?'

'The last Society of Authors survey showed that the average novelist makes way below the national minimum wage.'

'I certainly don't think Lesley was making very much. If anything,' Fidelis said. 'She seems to have had nothing but rejection slips for years. The ones that came out must have been in the seventies.'

'I checked,' Tina said. 'Published twenty years ago by Sayles, long since gone. It was a very small firm that did single editions in a small run for libraries. Never distributed, no authors you'd ever have heard of, I should think they printed five hundred maximum and sold three. Out of print in a few months, the stock pulped. I might find one at the British

Library and have a look.'

Fidelis didn't want to tell Tina, or anyone else, what she'd read at Catriona's place. Not unless she had to. Not yet. She said evasively, 'I'd guess her stuff would hardly be your line in literature.'

'No, but it's the best way to understand the writer. It beats that psychological profiling any day. If only Clodie . . .' Tina's voice tailed off. She could hardly express regret that Clodie had chosen Fidelis's specialism.

'Is that what's worrying you?'

'It's all connected, you can't sell that house too soon for my liking. Clodie's getting a thing about that man, I can tell—and I don't like it one bit.'

'His colour, d'you mean?' Fidelis asked mischievously, knowing it couldn't be that. Tina's own sexual adventures had been multicoloured, and her own third husband, the one before Clodie's ginger-haired Irish father, was an exiled South African from Soweto township.

'Don't be silly, Fidelis, I won't even dignify that with a reply. But what if he's really a murderer? Oh, how I wish she'd never gone in for that forensic option, I was always worried about the kind of people she'd be in contact with, the very most depraved and dangerous of all. They can be so attractive, some of those psychotic nutters, it's not the place for a susceptible young girl. I wish you hadn't

240

encouraged her, can't you do something?'

'Tina, please! What d'you think she'd say if I started interfering?'

'But she's only a child.'

What Tina meant, of course, was that Clodie was Tina's own child. If I argue, Fidelis thought, she's so out of it that she'll probably just tell me I can't understand because I've never had any of my own.

The traffic was clogged between west London and the City, where the two women were due at an awards ceremony. 'Apparently we get around more slowly nowadays than they did before the internal combustion engine,' Fidelis remarked, but Tina was not deflected.

'She does such dreadful work,' she went on in a quick, high voice very different from her normal, leisurely, almost lazy tone. 'That's what gets me, she has to deal with such awful people, murderers, rapists, serial killers, the absolute dregs of humanity. I've been nervous ever since she told me about going on that training course with the FBI in Virginia.'

'The Behavioral Science Unit.'

'Yes, at Quantico. She was so excited by it, she sent all those emails, you remember I told you about it—'

'Yes, she mailed me from there too.'

'All about how they drew up profiles describing the kind of person the criminal has to be to have done those things, and they were all sex crimes, rapes, murder. And then the forensic team immerse themselves in it, they create some peculiar kind of mental rapport with the dregs of society, people who've done such appalling things—you have to see, Fidelis, even you, that really is not the kind of subject one wants a pretty girl immersing herself in.'

'One learns to harden oneself very quickly, you know, you couldn't do the job otherwise, but medicine's often dirty and defiling, especially psychiatric medicine. What d'you expect?'

'Well, I just don't want my little girl spending all her time wallowing in other people's filthy, depraved minds, it can't be good for her.' Tina, stuck in an immobile queue to get across the Edgware Road, turned off the engine, murmured, 'We're going to be terribly late,' and, taking a lipstick from her ashtray, smeared scarlet goo in an accurate cupid's bow without looking in the mirror. Then she added, 'And anyway, it's all just fashion. Just like this year's colour—what is it? Opium Poppy,' she read, squinting at the words written on the little gilt tube.

'Fashion?'

'Yes, this year's theory. I don't see why your so-called profiling should be any more accurate than the Italian who had theories about criminal tendencies showing in thick hair and scanty beards or that Frenchman who made plaster casts of prisoners' heads to demonstrate degenerate features of the skull's structure.'

'How d'you know about Lambroso and Lauvergne, Tina?'

'I once edited a book about them.'

'Of course. Silly question,' Fidelis said, laughing.

'Oh Fidelis, I'm so relieved!' Tina burst out.

'Relieved? You just said you were so worried a moment ago.'

'Relieved about you—look how much more cheerful you are now. Clodie thinks you're miles better, thank goodness, we were so afraid you might do something silly before you had given yourself a chance to come—'

Fidelis stretched out for her bag, and, ignoring a brief compunction about the incompatibility of her velvet coat and the pouring rain, reached for the door handle.

'Sorry, sorry. Not another word, I promise. I'll change the subject. Tell me, are you still playing bridge on the computer?'

Fidelis shoved her shaking hand into her pocket and breathed deeply to calm herself. It's funny how it still upsets me if anyone mentions it, she thought, considering I've made myself accept it. Next step, public admission. By now nobody's going to be exactly surprised. But for the moment, *I dissemble* still. She said, 'I haven't logged on to the site for ages. But I haven't told you the most extraordinary thing—d'you know that

Lesley Cameron found me there?'

'What d'you mean?'

'She read in an article about me that I played cyberbridge, in a cyber-club which she happened to belong to herself, and managed to work out from my pseudonym who I was. And the email address I keep for strangers.'

'I didn't know you had more than one.'

'Oh yes, one for people I trust and one for sites that make you register, you don't want to be traceable. But that one gets drowned in junk mail, I never check it.'

'Never?'

'Well, not for a very long time. More than a year, I should think, it could have been disconnected for all I know.'

'So you wouldn't know if Lesley wrote to you directly.'

'No,' Fidelis said slowly. 'Nor I would.'

The idea niggled throughout the evening, as they eventually achieved the grandiose hall where the book awards ceremony was being conducted. It was a blatant public relations exercise designed to advertise the donor. Tina and Fidelis queued in a reception line and listened to predictable speeches, but were glad they'd made the effort when one of Tina's authors, a former colleague of Fidelis, won a prize. She had recommended the one to the other and was genuinely pleased for them both. But throughout the evening the thought of those unexamined emails niggled at her mind and when Tina dropped her back at the flat the first thing she did was switch the computer on and go on line. Her home page was set as her proper email inbox: fidelisberlin@medic.com. Yossi Lang had already replied—quick work, she thought, clicking on the message and thinking that either it had been very easy for him to find out what Fidelis had asked or he did indeed have contacts unavailable to most people.

The answer was simple. There had been a hit-and-run in the Negev on 30th September 1972. A girl of eight had been left dying by the roadside.

Oh God, it was really true. Fidelis flashed on the image of the young Murdo, with his bright colouring, that clear blue gaze, the ripe-corn hair—'I can't deny that my boy looks like a matinée idol,' Catriona once said. Fidelis had told her the expression she wanted was 'pin-up' or 'heart throb'. What would it be now? Dream-boat? No, that was long gone. Dish? Oh, what does it matter? That beautiful boy had done something dreadful and shameful. Nothing was unforgivable to someone in Fidelis's profession since her metier was to understand, but what Murdo had done came close.

She was shaking so violently that it was hard to use the computer mouse accurately. And it was so long since she'd logged into the Hotmail site that she had to look up the password, recorded in a simple code, that she'd put at the back of a previous address book in preparation for the inevitable lapse of memory. But here it was. Fberlin@hotmail, password *valkyrie*. Guess what I was listening to when I set up this particular account, she thought. She had to go through Microsoft's slow process of reviving the dormant address, but eventually her list of messages received flashed up on the screen.

The 'bulk mail' folder was full even though it was automatically emptied every few weeks. The 'inbox' contained some junk, but it also listed communications from cyberbridge, from some newspapers which Fidelis used to read on line, and various, apparently random messages she would not bother to look at. And it was all listed in date order, a list of ancient, time-expired communications that had never mattered in the first place and now were obsolete, as dead as—as Lesley Cameron, who could not have written after March '99. And there she was: Elsie@hotmail.com.

Unaccountably nervous, Fidelis clicked on the incoming message. And there it was.

He has become a judge. A High Court judge. One of Her Majesty's Judiciary.
How is it possible?

And the rest. The whole text of the document named Q.

246

Fidelis thought, What on earth am I to make of this?

She must have expected me to read it the day she sent it in March 1999.

What did she think I'd do? She knew I knew Murdo, but there's nothing in her document to tell me who she is. If I'd read it then it wouldn't have meant anything to me, it's only because she's dead and left me her stuff that I know. Elsie@hotmail wouldn't have told me anything. This Microsoft Hotmail was an email system which asserted that anonymity was not allowed, but there was no check what name one tapped on to the form. Innocent Fidelis had repeated 'F Berlin'. Lesley was more careful. As 'sender' she'd put L. See, which would have been meaningless to Fidelis if she'd read the message last year. Not that she would have done, actually. Knowing that computer viruses existed but understanding nothing at all about them, Fidelis never opened an electronic message unless she knew who'd sent it.

Lesley sent me this because she kidded herself I was a trusted confidante. Or—the new suspicion again—because she'd settled on me as the audience for her story. She must have expected a reply, an email back asking what it was about, who she was, shock horror from Murdo's friend. But I never sent one; and if I had, she'd have been dead when it arrived. And her killer got rid of her electronic

247

archives, as well as all her paper ones.

I only know one thing, Fidelis thought, that for some reason of her own Lesley settled on me as her target and made damn sure the message would reach me. Maybe there are more copies of it somewhere else, on some other system, eternally stored unseen in the ether.

She ran the cursor down the text. And there was something else—an extra section that hadn't been on the floppy disk.

So this is what I'm going to do, because I think he'll kill me rather than have anyone know what I know. I'm afraid. It was a mistake to write to him. But what else could I do? When I rang his home he hung up on me. When I tried at the law courts they wouldn't put me through. And he wouldn't recognize me in the street. I went to his home in Islington, I waited till he came out of the front door and followed him down the road, but first he cut me dead and then he hailed a cab and leapt in without looking at me. I tried in Parliament Square, thinking he'd have to take some notice if all the other judges were there, he wouldn't be able to look through me so snootily then but it didn't work, I was just dragged away like a criminal, very humiliating it was too. So then I wrote. A copy to his home, another

248

to the court, both envelopes plastered with 'strictly private and confidential' in red ink. Maybe he never got the letters. I thought maybe they were destroyed before he saw them.

Very likely, actually, Fidelis thought. Anything in red ink, or capital letters, or underlined was always assumed to be from a nutter.

But they weren't. He got them. He rang. He said I mustn't tell anyone what I knew until we'd had a chance to talk it through. Promise? And I promised. He's going to come here. To my house.

I'm scared. I know he wants to stop me telling. What will he do to shut me up? What if he finds all these notes I've made? It's not safe here. He could find everything on my vulnerable little laptop, and even the hard copy I printed out, neat pages in a ring binder like I was writing a novel. There aren't any hiding places in this grotty little house. No secret drawers or safes behind a picture or lockers under a floorboard. I bet he has all that stuff in his posh homes. And burglar alarms.

I think I've got to back up the file and hide it. Get it out of the house. Somewhere it will be found if anything happens to me.

Me, Fidelis realized. She left the floppy disk for me.

Seeing those words on the screen in front of me I feel sort of embarrassed myself, like I'm self-dramatizing. Come on, Lesley, you don't really think a High Court judge is going to do anything to you? Like . . . hurt me? No, I don't really believe it. But he is coming here. It would be silly not to prepare. I'm going to make three copies, one in the bank, one with Mr Mahatir. After lunch I'll deliver the sealed envelopes to the bank and the lawyer. Then I'll be safe.

I wonder when he'll come.

But I've had another idea. If I leave something over at Gavin's place they'll hand it on in accordance with my will if I die. I'm going to scratch the wooden lid of Mother's writing cabinet. I'll rub some dirt in so it won't look too recent, and I'll tell Gavin it wants restoring. I'm just going across to see him. I'll say there's no hurry.

Fidelis put the file list back on the screen, but no list of dates appeared. But that was the day it happened. After she'd taken the box to Gavin, before she'd had the chance to deliver the other security disks to safe keeping. That's when he came.

CHAPTER THIRTY

Yossi was expecting Fidelis's call.

'Yes, my friend, I managed to find this out after emailing you last night. The girl was a Bedouin, Fidelis, not a Jew. D'you know what that means?'

'Some kind of Arab?'

'Muslims, usually, certainly, but they're wandering people, nomads, and they live in harmony with us even now, the second intifada is passing them by, like the first. They are better off under Israel than Palestine. When you come you'll see for yourself, their angular black tents with hangings and carpets inside, all very colourful, and their flocks—the traditional Holy Land scene, you know?'

'Would there have been less investigation of the accident because she wasn't an Israeli?'

'Firstly, Fidelis, the child was an Israeli, a citizen like other citizens, and secondly—no, you are wrong to suggest that, for such crimes are always investigated. But the circumstances were difficult. The day was a Saturday, the Sabbath, so there wouldn't have been many people on the road in normal circumstances and that day there was a bad khamsin, nobody goes out in that unless they have to.'

'Is that the same as sirocco or foehn, the high wind?'

'It's much more than just a wind, it's very hot, from the south and straight off the desert, so it's terribly debilitating and irritating at the same time, people are not themselves in such weather.'

'I know there's a myth that you can use it as an excuse for murder.'

'Well, it makes one feel murderous, believe me. But it isn't just the discomfort and restlessness, it's the dust—the wind carries the desert's surface with it, so while it blows you're in a filthy cloud, it gets in your ears and eyes and views are blotted out. The little goatherd must have had trouble keeping track of her flock that day and she wouldn't have been easy for a driver to see either.'

Fidelis knew that Yossi's whole career had consisted of keeping secrets. Surely she could trust his discretion. She explained cautiously:

'What this is about—it concerns an old friend who's in a prominent position. The document that's come into my possession—I only sent you the relevant section—it was written by someone who died last year. I don't know what to make of it.'

'A confession?'

'You remember she said my friend was driving and also that he was the one who insisted on running away against her will.'

'So, an accusation.'

'I won't bore you with the reasons, Yossi, but I really need to know if it's true—did they kill that little girl?'

'You're going too fast, my friend. Approach this question in a logical manner. Firstly, are you sure this pair were really in Israel at the time?'

'Not entirely certain, no, but the dates fit. Mur—my friend was certainly on his travels that summer, he was just finishing as a pupil—as a student, I mean.'

Yossi was not only razor-sharp, he was also the product of an English education and knew perfectly well which profession had pupils rather than trainees or apprentices. He said, 'Ah. A barrister.'

'Oh dear, I didn't mean to—'

'Cool it, Fidelis, who would I tell? Next question. Did he have a car?'

'She said they hired one.'

'Possible, perhaps, but not entirely likely unless your friend was a mature student.'

'What d'you mean?'

'It's almost impossible for anyone under the age of twenty-five to hire a car, and was then too.'

'He can't have been more than twenty-two.'

'Was the woman older?'

'No.'

'So that's your first improbability.'

'Oh Yossi . . . are there any more?'

'Well, let's go on. Assuming they did manage to hire a car, or borrow one—I take it theft is unlikely—that car would certainly have

253

been damaged by the impact. And this is a small country, the size of Wales and smaller still when you leave out the uninhabitable desert. It wouldn't be easy to hide a person or a hunk of damaged metal, especially not if you're a foreigner. And you couldn't get away with returning a car to a hire company with that evidence on it.'

'But someone hit that poor child and ran, it happened,' Fidelis said.

'A lorry . . . tractor . . . something already scarred with previous impacts—that would be more likely than a foreigner in a little car. On the other hand, you say you have a first-hand account of the accident. It's hard to think of a reason for inventing such a thing.'

'Yes.'

An expensive pause for thought, as the telephone bill ticked upwards. Fidelis could visualize Yossi's dark face and thicket of white hair. Victoria said his left side was damaged by the last stroke. His voice did not sound different but she wondered what he looked like now, his vigorous features blunted and unresponsive. She thought, At least you can't see what's wrong with me in my face.

Yossi broke the silence. 'A reason for such an invention—there might be one, but you haven't said enough for me to guess at it. But the fact is, it could be done plausibly. Maybe the crime wouldn't be proven, but some mud would stick, there'd always be a doubt. And I

254

was not the first person to inquire about this incident in recent times.'

'Tell me.'

'My first inquiry was where you'd have gone yourself, the newspaper archives. After that I found information you'd never have access to. But the archivist was helpful, a nice woman called Ellina. She had to go back to microfilms and even paper, it's not all on line yet, but I could give her dates within a few weeks. She said it was much more difficult the time before.'

Fidelis made a questioning murmur, and Yossi went on:

'The previous inquirer was from the UK, Ellina told me that straight away though I didn't say I was asking for a Brit. And that time the query was not specific.'

'What d'you mean?'

'She thought it must have been quite early last year, the woman asked if there were records of any hit-and-run accidents during September 1972. She didn't say where, or what kind of person was the victim. She was interested in all three that Ellina told her about, a soldier knocked down in the Galilee, a tourist in Jerusalem and also the Bedouin child in the Negev. She asked for faxes of all of them.'

'How very peculiar. Can you think of an explanation for that?' Fidelis asked.

'Perhaps, when I also tell you that she

255

inquired the outcome of all of them, at the central criminal registry.'

'Did they tell her?'

'My dear, this is not your bureaucratic, secretive Britain. This country is a democracy, we are open and—as people were saying in the period we're discussing—we let it all hang out.'

'Fidelis?' That was Victoria's voice, she must have snatched the phone from Yossi.

'Hello, Vicky.'

'I'm just interrupting to say, look who's talking. Honestly, Yossi, for you of all people to pretend there aren't secrets here—but carry on, carry on—just, Fidelis, take it all with a pinch of salt.'

'Give me that phone, woman. Fidelis, we are only secretive where secrets are necessary, that's the difference. And in this case, they weren't. Your nameless inquirer was told the truth. The soldier in the Galilee wasn't dead and when he was compos mentis—which took some weeks—he admitted he'd been larking round in the back of a truck and just fell out. As for the tourist in Jerusalem, a delivery driver was arrested in March '73 and eventually confessed. He'd run the woman down while under the influence. So only one remained unsolved.'

'I suppose she could have asked for any such cases as a blind, to conceal her interest in one of them.'

'It's possible. But so is a different

256

explanation. She could have been looking for an unsolved crime at a time when she knew the man concerned had no alibi.'

'What are you saying, Yossi?'

'In order to pin it on him.'

CHAPTER THIRTY-ONE

When Clodie nipped back home in the lunch break, all was quiet in Knighton Drive. Nobody was loitering, and Gavin's house, with its closed windows and doors, looked dingy but secure. It was during the afternoon that she heard one of the ward maids talking to a charge-nurse in the locker room. At first she thought they were discussing the previous night's television. But their whispers and giggles didn't fit and when she heard the word 'Knighton' she paused, her hand on the door, to listen.

'They got rid of those fuckers in Portsmouth right enough.'

'Paedophiles.'

'Way to go.'

'I've never been on a demo,' the girl said.

'We need action.'

'You mean, take the law into our own hands?'

'There'll be some fireworks, I shouldn't wonder. Better than Guy Fawkes.'

'I'm not sure . . .'

'What d'you mean?'

'Well, we're, like, we're meant to be taking care of people, here, that's what the job is, right?'

'Oh, we'll take care of him, don't you worry. I've got two kiddies at home, me, and they gotta come first, right?'

Clodie went thoughtfully onwards to the day room where her patients, flashers, fondlers and other inadequates, as well as a few killers, were in the period of 'association' that was supposed to help socialize them. The usual outbreak of whoops, whistles, catcalls and unspeakable suggestions greeted her entrance. She reacted absently, her mind still on the conversation she'd heard. Could she ask the nurse? He was an experienced man, a former prison warder who had retrained as a psychiatric nurse. She suspected him of petty cruelties to their charges, perhaps of worse; and he had already made plain his disapproval of her appointment.

'All very well for the admin and the medics to go in for political correctness,' he'd told her. 'We're the ones who pick up the pieces when you've got the poor buggers all unsettled.'

'Unsettled?'

'Just take a look in the fucking mirror, why don't you?' he'd spat out.

Clodie did not pretend she didn't understand. But her first boss had believed, and taught her, that patients like these, both male and female, were often more relaxed and less hostile with a young, pretty woman doctor who seemed to present no threat. Clodie was not of a generation that thought it still needed to fight feminist battles. She just marked this nurse down as yet another time-expired, frustrated traditionalist.

But there wasn't much she'd put past a man like that. He seemed as untrustworthy, in his way, as the patients he was in charge of.

The ward roster showed he was on till eight. And then . . . ? She was nervous, tense and excited, like a soldier the night before battle.

She knocked off early. Having taken in Fidelis's belief that it was tempting fate to say you were ill if you weren't, she decided to risk a filling or even root canal and told the administrator she had a dentist's appointment. She filled up her car on the way home, and checked the oil and tyre pressures, just in case. She turned off the main road into the darkening street. The street lamps were warming up, casting a pink glow on to the gale-battered branches of the lime trees. The road surface glistened greasily from an earlier heavy shower. Not many of the houses had lights in the windows yet, but there were more people around than usual, some kids on foot-platform scooters, a little group of women outside the corner shop, a military-looking man with a clipboard who reached her as she got out to open the garage doors.

'That's right, lock it away,' he said. 'Batten down the hatches, right?'

Prepare for a siege. Clodie's heart was beating uncomfortably fast. She wished she knew if there was something to worry about, or if the whole thing was her misunderstanding. This was England, not downtown Boston. All the same, having parked in the little garage, facing outwards for a quick getaway, she bolted the up-and-over door, and went in through the side door of the house.

The plan had come to her fully formed, as her schemes usually did. She put her necessaries on the chair in the hall. Then she dialled Tina's number.

'Mum?'

'Clodie, brilliant, just the person. I can't get hold of Fidelis, she isn't picking up the phone, but you'll never guess what I've got in front of me here.'

'No, but—'

'It's a book by Lesley Bowhill, Lesley Cameron. I'd mentioned her to an agent I know—Jocko, d'you remember him? Debbie's ex. Anyway, the name rang a bell and he had a look and there it was, the typescript sitting in his slush pile. It's been there since she died, would you believe? I haven't read it yet—'

'Mum, I haven't got time, really. Listen, is it OK if I come round tonight? With a friend?'

'Darling, of course, and then you can have a

look at—'

'Bye, Mum.'

Clodie went out through the front door, leaving the lock on the latch, and waited till the kids had turned the corner and the clipboard man had gone inside a house up at the far end, before sprinting across the road and up to Gavin's door. She knew the bell didn't work. Crouching to the letter flap, now screwed down to let nothing more bulky than a thin envelope inside, she called through:

'Gavin, are you there? It's Clodie—let me in, please!'

He took ages to open the door and she began to hope he'd gone away, but eventually she heard the squeak of rubber soles on tiles and he opened the door a crack. Clodie slid inside and stood with her back to it, invisible from outside. In as bright a voice as she could muster, she said:

'Hi, Gavin, you OK?'

'Uh huh.'

'I was hoping you'd come over, there's something I think you should—'

'Having problems?' he asked. Clodie was about to say, 'No, but you are,' when she seamlessly changed tack. He was the sort of guy who'd be readier to help her than help himself.

'Yes, I'm really stuck with something in the house—I thought you might be able to help— if you wouldn't mind . . .' She tried to sound

261

fluttery and helpless, a manner she usually despised. He looked at her with a kind of weary distrust, like someone who'd learnt to expect booby traps. But he said:

'Might as well. When?'

'Well—would right now be OK?'

'Don't see why not. Do I need my tools?'

'No no, I've got everything.'

'I'll find my key then.'

'You might need to put something on—it's an outside job.'

He disappeared to the back of the house and Clodie pulled the door open and peered up and down the road, relieved to see the closest neighbouring houses were still dark. But the commuters would be back soon. 'Checking nobody sees us together?' he said, not joking. She was, but not for the reason he seemed to suspect. The coast was clear and— what a stroke of luck—the sky was dumping another load of heavy rain. He came towards her, shrugging on a zipped fleece. Like an officious female, Clodie pulled the hood up over his head and grabbed his hand.

'Come on, run!' They dashed across through the blinding shower and straight in through the unlocked door of Clodie's house.

'Home safe,' she gasped, slamming the door, turning the key on the inside and putting it in her pocket. 'I'm ultra security conscious.'

'So I see.' He was looking at her oddly. Suspicion had become his natural state of

262

mind, she thought, but this time, it was fair enough.

'Wait a mo.' She went into the front room without switching the light on and drew Lesley Cameron's mother's green velvet curtains closely across the window. Then she said, 'Come through. I could do with a cuppa, couldn't you?'

'I thought you wanted me to fix something out the back.'

'There's no hurry. Won't you keep me company? Look, I've still got some of this yummy cake my friend brought as a house warmer.' Clodie thought the kitchen shouldn't bring back Gavin's nasty memories. She'd not done much to the rest of the house, as she would be there for so short a time, but one had to have one liveable room, and the kitchen was it. She'd unscrewed the hinges of the door into the dining end and chucked it, and Lesley Cameron's heavy table and oak chairs, pulled up the swirl-patterned carpet and removed the chandelier light fitting. Then she'd spent a happy weekend with some cans of brightly coloured paint and remnants of gaudy material. You wouldn't want to live like this for keeps, she knew, but the shrieking colours in shocking combination certainly managed to banish any echoes of the previous occupant. Gavin hadn't seen it before.

'Wow,' he said. 'You're camouflaged, your hair's cancelled out by that red wall.'

'I guess I can do with toning down,' she said. 'Look, tea bags in that cupboard, pick your preference.' She liked the look of him in this brilliant cubicle, so very much not camouflaged, but his proud, regular profile standing out against the contrasting background. Somali, she thought, or Ethiopian, not West African, and wondered if he'd ever tried to find out. 'Look, mugs are by the sink, will you make the tea while I just . . .'

She did need the loo; but she also wanted to see what was going on from the front bedroom. Nothing yet. Or—wait a minute, what's that? Someone was standing in the shadow of a lime tree, two someones, lurking. It was just after five o'clock. Clodie thought, I'm going to keep him safely here if I have to chain him down.

CHAPTER THIRTY-TWO

It was time to reach a decision.

Fidelis looked at her answering machine— four messages waiting—and decided not to listen to them now. She ran her finger along the rank of compact discs, looking for something mathematical and intellectual, and settled on Rosalyn Tureck playing the Goldberg Variations.

Then she sat down to consider events and

their consequences in a logical sequence. If she had evidence about Lesley Cameron's death it was her clear duty to give it to the authorities. But was it evidence or guesswork? And if she let anyone know, even Clodie or Tina, that Mr Justice Wood-Wolferstan had the motive and opportunity to have taken the woman's life, even subsequent proof that he had nothing to do with it would not fully clear his name. The judiciary had to be, not cleared of suspicion, but above suspicion.

Did she believe he had really done it? And did she believe he had committed the crimes Lesley described, killed a child and run away? The first half of the story was horribly plausible, even if Lesley's sexual fantasies had made her embroider the rest.

If it wasn't true, why had he lied about going to Plowden, why had he told her he never spoke to Lesley after 1972?

'Ask him, why don't you?' Her own voice spoke aloud. There could be a perfectly reasonable explanation for it all, this monster she'd been building up in her head wasn't the man she'd known from his boyhood.

Yes, she decided, before anything else I must speak to Murdo himself.

Which turned out to be more easily said than done. Perhaps, Fidelis thought, in Israel—unlike bureaucratic, secretive Britain as Yossi had called it—it would be simple to ring up a High Court judge. Not in the UK:

she'd left messages on the unlisted number of Murdo and Gemma's house in Islington, but remembered Gemma had said she would be in Indonesia and the children were away at boarding school, so her voice was probably unheard. She spoke to an official at the Royal Courts of Justice in the Strand but he was either ultra-discreet or wilfully unhelpful.

'No, madam'—it would have been less infuriating if he'd not been so superficially servile—'I'm sorry, madam, I can't give you His Lordship's number. Email address? I really couldn't say, madam. No, madam, I'm not permitted to divulge his fax number either.'

'I know he's sitting in Ferriby. Can't I just call him at the judge's lodgings this evening?'

'I'm afraid that number's not in the public domain, madam.'

'Well, if you could tell him that Dr Berlin wants a word,' Fidelis said pessimistically. Filled with rage, she then remembered that one of her friend Elspeth Scott's last posts in the civil service had been a brief secondment from the Department of Health to the Lord Chancellor's Department. Fidelis tapped out her number in a fury and launched straight into a tirade about obstructive functionaries and a society deformed by obsessive secrecy.

'Stop, Fidelis, stop, you sound like a leader in the *Guardian*!'

'I might even write to *The Times* about it.'

'Well, do, if you think it would make a difference. But meanwhile, calm down, do.' Elspeth's role in her long friendship with Fidelis, which dated from their first term at college, was to give her sensible advice. 'I can get you the Ferriby number, no problem. Why's it so desperate anyway, is it poor old Catriona?'

'No, she's immortal, sadly. I'll tell you another time.'

'All right, I'll get right back to you.' And ever reliable, so she did.

Fidelis stared at the number she'd scrawled on her pad for a long time. She found it difficult to write legibly these days. Was that an eight or a three? Did she have to do this thing? A curious hesitation for Fidelis, whose working life consisted of taking responsibility, of doing things laymen would cringe from. She thought of some of the worst moments, compared to which it would be as nothing to ask Murdo Wood-Wolferstan if he'd killed a kid and run away. I'm the woman who told an adopted girl that her birth father had been the Butcher of Augsburg. I told a mother that her own birth son had turned into a schizophrenic rapist. I've broken plenty of bad news, medical and emotional, I learnt how to do it. Cringing for fear of confirming a fact she ardently hoped was a fiction, she lifted the telephone and asked the functionary who answered it to tell the judge she wanted to take up his wife's

267

suggestion that she should visit him on circuit.

He rang back almost immediately, sounding pleased. Innocent, surprised and affectionate.

'When would you like to come? Tonight as ever is? That's great.'

He told her to bring evening dress. Would she like to sit on the bench with him? There'd be a High Sheriff's reception. He'd be thrilled to have her company.

CHAPTER THIRTY-THREE

Two hours had passed in a flash. Conversation was so easy, their non-work interests so similar that Clodie felt as if she'd known Gavin for ever. Or no. That wasn't quite right, she corrected herself, you don't fancy blokes rotten if you've always known them. But it was funny how they'd liked the same films and gone to the same concerts, listened to the same music. When she put on one of her favourite bands he said:

'Great, that's Morcheeba, right?'

They were so caught up in a conversation that went way beyond words that Clodie was amazed when she saw the time. 'Just going to the—listen, don't move, OK? I've got a really great disc someone downloaded, I'll go get it, you'll love this one.' She went upstairs and across to the bedroom window but didn't turn on the light. The lime trees, even when bare, blocked a clear view of the road, but she could see there were figures on the far pavement. Just standing, with some kids running around. Others were walking up the road in this direction.

This is 'the community', she thought, neighbours egged on and ganging up with a shared purpose, it's exactly what politicians are always so keen on. People with one thing in common, never mind how wrong or dangerous.

But so far there was no harm done. Not yet.

She took the new disc back to the bright, cosy cave. The side door into the back garden was bolted, but someone could get a view of her kitchen from the rear windows of one house in the next street down. She hoped the shadows on the blind would be unidentifiable, but moved to one side all the same. Gavin joined her and they danced slowly and then more slowly, at arm's length and then closer and then touching, she was breathing in his enticing smell, for despite his evident failure to wash recently the sweetness was still there, she could feel herself glowing, softening, until his face, their lips, were nearly—

'What was that?' He sprang back, his enfolding softness suddenly rigid. The bang had been violent and sounded close but she said:

'Just a firework, they've been going off for

269

weeks.'

But she couldn't help hearing the other sounds.

'I've got to go and—'

'No, Gavin, don't, it's not a good idea to—'

'What's going on?'

'I don't know.'

'You do know! I'm—'

She grabbed his arm. 'No, don't, please!'

He shook her off and opened the door into her dark hallway. Clodie ran past him and stood with her back against the front door, her arms outstretched.

'Let me out,' he said.

'Gavin, listen—no, stop, listen to me. Please!'

'What is this?' His face was only just visible against the dark background, picked out in the gleam of yellow street lighting that came through the fanlight above the door.

'I heard some people talking at work today, they were discussing a—demo, they called it. But I think they were coming here, to you.'

'D'you mean you got me here for that? Let me—' He pushed her aside and reached for the door.

'It's locked.'

'Give me the key.'

'No, Gavin, don't—'

He was reaching for her. 'You don't think I'll hide here behind your skirts!'

'Let's look first. From the bedroom window.

Please, Gavin.'

Something—affection? An institutionalized obedience? Her own hard-acquired authority? —made him go up the stairs behind her. There was a crowd outside Gavin's fence now and spilling into the road. Men, women and children. They weren't drilled yet, arguing with each other, and with children treating it like an outing. Some of them had bangers left from 5th November; sharp cracking noises fired off irregularly. Clodie put her fingers to her lips and very carefully edged the window open a centimetre. The murmur of sound turned into words though it was hard to distinguish who'd said them.

'Out out out,' some people further away chanted.

Someone was using Gavin's outer doors as a stone-throwing target.

'Has he gone out?' someone called.

'Anyone see him go?' came the response. Clodie froze. If anyone had been watching—if they knew he was here . . .

'Nah, he's hiding out in there,' someone else shouted.

'Let's get on with it!' That was a man's voice. It could have been the nurse Clodie had heard earlier.

'Remember this is a peaceful protest!' a posh, female voice shrilled.

'Wait till the cameras arrive, Ron's calling the TV news,' a more demotic voice shouted.

Someone brought a car skidding to a halt in the middle of the road and got out calling, 'Here's the placards.' Hands reached out for boards and banners, black on white like a traffic stop sign. *No killers.* A longer piece of material stretched between two poles read **igger go home.* Clodie briefly wondered if the asterisk instead of a letter kept the phrase within the law, and immediately realized that the law had ceased to operate here. This crowd had reached critical mass.

'OK, time to get out of here,' she whispered, pulling Gavin out on to the landing.

'We should call—the cops'll turn out for you, don't say it's for me.'

'No time for that.'

'They'll have to come if you make the call.'

'I've seen a riot once and I don't want to again. Come on. This is what I was afraid of, we've got to get going.'

'You're not going out there beside me, they'll lynch you too. Give me that key.'

'They won't see us together. Come on.'

He seemed dazed. No wonder. But it was useful, because he followed Clodie without further argument. She put on her coat and took a moment to make herself look professional, pushing her fingers through her wild hair and smearing on some lipstick. Money, keys, her medical bag. Right, now for the plan, the best she'd been able to think of that afternoon. It ought to work. Nobody would be able to see what was taken from the house into the car and away.

No time to be nervous. She opened the side door that led directly into the garage. The noise outside immediately sounded louder. Beyond the usual smell of petrol and an unemptied dustbin there was something else, acrid and slightly sulphurous. She hoped it was just fireworks.

Clodie's car was an old, high-mileage hatchback Golf. The rear space had a flap which was supposed to hide your luggage or shopping. She'd counted on it being just big enough to hide a man.

Gavin balked, naturally enough. 'You kidding? No way. I'm not hiding in there while you face that lot!'

'They won't touch me, why should they? Please. Please do this, Gavin, I . . .'

She never meant to cry, but water rolled out of her eyes and she dashed the back of her hand against her cheeks.

'That's a dirty trick,' he said. 'It doesn't work on a man with two big sisters.'

'Oh for God's sake, what choice have you got? Go out there and let those animals tear you to pieces? Or come to supper with my mum.' The banality of the alternative offered made him utter a snort of amusement. In the dim light his teeth flashed a grin.

'How can I resist an invitation like that?'

'Your carriage awaits,' she said.

He could not fit in the space sitting or squatting, but kneeling with his head to the floor it was just possible. Clodie hooked the cover over him. 'It's not for long, just till we're out of Plowden,' she whispered, slammed the door down and locked it.

Now then. Look natural.

She made sure the three passenger doors were locked too, put the key in the ignition and turned the engine on. Then she went to unbolt and swing upwards the galvanized door. It made enough noise to be heard above the now very vociferous and angry crowd. Compared with the riot Clodie once saw in Boston this was low key, but by the standards of English suburbia, she thought, it was bloody terrifying. She got into the driving seat, locked herself in and moved the car forward. The people in her way looked at the car blankly. Were they stoned? Pissed? Or just high on the excitement of crowd behaviour?

A very fat, very muscular man with his arms folded across a T-shirt with a skull and crossbones on it came round to her side of the car. She wound the window down a little and smiled.

'You seen him today?'

'Who?' she asked.

'Him over there.'

'No, not for ages.'

'Sure?'

'I've been at the hospital all day. Look, can

you get them to let me out? I've been paged, I'm a doctor.'

He walked slowly round the car, peering inside. She watched the growing crowd. Where were the blue lights and screaming sirens, where was law and order?

'That your bag?'

'Yes, I told you, I'm a doctor—look.' She opened the leather flaps.

He doesn't believe me. He's going to make me open the boot. She shouted:

'They're bleeping me again, can you hurry up, they need me for a patient.'

At last he went back to the road and gestured enough people out of the way for Clodie to drive out. She went slowly along, aiming away from the crowd, away from the main road. She'd never seen the estate so animated. Residents from every one of the parallel streets seemed to be making for Gavin's home. Clodie wiped her sweating palms down the front of her coat and the back of her forearm over her wet forehead. Just as she reached the far end and was turning out of Knighton Drive she heard a whoomph like a giant's gasp and then his belch, and a dazzling light exploded in the rear-view mirror. Petrol bomb, she thought. Putting her foot down, she drove quickly to the furthest end of the Knighton Estate. There was Mrs Roberts' place. Wonder if she's in the crowd with her petitions? At the end, Clodie turned towards the main road and saw in the distance the blue lights and sirens—and about time too. But she didn't stop till she'd driven a long way north and west, far enough away for it not to matter if anyone saw her park, and get out and open the hatchback, and wait while a tall, thin, black man got out of the rear of her car to sit like a citizen and let her drive him home to Mum.

CHAPTER THIRTY-FOUR

'Let the housekeeper know which train,' Murdo had said, which only went to show that some judges were still out of touch with real life. This was a winter of discontent, in which a train crash was followed by act of man, in closing down the railway tracks, and act of God in sending unprecedented rain and floods. The train service had been disrupted for weeks and when Fidelis tried to find out the timetable for Ferriby an exhausted Indian voice told her there wasn't one, she should go to the mainline station and wait till a train turned up. How long would it take? 'That is unknowable. It is on the lap of God.'

So like everybody else, Fidelis went by road, wondering if all the travellers on that over-used motorway were as appalled by the speed and aggression of the heavy traffic in a torrential downpour on a surface that looked like a lake. She'd been an intrepid driver in her big Jaguar, but in this light little automatic had to tell herself fiercely to stop cowering in the inside lane like a little old lady, get out there, keep up with the big boys. And my God, were they big, lorries the size of apartment blocks, trailers the length of the non-running trains.

There was a stationary queue to turn off at Ferriby, a nose-to-tail crawl to the town centre and a puzzle to find the unmarked judge's lodgings, which were eventually pointed out by a homeless *Big Issue* seller who said in a disconcertingly posh drawl that what she was looking for was the only old house left in the city centre, 'up there, straight on, can't miss it, a pig on the doorstep'. Fidelis gratefully bought six copies of the magazine and went cautiously on over the brick surface of a semi-pedestrianized town centre, until she reached a tall, pompous, gaunt grey house which did have a policeman outside as well as a man on the inside of the door, who said, 'I am the butler, madam.'

This was not a way of life Fidelis was accustomed to, but His Lordship had spoken and his guest was expected, one minion waiting to park her car in a secure pound and the other to take her up a wide, chilly staircase into a large chilly bedroom. His Lordship was still in court, she was told, but a list had been provided, lying on the lace-covered dressing table. It was a piece of heavy, cream-coloured

277

paper on which somebody had typed a timetable: 6.30 p.m., cocktails in the drawing room. 8.00 p.m., dinner in the dining room. The Lord Lieutenant, the Bishop, the chairman of the council. Evening dress will be worn.

The absolutely last thing on earth that Fidelis felt like was a formal dinner party of strangers, but she changed into her own version of evening dress (a black velvet trouser suit) and went down punctually. The butler bowed her into a large, gaunt box whose inadequate light came from a high, central chandelier. It was impersonally decorated with municipal discomfort and a very large oil painting of a florid man wearing black clothes and a large chain of office. A tall youth in a dinner jacket stood nervously folding his hands over and over; when Fidelis shook one it was clammy. This was the judge's marshal, a young barrister attached to Murdo for the duration. Fidelis made automatic putting-the-young-at-ease conversation and learnt that this house was notoriously the least comfortable lodging in England, she should see the gorgeous stately home somewhere in the north-west or the lovely house in the West Country whose owners moved out three times a year to accommodate the visiting judge. A hotel? Oh no, that would never do. The judge depended on his privacy and security. In any case, there had to be three separate lots of dining and sitting rooms, bedrooms and bathrooms, to let the judge and his wife, if she came, the marshal, and the cook and butler all live without getting on top of each other.

The butler opened the door and Murdo entered the room. He hugged and kissed her, whispered, 'Ghastly, isn't it?' and as the sounds of arrivals came from the hall added, 'Don't worry, they won't stay long.'

It felt long. Sherry, standing around in the chilly room, a stuffy, four-course dinner in a bleak dining room, with grace said and tasteless, conventional food. There was formal conversation, mostly about Ferriby's local affairs, and an excess of deference all round. At one stage the council chairman mentioned his pride in the building they were in. 'A real piece of old Ferriby.' The ladies were conducted by the wife of the chairman upstairs to a sad bathroom. In her bedroom, not so much to apply new lipstick as momentarily to escape, Fidelis heard her mobile phone.

'Where are you?' a high voice shouted.

'Oh, hello Tina. I'm at the judge's lodgings in Ferriby, of all places.'

'What on earth are you doing there?'

'I've got to talk to Murdo Wood-Wolferstan.'

'God, Fidelis, you haven't been thinking that he—'

'I can't talk now, I've got to go downstairs.'

Fidelis joined the uncomfortable gathering

279

for acid, lukewarm coffee in the drawing room. And—what a relief—as predicted the guests left on the dot of ten.

'Thank God for that,' Murdo said, coming back from the front door. 'Phil, you can go to bed if you like.' The young man took the hint. 'Not a good choice, for marshal,' Murdo told Fidelis. 'What I need is someone who'd cheer up this morgue, last time I had a very jolly young woman. Thank God this'll be my last circuit, I heard today that I'm definitely going to the Court of Appeal in the New Year. It's a secret, Fidelis, you're almost the first to know—wouldn't my mother have been pleased.'

'Yes indeed.'

'God, I'll be glad to stop all this flummery. You'll see in the morning, processing through the streets in all the gear—some judges like it, but not me.' He undid his black bow tie and unfastened the collar stud. 'Come on, there's one habitable corner, we'll have a proper drink.' He led the way to a small room on the first floor, set up as an office, with a laptop winking on the desk beside a silver tray with decanters and heavy cut glass tumblers, and two deep chairs. An antique and possibly dangerous electric fire blazed heat from its two radiant bars.

'Whisky? Kill the taste of that appalling meal, help yourself to water. Cheers.'

Fidelis swallowed welcome gulps.

He said, 'Come on, Fidelis, spit it out. What's the problem? We've known each other too long, I can see there's something wrong. Is that why you came? Is there anything I can do?'

'No, Murdo, I came to ask you something.'

'Anything.'

'It concerns Lesley Cameron.'

'Oh, her again. Poor Lesley.' He pulled the heavy chair forward. 'Here, come nearer the fire, you're shivering.' Fidelis huddled over the electric heater. As Murdo had observed, she was shaking like a leaf, and although she wasn't cold she'd prefer him to think so.

'Murdo, why did you tell me you never met her again, after you stopped going out together?'

His face was suddenly wet. He pulled the silk handkerchief from his breast pocket and mopped his forehead. 'I never could pull the wool over your X-ray eyes,' he said.

'Oh Murdo.' She felt suddenly weak and aching like someone with flu. The liquid was slopping round in the glass. She knew she wouldn't get it to her lips, so pushed it clumsily on to the footstool.

'D'you know,' he said meditatively, 'I'm not sure that isn't the only real untruth I've ever told—apart from social compliments and excuses. It's something I've always prided myself on. Self-interest, really, it means no little snoop of a journalist can fling something you've said back in your face.'

'Lies of omission are no better.'

'Why d'you say that? This was a lie of commission. I told you I hadn't seen her and I confess, I actually did. Once. It was shortly before she died and when I heard she'd been murdered I decided to say nothing, it was best not to be associated with it at all, keep my name entirely out of it—in my position, you understand.'

'You saw her. You were in that house. Murdo, tell me—'

'Yes, if you like, it was all so ludicrous that if the poor woman hadn't died so horribly you could only laugh. She'd got in touch, as Gemma told you, she called when we were in the country. It was some months after she'd made that public exhibition of herself, and it took me quite a while to remember who she was. She said something like that she couldn't keep quiet any longer, the secret would have to be out, her conscience was troubling her, stuff like that. Well, I hadn't the remotest idea what she was talking about. I'd never denied we had a relationship back in the early seventies, Gemma knew, it was before I met her. D'you remember I took a long break? Down through Europe with a backpack, those were the days. I didn't care who else knew about it either, it was no secret. But she went on and on in the same vein and eventually I realized I'd have to go down there and talk to her.'

'Yes.'

It was spring, last year, we were in London for the weekend so I went down on the off-chance. Bloody long way, those outer suburbs, took me hours. So I called at her house, she lived opposite a bloke who was doing lovely woodwork though I read later he was the one they charged with her murder, sad story. I hardly recognized Lesley, she'd aged badly and obviously didn't have much money for hair and facials and all that stuff other women do. And she was quite out of it, absolutely barking. She kept going on about something she said had happened that summer when we were travelling round the Near East together, claimed there'd been a car incident—well, bluntly, Fidelis, the woman accused me of hitting a child, and driving away. I mean, I ask you!'

'Was it not true then?'

His face grew drawn and pale. You could see this man might be terrifying. 'Fidelis, I have to tell you, I cannot believe you just said that.' The blood rushed back through the veins, mottling the cheeks. Sweat glistened on his brow. 'How can you even ask? Of course it wasn't true. For Crissake, you've known me most of my life, you don't seriously think I could do such a thing? Leave a wounded kid to die, just to save my own skin!'

'Are you saying she made it up?'

were "the actual pillars of the state."

Smith (1776:9) hinted at this contradiction in *Wealth of Nations*, but he downplayed its significance by arguing that while a peasant may look humble in front of a European prince, the peasant's living conditions exceeded that of "many an African king, the absolute master of the lives and liberties of ten thousand naked savages." By comparing and contrasting the relative deprivations between the poor of one nation and the affluent of another, Smith concealed what Colquhoun was at pains demonstrate. Poverty compelled labourers "to exercise their industry", he wrote, constituting the driving force of the capitalist economy since capital was fed by labourers who had only their labour-power to sell. But despite his apparently sympathetic tone, Colquhoun was no Marxist before Marx and he set himself the task of theorizing and implementing the successful exploitation of labour through techniques of police. At a conceptual level, this entailed classifying the poor. Labourers, despite being "pillars of the state" were also the likely sources of crime especially when indigence prevented them from working as wage labourers. Colquhoun constantly referred to those who were unable or unwilling to work as the likely culprits of highway robberies and burglaries. Indigence also produced the more depraved class of thieves – "servants, ostlers, stable and post-boy[s]"—that preferred "idleness" over hard work and thus took up "the profession of thieving." Even "idle and disorderly mechanics and labourers" who due to their thieving had "lost the confidence of their masters or employers" were, according to Colquhoun (1800b:95-6), part of the same general problem of idleness found among those "persons who being imprisoned for debts, assaults, or petty offences, [had] learned habits of idleness and profligacy in goals" . Thus, the problem of idleness is a recurring theme in Colquhoun's account of crime. Neocleous (2000:55) notes that "the general idea" in Colquhoun's plan for police then, "is to put the poor to labour, to make the working class work." Indigence was "merely coda for any attempt to avoid wage labour, to refuse exploitation."

A major thrust of Colquhoun's thinking was to classify, manage, and survey the poor so that they did not descend into indigence. Colquhoun identified five classes of poor: the useful poor, the vagrant poor, the indigent poor, the aged and the infirm poor, and the infant poor. While there seemed little hope for the vagrant poor, who were able but unwilling to work, particular attention was given to saving the indigent poor and preventing their slide into criminality. Colquhoun thus argued that a "first consideration" ought to be vetting those able to "reoccupy their former station among the labouring poor." His goal was to "restore them to [the] first class" of useful poor as soon as possible so they could "resume their former employments" to best "help themselves and their families" (Colquhoun 1800b:363). The poor, in Colquhoun's view, required identification, oversight and intervention to prevent their degeneration into a

'As it's not true, presumably she invented it all. I do remember she was a story-teller, she was always embroidering on what happened.'

'But why would she invent such a thing? What was it all for?'

'Blackmail? Extortion? I don't know, I left before she could go any further—she was either mad or bad and I just wanted to get clear.'

'But the story would have done you damage if there was even a rumour of it.'

'Too right. I shouldn't say so, but it was lucky for me that someone broke in that day.'

'But she left a kind of memoir, Murdo.'

'What!'

'I've brought you a print-out.'

'If that story's repeated, it's all fiction, you do know that, Fidelis. She was a fantasy merchant. Don't tell me you believed a word of it.'

Fidelis went to fetch the folder. She watched him put on half-glasses to examine the document, speed-reading down the pages. A bell rang somewhere, long and loud and then repeated, but it wasn't their business and Murdo ignored it, his face severe and concentrated, the judge at work. Someone was banging on the front door.

'Ought we to—'

'Someone will see to it.' He tapped the pages into shape and put them into the folder. 'Of course this whole thing's an invention.

Fiction from beginning to end,' he said. 'In fact, a straight, unadulterated lie. Very little she describes actually happened. I certainly never had or pretended to have the remotest idea of marrying the woman. And as for this cock and bull story about a hit-and-run—'

There were angry voices on the stairs.

'But Murdo, I've checked it out, a child did die in exactly that way exactly at the time she says, and you were there in Israel then.'

He mopped his face. 'This could do a lot of harm, you do realize that?'

'Not if the story's all invented, surely.'

'But you know it's not possible to prove a negative. I certainly was in Israel about then, it was after I'd done my year as a pupil and they didn't want me back in chambers till the start of the new term so I took a long break. And it's also true that I was there with Lesley Bowhill though we never hired a car. In fact I might even have been in the Negev desert, though if you asked me to give a date I'd have thought it was earlier in the month than that, but I didn't keep a record. There might just be a postmarked card from Masada saved in my mother's papers because I'd certainly have sent her one from there. I brought her some souvenirs when I came home.'

She thought, He's quite forgotten what happened between us then.

'I might even have sent you a card. It's a wonderful site, most impressive. I was there again a few years ago with the Bar Association. But as for the rest of it—'

Some altercation was going on outside the door, which was burst open at this point.

'Sir. My lord.' The marshal and the butler, one in a dressing gown, the other in old flannels and a T-shirt. 'We couldn't stop her, she just—'

Behind them, pushing past into the room, was Tina Svenson. And following on behind her came Clodie, hair and cheeks both flaming, hanging on to—in fact dragging behind her—an embarrassed-looking man: Gavin Rayner.

CHAPTER THIRTY-FIVE

'Sir, my lord, I asked the lady to wait in the hall but she—' The butler seemed to be genuinely frightened of the judge.

'What's going on?' Murdo demanded. His marshal interrupted.

'Security's on the way. Ah, there they—' Heavy footsteps galloping up the stairs. An official in uniform with, Fidelis saw, a hand gun in a holster, pushed past the other men, his eyes going first to the judge, then quickly round the room and straight to Gavin, who was standing still and embarrassed. Smoothly and neatly, the officer had Gavin with his face to the wall and his arm in a lock.

'Murdo, don't let him—these are my friends.'

'Your friends?' The judicial calm, which could have been mere slowness to react, seemed undisturbed, although he had managed to get himself behind the desk with his hand on a heavy glass paperweight.

'This is my old friend Tina Svenson, though God knows what she's up to, and my god-daughter Clodie Byrne.'

'And this is Gavin Rayner,' Clodie announced.

Tina said, 'Sorry to burst in on you like this, but there's something you need to know, Fidelis, before you go any further and—'

Fidelis interrupted before Tina could say anything compromising. 'Murdo, I don't think there's any need for the officer to restrain Mr Rayner.'

'You may release him now,' Murdo commanded. 'Thank you, officer, I'm grateful, but it seems there's nothing to worry about.' He shooed his protectors from the room and added once the door was closed, 'You could have assassinated me in the time it took him to get here, Mr Rayner, if that had been your intention. I hope you aren't hurt.'

Gavin shook his head mutely. Though he was obviously a man who'd been through a trauma, Fidelis thought, seeing the way he looked at Clodie, and she at him, it was not difficult to predict that there was an enjoyable period of rest and recreation ahead for them both.

'But Fidelis, look how you're trembling,' Murdo said in a tone of real concern. 'It's all right, my dear, there's nothing to be afraid of now.'

'It's OK, I have a neurological disorder. It makes me look shaky but please take no notice. I'm fine,' she said, and realized to her own surprise that what she had said was true. Clodie smiled brilliantly at her and made a gesture with her free hand. *Way to go!*

Tina said, 'I do apologize that we've intruded so unceremoniously, Sir Murdo, but I had to catch Fidelis before she started suggesting you're a criminal.'

Gavin flinched and Clodie reached out protectively for his hand. He must be frightened of the legal system and everyone concerned with it now, Fidelis realized. Confrontation with a judge might be something he'd dreamed of when he was inside, but probably only in nightmares.

'The child's death would be manslaughter, from what I've read,' the lawyer said. Then he added, 'But the story's not—' He looked surprised when Tina interrupted, no longer an experience he was accustomed to.

'I meant Lesley's own death.'

'You can't possibly have imagined I was responsible for that?' he exclaimed. 'Fidelis, did you? Just because I went there!'

'I thought I recognized you,' Gavin said.

Murdo went on, 'Really, Fidelis, I knew she'd been killed, but what could make you suppose I had anything to do with it? In any case, a man was charged, surely?'

'And acquitted,' Gavin said softly.

'Ah, it was you?'

'I never touched her.'

'I meant, you were the man accused, yes, you're the woodworker. We've met before.'

'Yes, I saw you, the times you went to Knighton Drive.'

'No case to answer, wasn't it?'

'That's what the court said.'

'Murdo,' Fidelis said, 'you know she was frightened of you, you read that just now. And she was waiting for you to visit her, on the day she died. It's all in there, that document, you've read it yourself—what could I think?'

'The suspicion's unworthy of you,' he said, offended.

Tina spoke loudly. 'Fidelis, stop. Let me tell you what I found, that's why I came.'

Unhitching a leather tote-bag from her shoulder, she rummaged in it and brought out a large brown envelope. Out of that she drew a large brown cardboard folder stamped with a label which said, *Petra Damiano, Literary Agents*. There was the word 'received' and a date scrawled below: 25th March 1999.

'Look.' The top page read,

The True Story
by
Lesley Bowhill
author of *Dog Days, The Jackdaws' Parliament*
and the highly praised *Catwalk.*

'Look, she's put in a photocopy of its dustjacket,' Tina said, and read the blurb aloud. '"When famous star Hermione Elphinstone learns she has only a short time to live, she determines that her death will not be in vain. She plans to take her own life and do it in a way that ensures that the man who used and spurned her, the villainous Sir Gervase, is suspected of committing murder. Later she is found dead from an overdose of barbiturates and suffocation."'

'That's how Lesley died, as far as I recall the details her solicitor told me,' Murdo said.

'Except that it was temazepam,' Fidelis said, and Clodie added:

'She only had a short time to live too, the post-mortem showed a primary pancreatic cancer and extensive secondaries, poor woman.'

'How do you know that?'

'I'm a doctor, Judge. I've seen the path report.'

Tina said, 'Wait, do listen, because I've read this manuscript. I think I'm the first person to look at it.'

290

'Surely the literary agent did.'

'Doubt it.'

'Didn't read it at all?'

'Well, tried the first para and then tasted at random, maybe.'

'Is that usual?' the judge asked.

'Unsolicited manuscripts go on to a slush pile. Someone would get round to reading more of it eventually. But there's not much hope for a third or fourth novel by an unheard-of author. What's going to be marketable there?'

'It's been nearly two years, why didn't they send it back long ago if they weren't interested?' Fidelis protested.

'They would have done sooner or later, no doubt.'

'But they might have missed a masterpiece!' Fidelis exclaimed.

'Don't worry, they didn't,' Tina announced. 'Far from it, in fact. But it's very interesting all the same. You need to hear about this book which she called *The True Story*, it's about a woman who makes up a story about a famous ex-boyfriend. She finds out where there was a hit and run accident, years before, one that nobody was ever caught for, she claims he did it when they were going out together and there's no way he can disprove the accusation.'

'My God!' Fidelis cried.

'Ingenious,' Murdo remarked.

'But that's not all. She put a twist in the tail,'

Tina said.

Murdo went to the door, opened it and said, 'Are you there?' The marshal must have been lurking just outside. 'Tell Harden to bring more glasses, would you please? I'll be with you in a moment.'

'He's not getting security back, is he?' Clodie said, clutching Gavin's hand tightly.

'Having a pee, I should think.'

Fidelis was right. As the butler entered the room with another silver tray, Murdo came in after him.

'I brought up some wine for the ladies, my lord.'

'Right. That'll be all for the moment, thanks. Now ladies, you'd like a tot? And you too, Rayner. Let's be comfortable.' He gestured to the two armchairs. Clodie sat on the arm of her mother's, Gavin stood close behind her and Murdo took his place behind the desk and put his reading glasses on again. He rubbed forefinger and thumb against his temples. He looked unfit and weary, and Fidelis felt a pang of sadness for the beautiful youth he'd once been. 'Now Ms Svenson, go on. What is this, if not Lesley Bowhill's last novel?'

CHAPTER THIRTY-SIX

Will they reach these last pages? I doubt it. I bet they never even read the book at all. Agents, publishers, the self-created gatekeepers between me and the reader. Creative writers get shafted and nobody cares. I've never been properly valued.

So this is my gamble. My punt on posterity. I won't be forgotten in death as you all tried to make me in life. If you've got to this page you'll understand how ingenious I am, how skilfully I plot, how cunningly I set up my clues. You should have appreciated me sooner.

And if nobody does read this? Then serve them all right. Serve Murdo right for spurning me, sucks to Petra Damiano and the publishing conglomerate that bought up Sayles. The story of a lifetime is handed to them on a plate—and wasted.

They have always underestimated me. I can count on the fingers of one hand the reviewers who wrote about my work, and just one who appreciated my cleverness and ingenuity, my clever plots and intricate manipulation of the events and characters. I should be famous, with a seat in the House of Lords like P.D. James or Ruth Rendell, or festivals named after me like Agatha Christie or Daphne du Maurier. What makes them any better than me except that they got their chance? Fame and success are due to pure luck, it's as simple as that—and knowing the right people. If I'd been the wife of a prominent lawyer I'd be right up there too. Murdo Wood-Wolferstan should have married me. He did me a bad turn, leaving me to make my own way in life like that. But he'll be sorry. They'll all be sorry. And if they can't even be bothered to read my work, they deserve all they get.

It will even things out just a tiny little bit. It's all so unfair. After all I went through, looking after the old woman, slaving, suffering her bad temper and fits of shrieking and groaning, the smells, the hard labour heaving her round, all the degradation of nursing, and for years— now for me to get the same illness is fate's last cruel trick. They say it's not infectious. Hereditary tendencies, they think. Trust her to leave me something like that.

'I'm afraid there's little we can do,' the oncologist said and talked about palliative measures and the hospice.

'How long have I got?' I asked.

'We never like to say.'

I wasn't going to let him get away with that. Not after watching my mother's last few months. I'm not going through that agony, no way, especially when it's all for nothing.

'Is there any chance you're wrong?' I pressed him and he shook his head. He didn't use the word. But it was there, hanging in the room. Death. I'm dying.

I've just deleted some pages about that. You don't need to read them. All you need to know is that I'd have gone straight off to jump into the Thames if it hadn't been for meeting Fidelis Berlin. But seeing her reminded me of so much. The wasted years. My dashed hopes and ambitions. I was in a daze going home, terrified, just plain terrified. And the next day, angry. Why should I be doomed to fade out leaving nothing behind me except three forgotten novels? Months of agony, and then oblivion. I'll be gone as though I'd never been.

I *will* make a mark.

It's poetic justice that it's only because my book sunk like a stone that I can carry out the plan I invented so ingeniously all those years ago. Nobody remembers *Catwalk* now. Which will be their bad luck. I sent it to Murdo when it came out. If he had the grace to read it then he'll be able to wriggle out of the snare I'm going to trap him in. And if you have had the simple professionalism to read this manuscript by a writer who used to be one of your own

295

clients, if you've got this far, I take it all back. My voice will forgive you from the grave.

Otherwise, Fidelis will read the 'journals' I've concocted. She'll know it's true and she'd never keep quiet about something like that. He'll be accused of killing me to keep me quiet about the crime I've invented and describe him committing all those years ago. He'll never be able to prove it's not true. And suspicion's all it will take, in his position. He won't be able to discount me then.

Tina, once a good amateur actress, had read the words in a self-pitying whine that made them carry disgusting conviction. 'There's more, several pages,' she said in her own voice.

'I think we've got the gist.' Murdo sounded like a man who felt sick.

'It's perfectly clear,' Tina said. 'And peculiarly nasty and sad too. Tragic to think of her, knowing her whole life's been an empty failure, brooding on it, telling herself it was all someone else's fault. You can see how she'd remember the plot she'd concocted all those years before. Mad, of course—'

'But isn't suicide insane almost by definition?' Murdo said.

Tina went on, 'But just imagine having the resolution to do it! She must have been terribly brave. I mean, I can understand planning to die quickly and get revenge at the same time, it's the kind of thing an ingenious writer would invent—but actually carrying it out! I know I couldn't.'

'I don't understand why she wanted revenge on me,' Murdo said. 'I never harmed her.'

'Didn't you use her and spurn her, like the wicked Sir Gervase?' Tina's cheeky question was somehow made permissible by her charm. Good Lord, she actually fancies him, Fidelis realized, this room is full of sexual undercurrents.

Murdo was regarding Tina's light, bright hair, her sharp aquamarine eyes and her general air of adventurousness with approval too. His voice was more conversational than judicial as he replied, 'Certainly not.'

'Are you sure?' Fidelis asked. 'Sure she didn't read more into it than you meant? Sure she wasn't waiting for proposals and wedding bells?'

'I bet you she was, I see her as exactly that kind of woman, always waiting for someone else to sort out her life,' Clodie said.

'What happened after the Israel trip?' Fidelis asked.

'It was the end of a long summer and I had to get back to work. When we got to the airport all the flights were full—it must have been Jewish New Year—so we had to fly home separately. You know, we're talking about a very long time ago and I'd find it impossible to give sworn evidence about the details but I don't actually remember any emotion here, it wasn't a passionate parting. You've got to understand, we weren't serious. She was a sweet girl in those days, pretty, lively, game for anything, we had a good time that summer, but when it was over it was over.'

'That doesn't seem to be what she thought,' Tina said.

'She thought you dumped her,' Clodie said.

'I can see her building it up in her mind, those last months, looking back on a life that turned out disappointing and wondering what it was all for, where it all went wrong, why she was going to die alone.' With those last few words, Fidelis felt Clodie's hand grasping hers, a warm, meaningful grip which implied 'Don't worry, you're not alone.'

'She once told me she hated living by herself, she was scared,' Gavin said. 'She said it made all the difference that I'd help in emergencies.'

'Some gratitude she showed then, setting you up on a murder rap!' Clodie snapped.

'I thought it was me she was trying to set up,' Murdo said.

'Oh, right, which is why she got blue fluff from a fleece under her own nails.'

'I'm not the only person with a navy blue fleece,' Gavin murmured.

'What were her arrangements, exactly?' Tina asked.

Clodie enumerated them, recalling her work on the case documents. 'She made it look like intruders had cleared the place of her stuff, like someone didn't want any info she had to come out. She loads everything into her car, hidden, like we were tonight, Gavin, and takes it all off to the dump.'

'I saw her driving in and out lots of times, those last days,' Gavin said.

'She makes sure you get it that she's afraid of someone. She does some stuff to look like she's expecting to be there for keeps. That's the party invites and ordering new curtains or whatever. She fixes up a bridge four, so someone's sure to find the body, and makes like she was interrupted in the middle of cooking a meal. She scrapes some trainers on the carpet to make it look like there was a struggle. Then she gets rid of the trainers, the packaging for her meds and the whisky bottle and the packet of dustbin bags and all that. She's saved up things with unidentified prints, and one of them's a glass, all smudged, she's rubbed them around a bit—pity you innocently superimposed your own, Gavin.'

Murdo's and Fidelis's eyes met. Without a word spoken they agreed not to mention that Murdo had been to the Cameron house and some of the fingerprints were his.

Clodie went on, 'And when she does those final things, swallows the tablets, pulls the bag over her head, she has the inside of the plastic over her hands to keep her own prints where they'd plausibly be.'

'That's sick,' Gavin said loudly. 'Really sick.'

'What a way to go, that poor, pretty girl.' Murdo wiped some moisture from his cheeks and then yawned uncontrollably. 'I'm sorry, it's been a trying day, what with one thing and another.' He moved to the window and pulled the heavy red curtains back. Fidelis went to look out beside him. The judge's lodgings were isolated amid buildings put up in the twentieth century's least sensitive architectural style, slabs of ugly brick above display windows and neon signs, all illuminated by unflattering yellow street lamps. The area was technically pedestrianized, but at this time of night drivers headed straight through it, scattering groups of drunks, ignored by the recumbent forms of rough sleepers. A man was vomiting all over a built-up brick flower bed. Three women in tiny skirts and stiletto heels lurched into an underpass. 'Thank God it's only two weeks,' Murdo murmured. After that he would be back in London, in the rarefied atmosphere of the appellate courts and safe forever from close contact with the people on whose lives and behaviour he pronounced, accessible to them only from afar as he processed in protected dignity on to his bench or past an awestruck crowd.

CHAPTER THIRTY-SEVEN

The other judge who was on circuit in Ferriby's courts during this fortnight refused to spend longer in lodgings than the rules required. She'd slept in her own bed and turned up for breakfast. The butler had been sulky and unwelcoming to the unexpected overnight guest since Tina, on Murdo's invitation, had occupied the room made ready in advance for the Mrs Justice. He was deferential to the new arrival. Senior to Murdo in date of appointment, she took her seat at the head of the table, but was preoccupied. She gulped down a cup of coffee, said, 'Ugh, I'd forgotten—Cheryl, you'll have to buy some proper coffee and a Gaggia later' to her young marshal and stood up. So, in formal politeness, did Murdo and both marshals, copied, awkwardly, by Fidelis and Tina. 'See you on parade,' she said, and left the room followed by her attendant.

Tina's mobile rang. The marshal looked appalled and made a 'turn it off' gesture but Tina answered anyway. 'Darling, you got there all right—what? You don't mean it—that's dreadful—yes, I suppose so, that's some consolation, but listen, you get your stuff out of there and come back to my place, you're not spending one more night in—yes, of course you can bring him too—tonight.' Still talking, she pushed her chair back and went to the door, making an apologetic gesture to Murdo.

'You start getting things organized,' Murdo told the young man. Alone with Fidelis, he said:

'I've been thinking about poor Lesley. How odd it seems, that all these years later she should pop out of the woodwork and claim—well, you read it. I seem to have been part of her life, while I'd completely forgotten her. A salutary reminder.'

'Of what?'

'That nothing one does is without its consequences.'

'How did you leave it with her, after the Israeli trip?' Fidelis asked.

'I've been trying to think. Things were casual in those days, I don't suppose we made any particular plans. I went to visit my mother—'

'Yes, I remember,' Fidelis said.

'After that, I started in chambers, got caught up in work—you know how it is for a successful young barrister, it takes your life over.'

'In other words, you dumped her.'

'We just didn't happen to get together again.'

'But she'd thought it was serious, you'd made plans together.'

'Not real plans, it was just talk. Fantasies.'

'You led her on, Murdo.'

'But I never meant to, that's what I tried to make her understand.'

'When you went to see her?'

'She wouldn't listen, went on about this fictional incident. In fact, Fidelis, I'll be frank, she told me I was capable of killing and so now I had to help her kill herself. It was perfectly grotesque.' His tone was full of convincing indignation.

'You must have tried to dissuade her from the idea of committing suicide.'

'I didn't think she was serious, it was all an act put on to trap me. I should never have gone near the woman, not in the seventies, not last year, she was bad news.' Hearing his own unguarded voice, he added more gently, 'Poor, deluded woman.'

'Murdo, Gavin said he saw you the times you went to Knighton Drive. Times, plural.'

'Is that what he said? I didn't notice.'

'Did you do as she asked?'

'Fidelis, please, how can you even suggest such a thing? You'd never have asked me that in the past. It must be your condition speaking. I can see you aren't well.'

'Parkinson's disease only affects the body, Murdo, the intellect is unimpaired,' Fidelis said. She named it, acknowledged it, accepted it. *About time too.*

'Is that what you've—my dear, how dreadful, I am so very sorry.'

'Did you help Lesley, Murdo?'

'You cannot be serious. How can you even ask that question? I'm a judge.'

'What's that got to do with it?'

'Assisting a suicide is a criminal offence.'

She stared at his bland, closed features. A stranger. 'Did you, Murdo?'

'My dear, *would* I?'

It wasn't a denial.

Was that Lesley Cameron's final legacy— the miasma of distrust amid a destroyed friendship?

Tina came back into the room. 'Fidelis, Clodie's moving out of that house right away, it's not safe. There's been a fire, arson— Gavin's house has been burnt out, it's not safe for them there.'

'Oh no, poor Gavin!' Poor Gavin, whose word would never be trusted again. Had he seen Murdo go there twice? Even Fidelis didn't know if she'd believe him rather than the man she'd known so long, and yes— respected. A just judge. An upright man. A little cold, insensitive, careless of weaknesses, but you couldn't blame him for leaving a onetime girlfriend behind, the way so many men did. I've done the same myself, Fidelis thought, often enough. What would I do if the partner in some long-forgotten fling turned up out of nowhere and claimed I owed him something? I'd have the right to protect myself. If that's what Murdo did. *Stop it.* It was

304

absurd to build this flimsy construction on the basis of one, perhaps misunderstood word. Time or times. *Forget it.*

Tina was saying, 'She says he's got heaps of insurance, his sister kept it up all the time.'

'All the same . . .'

'Poor chap, the locals will always think he did it really even when there's a suicide verdict,' Tina said.

'He needn't go near the place again, need he?' Murdo said. 'Nice chap, I thought. He said something about Nairobi before he left last night.'

'No, that was Clodie, she's been offered a post there. Of course they might go together.'

'Judge, it's ten past nine,' the marshal said.

Murdo stood up. 'I'll have to get on.'

'Murdo.'

'Sorry, Fidelis, it'll have to wait.'

'Just tell me quickly. Did you go to her house a second time?'

'I drove there that morning, found her house, saw that the curtains were closed with milk on the doorstep, decided it was too early and went off to fill in some time. I had coffee, looked round the district a bit, came back, bought a piece of that chap's woodwork, then I noticed the milk had been taken in so I rang the bell and Lesley opened the door. I was in her house once, Fidelis. Just once.'

'Judge, it's really—'

'Right. I'm coming.' He didn't kiss Fidelis

305

goodbye. She couldn't blame him. His cheek met Tina's, his hand lingering on her a fraction too long. Fidelis, who had heard the floorboards creak outside her door in the small hours, thought, if we were a few years younger I'd ask her about last night. Or she'd tell me.

But all Tina said was 'Let's stay and watch, I've never seen any judicial pomp and circumstance before.'

Standing in a small group of curious onlookers, Fidelis felt a sense of relief at the sight of the judge in a wig and red robe, a man disguised as objective, impersonal justice. What would she have done about it if she'd learnt without any doubt that Lesley's story had been true? Don't go down that road, she thought, and began trying to tell herself she hadn't believed it for a moment. Not really. Not of Catriona's Murdo. Not of someone whose life consisted of upholding the law.

I must ring Yossi, she reminded herself. I'll tell him I'll come for a visit as soon as the weather's a bit warmer. Next year in Jerusalem.

The judges were conveyed to Ferriby's cathedral in a shiny black limousine, driven very slowly across the cobbles of the pedestrian precinct. There were trumpeters. There were other, lesser members of the judiciary and bar, in full bottomed wigs and purple or black silk; the Lord Lieutenant, whom Fidelis had met the previous evening, transformed from a pompous businessman into a romantic figure in a gaudy scarlet and ultramarine uniform, with a sword. The High Sheriff, a stout woman in a frogged dark green velvet coat and a hat with an ostrich feather; the under-sheriff and civic officials in wigs and black gowns, the Lord Mayor in a vermilion cape, with a cockaded tricorne hat; the Bishop in an embroidered cope and mitre.

'Remember St Spyridion's procession last summer?' Fidelis said.

'I'm going to make our booking for next year soon,' Tina replied. Her voice was uncharacteristically tentative, its rising tone an implicit question.

No more dissembling.

'I might need a wheelchair at Gatwick,' Fidelis said.

Tina replied without surprise, 'That's fine, I'll fix it.'

'And an arm down to the beach.'

Tina took Fidelis's shaking hand in her own warm grasp. 'Whatever it takes,' she said.

A fanfare sounded from the cathedral steps as the judges went in.

'Next year in Greece,' said Fidelis Berlin.

We hope you have enjoyed this Large Print book. Other Chivers Press or Thorndike Press Large Print books are available at your library or directly from the publishers.

For more information about current and forthcoming titles, please call or write, without obligation, to:

Chivers Press Limited
Windsor Bridge Road
Bath BA2 3AX
England
Tel. (01225) 335336

OR

Thorndike Press
295 Kennedy Memorial Drive
Waterville
Maine 04901
USA

All our Large Print titles are designed for easy reading, and all our books are made to last.